CARNIVAL

Also by Rawi Hage

De Niro's Game
Cockroach

CARNIVAL

RAWI HAGE

ANANSI

This edition published in 2012 by House of Anansi Press Inc.
110 Spadina Avenue, Suite 801
Toronto, ON, M5V 2K4
Tel. 416-363-4343 • Fax 416-363-1017
www.houseofanansi.com

Distributed in Canada by HarperCollins Canada Ltd.
1995 Markham Road
Scarborough, ON, M1B 5M8
Toll free tel. 1-800-387-0117

All of the events and characters in this book are fictitious, and any resemblance to actual persons, living or dead, is purely coincidental.

The author wishes to thank the Conseil des arts et des lettres du Québec and the Berliner Künstlerprogramm (DAAD) for their support.

The story of the Magdalena girls has its seed in an interview conducted by Jean-Luc Hennig with Grisélidis Réal in *The Little Black Book of Grisélidis Réal: Days and Nights of an Anarchist Whore* by Jean-Luc Hennig (Paris: Semiotext(e), 2009).

House of Anansi Press is committed to protecting our natural environment. As part of our efforts, the interior of this book is printed on paper that contains 100% post-consumer recycled fibres, is acid-free, and is processed chlorine-free.

16 15 14 13 12   1 2 3 4 5

Library and Archives Canada Cataloguing in Publication

Hage, Rawi
Carnival / Rawi Hage.

Issued also in electronic format.
ISBN 978-0-88784-235-1

I. Title.

PS8615.A355C37 2012   C813'.6   C2012-902914-9

Jacket design: Brian Morgan • Jacket Illustration: Lorenzo Petrantoni
Text design and typesetting: Alysia Shewchuk

We acknowledge for their financial support of our publishing program the Canada Council for the Arts, the Ontario Arts Council, and the Government of Canada through the Canada Book Fund.

Printed and bound in Canada

For Madeleine Thien

True open seriousness fears neither parody, nor irony, nor any other form of reduced laughter, for it is aware of being part of an uncompleted whole.

— Mikhail Bakhtin, Rabelais and His World

◡ ◡ ◡

Those who are motionless on the wandering
earth: the voyagers.
Those who flee over the motionless earth: the
stay-at-homes.
But those who flee over the wandering earth,
and those who are motionless on the motionless
earth: what should *they* be called?

— J. M. G. Le Clézio, The Book of Flights

ACT ONE

MOTHER

I WAS CONCEIVED on the circus trail by a traveller who owned a camel and a mother who swung from the ropes. When my mother, the trapeze artist with the golden hair, tossed me out of her self to the applause of elephants and seals, there was rain outside and the caravans were about to leave. She nursed me through the passages of roads and the follies of clowns and the bitter songs of an old dwarf who prophesied for me a life of wandering among spiders and beasts.

But the owner of the circus already had plans for me. We are missing a strongman and a lion tamer, he said, and took me out of my mother's arms to feel the size of my thighs and the shape of my head. But I grew up to become a knower and a guesser in the world of tents, amid the shouts of the barker in the midway shows, who lifted his long hat and banged his cane on the outdoor stage and shouted: Step right in, ladies and gentlemen, and meet the Surmise Child! You'll get your money back if this kid fails to guess your weight, if he doesn't guess your age and the remaining number of your living years before you rest under a stone. And I, who learned how to weigh lives by the size of feet, by the strangles of belts, the heaviness of eyes, and the expansion of cheeks, grew to become a watcher who saw my mother hang and my father fall under the weight of his own beard.

After my father's departure and my mother's death, I was left to the circus, to roam between the ankles of gentle giants, the brief hands of midgets, and the loving nature of freaks. At an early age, I learned how to pull the ropes and tie the monkey's bow tie. I learned of smiling dragons by stretching the skin of the tattooed girl, and I played with the average son of the world's smallest woman and the world's tallest man. I grew within those circular tents and the rotation of their acts and I was carried by the trunks of elephants across borders and foreign lands.

I also learned how to guess and how to kill.

Sunrise Child, as the fat lady once mispronounced my name, you just made my day, because you guessed the lightness of my spirit under the burden of my weight. And she kissed my bright face and stepped right out of the tent, feeling the clouds on her hair and caressing the gliding birds in the sky. But when winter came and the tents were dropped and we all starved in the circles of cold, I killed a horse and fed it to the beasts.

RODENTS

FOR THE PAST five years I have lived in a building that hums with strange people, rodents, and insects who come and go as they please. In the next-door apartment on my left lives a Romanian woman who once was a gymnast, and now that she is in need and alone, she occasionally offers herself to a big old doctor who has a beard and cars that never cease to change and grow.

I know him from the neighbourhood clinic. On my last visit, he asked me a few questions about my family's medical history, invited me to settle on the paper surface of his table, and then got busy tapping my back, pressing my tongue with a disposable stick, holding my testicles until he forced a cough or two out of me. He frowned as he added something to the pages of my medical file.

He shook his head, but before he could tell me the news, I said, Doctor, I know, you don't have to say a word. I guess that I have to lose a bit of weight, believe me, I know, Doctor... because I looked at my ankles this morning and examined my cheeks in the mirror... we all have our vices, Doctor, it could well be gluttony in my case. One out of seven sins is not that bad. Not to be religious or anything... I tried gambling and it never paid off, women make you suffer, and greed has no end... I guess I have to change jobs, you seem to be saying, Doctor. Driving a cab for these long hours without a rest, or exercise. It dulls your mind, staring at the road like that... all I think of sometimes is my fate... I said fate, not fat. What a joker, Doctor! What a wasted life, what a wag I am... it is not my fault, Doctor, and who can resist? I am attracted to all those banners, the ballyhoo that draws me inside those places of gigantic pizzas, double Siamese cheeseburgers, eyeless four-legged chickens calling to me in their yellow costumes, and let's not forget those milkshakes straight from the triplicate nipples of newly cloned cows... but I still say fresh milk goes very well with a dozen of the largest doughnuts in the universe...I should have known better, Doctor. I guess, I can guess, but I never know...

Well, said the doctor, what I detect here is some malfunction in the brain. Judging from the jerking movements of your hands and the shifting of your eyes, not to mention your long monologues and your fancies about librarian monkeys conspiring against the world, I say we had better check your head. Now, what I suggest is that I put you in touch with a psychiatrist who can assess all these wild thoughts of yours. What do you say? I can give you a referral today...

The doctor recognizes me when I encounter him on the stairs of our building or when he parks his car along the garage wall underneath my balcony during those lunch hours when he goes up to see the Romanian woman next door.

I watch him coming up the stairs, almost ready to drop his pants under the patient watch of the spiders. As soon as he steps into the building, the dog bitches howl to the rhythm of their own heat, the jaw of the lady across the road clinks to the hiss of the gossip of rattlesnakes, and the hoofs of the horses next door tap dance to the beat of the shoemaker's hammer down at the corner of the street. It is mating season every day!

So, Doctor, I think this is what it comes to after years of being studious, after memorizing thick volumes on the inflation of the lungs, the deflation of the kidneys, and the meticulous classification of bones, veins, anuses, Fallopian tubes, hearts, and genitals. This is the reward for not fainting or barfing in class in the presence of slashed pale corpses on autopsy tables. I say, doctors are the profiteers of death and unclaimed cadavers that were once inhabited by homeless and wandering poets! Doctors are the final custodians of those

delusional walkers who roamed the streets, reciting monologues to imaginary friends, their long orangutan arms peek-
ing out from magician's cuffs and reaching inside the bellies
of city barrels to make food appear and cans disappear and
recycle into metal tables displaying the wretched of the earth,
the unclaimed dead, in open chests and torn shoes.

ABOVE ME THERE is an old Polish woman who survived the
Second World War camps. Her son, the building's janitor,
owns a Harley, long boots, and a black, mean jacket. He is an
ignoramus who talks and talks and looks at his aging face in
the hallway mirror. He straightens his leather pants before
fixing his windy hair. At times, when a pipe is leaking in my
apartment, or when the window is precipitating water and
air, I knock at his door. He opens it and frowns at me with a
Leave a note in the box at the door and I'll look at it later.

When I leave the janitor a letter, I make the situation
sound urgent, with apocalyptic consequences. I write in a
poetic, wrathful, religious style with a hint of menace to his
own well-being and to the collective welfare. I try to explain
to him that everything is interconnected. Even a small, innocent leak of air from a window can tip the balance of warmth
in a building and lead to microcosms of small global infernos.
I remind him that our nature is a fragile one.

Like I said, he is an ignoramus, and he never gets the hu-
mour of my literary, sardonic style. His speed machine has
made him lose all interest in history and humankind.

But, nevertheless, he ends up by appearing at my door
waving my letters in his hand: What exactly is wrong here?

You are not a little girl and should not be afraid of spiders. And what do you mean by the words *juridical rivers of blood . . . welfare and warfare . . . licit and explicit . . .* Are you trying to scare me by using big words? I ran your letter by a lawyer, pal. I say you better be careful what you write, because my lawyer can drive you up against the wall. If you keep threatening me and writing letters in red ink with "buccaneer flags" . . . I might have to double the rent or kick you out altogether. I don't have time for this! And your apartment is cluttered with books and papers, and that, my friend, brings all kinds of insects and rodents. So you might as well make peace with me and accept the spiders as pest control. And now, where is that flood you wrote about . . . and who is this Mr. Moses, is he staying with you here . . . ?

LANTERN

BENEATH ME THERE is an agitated student who complains that my sluggish steps, the ship-like commotion of my hips against my ever-insomniac mattress, and the ultrasound fretting of my flying carpets are forbidding her from excelling in her studies, ruining her future life of grand diplomas and her prospects for a large car, a big house with a pool, a husband on a leash, and a free-range poodle mowing the lawn. A few times, she threatened me with the police. When she appears from below, she is usually in her pyjamas, her Mickey Mouse slippers frowning up at me, her hair looking like she's gone through a psychiatric treatment or homegrown electric shock. I always promise that this is the last time she'll hear a noise; I blame it on a pile of literature that fell on the floor and bounced for a while because of the lightness of the writing inside. She never gets the joke, maybe because she is studying to be an engineer, and falling matters are never a light matter.

Beneath it all, in the parking garage, there is my car, its meter and its long oval rearview mirror, and the lantern on its roof. In my car, on the dashboard, between the glass and the steering wheel, I keep a Kleenex box that I use, on occasion, to scoop dirt and stop spills and the slow movement of liquids extracted from running noses by bare, sweeping hands. I also use it to cover my nostrils from the assaulting smells of the poor and the drunks and the unwashables who ride in my car with the stiffness of floating corpses and the miseries of the underground.

When all is calm, after all the strange creatures in my building have settled down, retreated to their stoves to feed themselves, and then moved towards their televisions to receive their daily allowance of vitamin D from the eminent face of the news anchor, I get in my taxi and go out into the night.

SPIDERS

THERE ARE TWO kinds of taxi drivers: the Spiders and the Flies.

Spiders are those drivers who wait at taxi stands for the dispatcher's call or for customers to walk off the streets and into their hungry cars. These human insects can be found on city sidewalks rolling newspapers, comparing cars, recalling customers and their own lives. They wait on corners for things to come and ages to pass. Nameless they have become, reduced to machine operators who identify each other and themselves by the number of their car: 101 had a fight, they might say; 56's wife is pregnant; 97 just passed by...

But I call them the Spiders.

Flies are wanderers, operators who drive alone and around to pick up the wavers and the whistlers on edges of sidewalks and streets. They navigate the city, ceaseless and aimless, looking for raising arms to halt their flights, for the rain to make them busy, for the surfing lanterns above their hoods to shine like faraway ships leaving potato famines and bringing newcomers. No wanderer ever rests on the curb to play or feed. No wanderer chooses to travel the same road twice.

I am a wanderer.

IN THE EVENINGS during my shift, I often pass by Café Bolero. It is open twenty-four hours and many taxi drivers stop here to rest, eat, and socialize. I sit in the corner and listen to their stories and complaints. I find consolation when I assess their tired faces and watch their knuckles open and liberate themselves from the clutches of steering wheels, the handling of doorknobs, and the counting of change. I am an oddity among these charioteers but I observe their ways, hear their words, and follow their movements between the tables and the chairs. I also assign them names because I fear to forget their numbers.

Spiders come in many forms and shapes and colours. And here is the Sleeping Spider, ladies and gentlemen! Also known as Mr. Green, he takes a very short nap at every red light. He wakes up just as the light changes. Some drivers say he shuts his eyes and doesn't sleep but stays aware of everything around him; others say he has a colour sensor in his eyelids. But the truth is that when the colour green catches his eyes, he wakes up and thinks he is back home in the lush jungles of the south. It is said that once, in Café Bolero, he fell asleep in the middle of a meal, his head hanging over his plate, but when the daughter of the owner brought a green salad to the table, he was awake again. That is how he got the name Mr. Green.

And let's all welcome the Piss Spider, ladies and gentlemen, the driver who never leaves his car! He works twenty hours a day. He has a grand plan! He wants to retire to an island one day, with a house and a young woman to marry.

Since he never leaves his car, he hardly ever takes a shower. But, even worse, this spider always carries an empty antifreeze container and pisses in it. Going to the bathroom is a waste of time, he thinks. He is afraid to miss a dispatcher's call or a customer off the street. It is said that a young woman who sat next to him in the front seat asked him to stop the car and got out and puked on the side of the road. If I were a customer of his, I would leave the swine the change and never touch anything that touched his hands. I'd become a generous donor to help cease the epidemics of the world. That spider could plague you with typhoid, the plague, hepatitis A, B, and C, and the whole Phoenician alphabet.

The Piss Spider is a man who would win every fist fight. Just his grabbing you by the collar and pulling your nose towards his armpits would assault you with olfactory punches, give you instant menopause. A waft of smells stronger than a thousand filthy Crusaders would ravage you, and you would be begging for mercy and clean air, you would be on your knees chanting five Hail Marys and six Our Fathers. But he is also a Renaissance man. With his knowledge of the art and science of channelling and containing liquids, his great mysticism expressed through an ascetic lifestyle, his skills for long-term navigation, his capacity for alchemy and the gathering of gold, he is admired and feared by friends and foes. A real son of the European kings and nobility, I call him the Piss Spider, but he truly earned his royal status when he became known among his fellow drivers as Louis XIV, after the French king who never took a bath in his entire life. When the sun hits le Roi Soleil's dashboard, it turns into a fussy layer of dust, enough for ten fingerprintings at the border crossings. And every December he says, One more year of this and then I am off to my little bride on the beach, but then the massive layers of dust in his car turn to sand and beaches, and the smell of his seat becomes the smell of the old and familiar, and the cavity of his chair becomes a hole of misery and an opaque quagmire of greed, dirt, warmth, and even comfort.

IN THE EARLY mornings when my work is done, after I have mopped the streets and picked up a few owls and hyenas and a collection of nocturnal apes desperate to go home, I park my taxi in the garage beneath the building, count my fares, and hide the money under my long coat.

By the end of each shift, my car retains traces of things brought in and eaten, things lost and forgotten by clients who sit and shuffle their shoes and point their fingers in various directions. I've found hats, wallets, scarves, documents, change; also nail polish, makeup cases, knives, traces of drugs, and small or large umbrellas (closed but wet for the most part). The bottom of my car is a swamp where everything eventually rests. And inside my machine and between my car windows every word said, every gesture, complaint, suspicion, and laugh, is retained by the absorbent sponge of the air freshener that dangles from my mirror in the shape of a cedar tree.

These are the good times, when I excavate the traces of the night and all the things that were missed. People lose things and let go of things while they tell you the most sincere stories of their lives. I picked up a gambler once who wept and cried and blamed his wife for his addiction. Three nights he had stayed out playing cards and now he was going back home. When we arrived at his house, it was the middle of the night. He asked me to come inside with him. I will tell my wife to pay you and she will know that I lost it all, he said. I stood at the entrance watching the woman screaming and breaking dishes while his kids cried in their pyjamas under the archways of the doors.

ZAINAB

AND MY NEXT-DOOR neighbour's name is Zainab. Studious, forever calm, quiet and smiling Zainab, the librarian type with burning lava inside that could burst in your face, ignite you, and deform you into an anatomical wonder.

Zainab! Oh Zainab, who fears the afterlife, is never made up, hardly colourful, she plays the austere, the intellectual... she seems on the conservative side, but I know that behind it all, there is a riddle that has to be cracked. Everything about her seems to be saying, Listen, if you don't look attentively, if you don't go beyond my simplicity to detect the simmering volcano in me, you are not it. Carpet merchants, buffoons on ropes, caretakers with leather jackets, taxi drivers with eccentric mannerisms, and all those men willing to stick a feather up their ass and do the peacock rounds are entertaining, but not it.

I could be wrong, but I assume that Zainab is looking for the brooding type who goes to caves and mountains and waits for God's revelation through the smoke of a pack of cigarettes; or maybe even the concise type whose every word seems prophetic and profound and resonates with the majestical voice of heavenly trumpets. Or maybe a moustached man playing the lead in an Egyptian soap opera with his hair combed into a side part, posing in his castle with his long sideburns, dressed in a shiny nightgown, holding a cigarette, puffing and echoing, echoing, echoing away: *Masr oum el dounia*. Egypt, the mother of the universe...

I often cross paths with Zainab in the mornings. She and I chat a bit, politely, and then I tell her a story or two about my night on the job. She often giggles or laughs, or else just smiles and listens, and we follow this up by discussing books and such diverse topics as the savageries of histories and the make-believes of mankind, life and its absurdities, and then literature and other pretentious intellectual matters pertaining to death and migration, among other losses, and that is when her smiles turn into contemplative looks and she re-members that she has to go back to her books and her studies.

And usually, just before she leaves me, I ask, or insinuate, something about meeting for a coffee, or dinner and a glass of red wine at my place, or, to take things slowly, a meal at a restaurant of her choice, but each time she smiles and tells me that she doesn't have the time. She is busy with her job at the National Library, she explains, and her dissertation takes the rest of her days.

Zainab told me once that her degree is in Islamic stud-ies and that the word *jihad* comes from *ijtihad,* which means to apply oneself, to question, and to reform. She even noted down the names of some writers for me, Mohamed Abdo, Al-Ghazali, but before she could add others, right off the bat I said, But Zainab, darling, God is dead! The other day I killed him myself. I hit him with my cab while he was crossing the street on a red light. I say he should have known better, him being God and all... And just before he closed his eyes, just before he mumbled his last prayers to himself, he said to me: Son, it was an honour to meet you, son. It was good that you killed Me now, because this whole charade of popes with tri-angular buffoon hats and shepherd's sticks, not to mention the ever-multiplying lot of carpet kneelers and myopic seek-ers of long-vanished temples and lost tribes with a bad sense of direction, has become uncontrollable. And then, for no ap-parent reason, or maybe for an apparent reason, he switched to French and said, Look, my son, as you might well know, those desert lots of Semitic Arabs, Syriacs, Aramaics, Nestor-ians, Nabateans, and Jews got it all wrong, and the worst of it is, they took it north, south, and lateral. They made it all about food and pussy, like Hollywood fitness trainers putting a fading star on an exercise regimen and a strict diet. Those Abrahamic progeny are obsessed with nutriment mixes and covering and shaving and twisting women's hair to regulate the cycles of the cunt...yes, you heard Me, I said *cunt*, not *count*...They got it all wrong, that bunch of archaic literates, and now they are trying to patch it with bits of poetry and apologetic explanations because they can't see beyond the sand dunes on the tips of my giant sandals, which, I believe, as a result of this unfortunate or fortunate accident of ours, might well be found on the other side of the road...make sure to bury them with Me!

And Zainab, bewildered, smiled, chuckled, and shook her head in disbelief, and she left me once again to my own mind and its ever-swirling circuit of fires and hells.

MORNING

EVERY MORNING, AND I want to say to you every morning, after Zainab bounces down the stairs on her ever-bending knees, on her way to school under the call of distant minarets and the faraway sound of bygone calls to prayer, every morning I open my palm towards the sun, lie down on my father's carpet, and happily masturbate.

I am a good neighbour and a welcoming soul. In my early-morning dreams, I invite everyone to take part in my creation and recreation of world events: the universal injustices, the pounding motion of the stars, and all of this anthropophagical existence. In my fantasies, I unveil the ludicrous, the farcical, the senseless weight of histories. I have climbed donjons and walls, slain guardians and monsters alike; I have participated in battles and jerked my hand to the systematic rhythm of war drums, the bleak tunes of marching flutes, and the blowing flags of the vagina armies ready to conquer and duplicate the universe a millionfold. I pound and pound until I hear the humming abyss of the rosy holes, the cannibalistic cunts of mammals and dinosaurs, the leaping legs of the lady frog, the latent hazy breasts of promiscuous albino sisters liberating their kind from the condemnation of the *sanctus doctrinalis*...

There is always a box of Kleenex next to my bed, as there is inside my taxi. Also there are slippers, and mountains and mountains of books. When the fantasy is right, when the world is rescued and saved by the ecstasy of my creation, when every word is valued, every conversation timed, and every bullet hits its target, when the folly of history comes to a fitting end and short dictators are slain on Christmas Day by orphans with guns, it makes me happy and I can ejaculate far and beyond. I can spray-paint walls with thick, dewy rhapsodies and white dripping masses of abstract figures. Once in a while I ejaculate too far, hit my own eyes, and blind myself. Seeking water, I walk towards the sound of the clanging pipes, the rusty faucets of the old building, where I find myself again inside large prisons and filthy common baths, in showers devoid of soap, because it's war, and all the prisoners, barefooted, skinny, huddle in the cold, buried by the shouts of the guards and the barks of the dogs.

But luckily for them, those frail victims of history and man, when I finally reach the river and wash away the dirt that has got into my eye, I walk through the cold towards the barbed wire, a metal net lit from behind by the guards' torches, and I save those poor prisoners and free the girl. (Please note that it could happen that I jerk off more than once a day.)

But in my real life, when I meet Zainab on the stairs, we politely exchange politenesses, and with bashful smiles and downcast eyes and the distance of a few steps between us, not to mention the demarcation of a handrail to save us from temptation, I try to engage her in conversation and I ask her about her life and she asks me about mine.

Once Zainab asked me where I came from. I told her that I grew up in the circus, but one day my father, who was a flying carpet pilot, left us to go east on a pilgrimage to find his God and His ninety-nine adjectives.

She asked me if I was a Muslim, and I said, Yes and no, because I drink and lust, I caress performing dogs on holidays, I devour pink swine, and I never kneel to the east or to the west.

And your mother, Zainab asked.

My mother was a trapeze artist, I told her, a weaver of ropes, who loved for dwarves to nibble on the backs of her knees. She locked me in the back room when the clowns came to provide us with a little extra change for food and cotton candy. She told me that heaven is within our palms and that the inferno is somewhere between the desert and the northern pole.

And then Zainab asked me my father's name.

I forgot that long ago, I said. He left before I had the chance to see him on the ground. But I remember he wore a turban during his flying carpet show, and then one day his carpet came to a halt and crashed in front of a thousand people. And then he thought of humiliation and death and the meaning of life.

I still remember the tune that went with my father's flight. It was composed by gypsy Jews and played by a band of menacing Italian rabbits. It sounded like the music that lures snakes out of their baskets to be willingly hypnotized, pacified into doing volunteer work for the boon of the man in the turban and the entertainment of humankind.

I hate snakes and their wickedness, Zainab said.

I love the free-spirited snake, I said. I love it because it hangs from branches to offer us wisdom. It warns us of those confining, egotistical false demiurges who order us not to butt-fuck each other under the cactus tree (spikes are known to be painful), not to ejaculate in their kingdom and stain their carpets of fluffy white clouds and giant's pea trees. I love the snake because it dances looking us straight in the eye, it sheds its skin and leaves quietly.

And you, dear Zainab, I asked her. Was your father a roamer or your mother a weaver of ropes?

Yes, she said, my father roamed. He lost his home and became stateless at the age of eighteen. His land was taken and he wandered for a while. But when he met my mother, he stayed and worked and prayed and raised us well.

And your mother, I asked.

I won't talk about my mother or her ordinary life, but feel free, the next time we meet, to go on about yours. And with that, Zainab was gone.

BOAT

MY CAR, OR what I call my boat, or sometimes my airplane, my home, or my library, is always clean, always shiny and swept and taken care of, ever ready for passengers on their way to work or honeymoons, to catch a plane or join a cruise with dancing bands and a hospitable staff of bartenders, captains, and single doctors.

I take pride in the service I provide because I and the likes of me are the carriers of this world, the movers and the linkers. Just try to imagine the fate of any great dynasty without the donkey, the elephant, or the camel's back. I won't start about the horse, but do imagine where the Hyksos would be without their chariots, or the Mohammedan invaders without their hunchbacked servants, those magnificent porters of dates, swords, water, and goat's milk! If it hadn't been for the services of the camel, the defeated Byzantines would still be arguing and trying to determine the sex of angels while complimenting themselves on the intact orifice of Mary.

In my car, I hide an elaborate feather duster and a screwdriver. I leave the feather duster under my seat and the screwdriver at my side.

You see, I took the advice of my friend Mamadou, the Senegalese Spider who hangs out at Café Bolero. He said to me once, Never carry a gun, and don't carry a knife either. Carry a thick stick with ostrich feathers on top, to keep away the filth and the troubled, and a screwdriver to stab with when needed. That way, the police can't accuse you of violent intent. You can always claim that you were defending yourself with whatever happened to be lying around.

Still, I drove for years without carrying either, until my car started to collect dust and fall apart, everything started to rattle and shake, and I feared that the mirrors would fall off and the doors would swing open and the very poor would come in and beg for a free ride.

Like the homeless man I picked up once, on a night when the cold was so cold and the streets were desolate. The man looked as if he was going to collapse. He stood in front of my car, oblivious to the traffic, and the light changed over his shoulder and made him look like a glowing saint. He laid all his plastic bags in the middle of the road, raised his arms like Jesus, and begged me to take him in. I rolled down the window. He approached me and said: There, and pointed to the sky behind him, I am not going far, please, have pity on my old bones. It is cold, I have no money for the bus and I am hungry, I have to get to the shelter, they are serving soup.

I let him in. He sat in the front. He piled the bags on his lap and they covered the dashboard and crossed his seat's border onto mine. He had the smell of the destitute, and he talked about God and his angels. He said he had seen them that night.

Who, I asked.

The angels, he said, the angels. And he started to talk, and his lips flapped against each other like featherless wings, describing angels that land on a strip beside the river. His big black garbage bags rattled with empty cans, as if they were full of trapped devils and snakes. I dropped him under the bridge. He got out and immediately started to run, shouting, I will pray for you, I will pray for you, and his bags bounced off his rushing heels.

Minutes later, when I was making change for a client, I found that the man who had promised me prayers must have slipped his hand out from under his bags and stolen my cash. And the client, who had been telling me all about his kid's school and his wife, and who had been complaining about the high crime rate in this city, now started to go on about taxi drivers and how they never have change. I think you do it on purpose, the man said, you get a bigger tip that way.

Suspicious, I thought, people are suspicious, inconsiderate citizens.

They all come with large bills. They press them over our shoulders and wave them with a rich man's pride. They get all our change and we get tired of aligning our windows with those of our fellow drivers, flashing fifties at red lights, calling, Brother, do you have change, and we resent stopping at gas stations and buying candy bars to break bills and gain the right to wash our faces in dim, filthy bathrooms with curled toilet paper carpeting the wet floors like morning confetti in the aftermath of carnivals and fairs.

Another time, I picked up a skinny lad who wanted to go to the Garage nightclub. I knew that club. I'd been there once, but that is another story. He shivered and talked and shivered and sniffed. And when I looked in my rearview mirror again, I couldn't see him: I thought he had disappeared right in front of my eyes. And then I checked the bottom of my boat, because I knew that he was the lightweight type who would sink in turbulent waters, and I saw a needle in his hand ready to go.

He waited for the red light before he dove.

I stopped the car and watched over him, small and curled, his hand extending over the back of the seat. The car behind me honked and cursed, but a green light should be neglected at times. I dropped my anchor and my boat sat still, and the horns got louder behind me. But I waited until the needle penetrated his vein. I wanted this floating corpse to have his needle land with precision and not be wasted on muscle or bone, and I wanted him to finish and to leave my car and fly, dance, live, and escape for a short while. I don't judge those who can't dream, those who need to pierce their arms to create different worlds under their skin, because I am fortunate in the tools of my escapes. I could, at any minute, dock my car under a bridge and, like a comic book hero, have my freedom fighter suit slapped on me in no time, fly above the ruins of men, and let my happiness come right into my hand.

Pick it up, I said to him. Do not leave that junk in my car. Show it to me, I said.

He did, and then he opened the door, got out, and walked to the closest wall to embrace it.

GUNS

THERE ARE CERTAIN kinds of men that a driver has to watch out for: Quiet men whose paths have narrowed. Those who have been taken for long rides and sickening turns. Those who bring vomit, misery, lice, and stupor from the stained mattresses of crack houses and jails.

Last night, I picked up a couple.

The man looked like a mean motherfucker. His girlfriend had bags, many shopping bags. She talked and he kept quiet, barely nodding, looking at me in the mirror, then looking outside, closing his eyes, hanging his head under the weight of his girlfriend's babbles and complaints.

A full moon, she said. Tonight, baby, let's go on the roof and look at it.

And then some trivialities about girlfriends and dresses and so forth. The man asked her to shut the fuck up, but that made her shout and shake her index finger in his face. When we arrived, he paid me; he told me to keep the change and I thanked him. He barely acknowledged my thanks. Too cool, too generous, too wealthy, too above women's bitching and the fare's leftovers.

I drove away, arranging the cash inside my pockets, splitting off the large bills and sticking them inside the glove compartment, positioning the coins at my side. I hate it when my pockets jingle with money. Its heaviness reminds me that my thighs will be ground into the seat for many hours to come.

A few blocks later, I glanced in the mirror and saw the tip of a handle on the back seat. The lady had left her bags. I pulled over and searched through them. Everything was too shiny or too wide. If my mother were still alive I would have offered her the glittering outfits to wear on the ropes. If Pinky the clown were still around I would have given him the baggy pants, the baggy shirt, and the colourful hats. It is admirable how humans think of friends and family first in times of looting and quick grabs.

So I retraced my steps and I parked in the middle of the street, not quite remembering which house was theirs. It was late but I honked loudly at all the buildings, hoping that a head or a hand would appear, wave to me, ask me to wait, and rush down the stairs with joy and a reward or even some applause.

The woman came out with her blond, exuberant hair and high heels, and she rushed towards my car shouting, You good man! She opened the back door and grabbed the bags. He'll take care of you, driver. He will. Be generous to the man, Zee, she said to her boyfriend as he came out. Be generous now.

Sure enough, the man walked slowly towards the car and handed me a large bill. But before I could roll up the window, he tapped me on the shoulder and said, Why don't you work with a generous man like myself?

Where and what, I asked.

Right here. You stay in your car, your office, man, and you drive me around. I sit in the back like before and tell you where to go. A few hours a day and I will take care of you big.

Anything illegal, I asked.

Anything illegal, he repeated. What is legal, my man. What is? Is history legal, was Vietnam legal. What the fuck is legal in this universe? Stars eat each other, wolves eat the pigs, and Grandma fucks over Little Red Riding Hood.

Nothing is legal, I agreed.

No doubt, nothing.

I am in, I said.

Be here Monday night. Right here. At eight. And he surprised me with a big smile followed by a fist pound to his heart.

I left and drove for a while. The streets were wet and the water expanded under the pedestrians' stomps. Rain swirled like the halos of pebbles on the face of a pond. I drove in circles as the universe spun and exploded and filled itself with dust and liquid, oblivious to whether I turned left or right or whether I gazed at its prehistoric twinkles and its giant stars.

I drove but I scooped up no customers in this flooded city of the north. I consoled myself thinking that at this hour, sailors and men must be drinking inside bars, eating chips off counters while clouds of flies, giddy on the scent of roasting animals, swirled above the bald-headed, rug-like dizzy oval heads. Then I felt hunger and I stopped.

I entered a fast food joint and went straight to the bathroom. A policeman was taking a leak into the white fountain on the wall. I washed my hands and sensed him weighing me. So I entered the booth and locked the door, fearing that the state would slap me with a ticket for not washing my face, failing to move out of authority's way, or using too much soap that foams and grows bubbles that might pop like gunshots and cause panic and alarm.

I waited until he was gone. And then I left the stall with my belt still undone, looking for the hole in the leather. Finally I buckled up and washed my hands again, killing most of the germs. Some must have escaped, no doubt. I went to the counter and ordered a sandwich and a coffee, and then I decided to drive up the mountain and see if the moon was full or empty.

FATHER

THERE IS NO void, said the bearded lady who raised me after my father's departure and my mother's death. There is only motion, she added, and she asked me to fill a bucket and clean the caravan's wheels.

Your father, she said, led a camel when he first appeared

from beyond the dunes, and carried a stack of rugs and blue stones to chase away the evil eye. He was a merchant and a lover of flight. As soon as your mother laid eyes on him, she was swept away by his life-saving oasis of a smile. His long eyelashes tickled the backs of her ears; his thick, curved eyebrows sliced through her chest like Indian blades. Your father's carpets were always floating above the ground, he never laid his head on the floor, and his eyes were always on the stars. He shifted the wind with his turban and steered his flying rug with his whiskers, she said. He flew around the tent poles above the audiences' exclamation marks and dashes of applause.

My parents met high up on the trapeze, in a joint act that turned into a great success. My mother would fling her rope at his carpet and my father would catch it and shout, Hold on tight, Mariam! (He insisted on changing Mary to the original biblical version of that name.) And she would fly behind him as if gliding on water in space.

But one day, my father met another man with a beard and a long robe. The man, like my father, came from the east. They talked about life, death, and the danger of flight. And then, on a moon-shiny night, my father said that he had become a believer, and that carpets should be pinned to the ground. Carpets are for prayer and not for cunning artists and flying buffoons, the man had said to my father. Carpets are the sacred thin crust that stands between the earth and the heavens. My father put on his old clothing, saddled his camel, rolled up one of his non-flying carpets, and left us. After his departure, none of his carpets would stay on the ground. They swirled around the tents like little hummingbirds, they flew around and sideways and upward in the angles of angels and birds. The only photo of my father was a poster of him sitting on a suspended carpet, legs folded, his moustache curled against a background of clapping monkeys, smiling cats, and painted clowns.

After my father's departure, my mother took to the ropes, and for days she swung, cried, and wailed at the top of the tent. She wove a large web in the sky and trapped clowns and lion tamers, sword swallowers, and the one and only Alligator Man, and dragged them to our little trailer behind the main circus tent.

She would lock me up in a bed of cobwebs and try to hypnotize me to sleep so she could play, but I would wake in a daze, guessing at the arrival of the Wolf Boy or the Skeleton Man. And I would climb onto one of my father's carpets, fly below the ceiling and watch, with a bird's-eye view, my mother tangled in ropes with a fellow trapeze artist, chained beneath the magician's saw, or roaring like a lion under the long leather boots of the animal keeper. And I, who was flattered that the ringmaster was coming to our house, happy to be in the presence of this carnival of flesh, gasps, and pleasurable groans, would lie still on the carpet and watch my mother's acts and, imagining my father on his camel crossing the world, I would happily masturbate.

We always wondered whether he had survived his journey back. After all, the bearded lady said, a camel is a highly visible animal. Camels can't hide, camels are too sluggish to fly, and too patient, too curious, too opinionated, and too stubborn a creature to kneel for robbers, fall to dictators, or flee the cold.

Now when I remember my mother and her collection of bare-assed companions, when I lie back on one of my father's carpets and float above the world, I journey through those ancient lands of guns, trenches, and blood, the troubled lands of Slavs, Germans, Latins, Assyrians, Arabs, Turks, Kurds, and Greeks. In those nations where young men were drafted and women wept and populations were transferred and people starved and burned by the millions, I landed my carpet, I witnessed, I rectified, and I flew again.

BOOKS

How are you, Zainab asked as she appeared, with her books and her combed wet hair, from behind the entrance door.

Long night, I said. The world is a circus and it will always be. By the way, I have a book to show you.

Do you have it on you?

No, it is in my apartment, I said. Why don't you come up and I'll make you a cup of coffee before you leave. A coffee will keep you awake and attentive, because listening to God's words can be confusing, all those contradictions. Personally, I would be afraid to fall into an eternal boredom. Besides, I said, your hair is wet. Maybe you should cover it, or you could wait a bit, have a cup of coffee until it dries, and that way you won't catch a cold.

So considerate and sweet, she said, but I don't have time to come in and I am not done with the stack of books you left at my door last week. I am not sure why you think I would be interested in *The History of Court Jesters* or *The History of the*

Comic Grotesque. Are you trying to tell me something, Fly? My dissertation, may I remind you, is on religion.

But, yes indeed, I think clowns could be an essential addition to your thesis. Is there anything on earth or in heaven more potent than a good dose of mockery and laughter?

Oh, Fly, you take life too seriously, she said, and giggled at her own joke. And don't worry too much about my hair. It should be okay.

Have you or any members of your family been to the black stone for the pilgrimage? I asked her.

What an odd question for an early morning.

I was thinking of my father, who went in the stone's direction.

Is that what you call it now? Zainab asked. A stone?

Well, that is what it is.

What about what it represents?

To whom? I asked.

To some of us humans, she replied. Not all, but a substantial number. But who knows, maybe one day it will be all of us.

Submission?

Conversions, she said, frowning at me.

By love or by might?

Love would be nice.

But before I could bite she followed with, How was your night?

I told her about the man's proposition. She listened and then she asked, But why did you accept?

He said that nothing is legal in this universe and I agreed with him, so I said yes.

There need to be some laws, said Zainab, or everything will go to chaos.

God's laws?

Man's laws, she said, or God's laws, nature's laws, some guidance by something bigger.

Man's laws are self-serving, nature's laws are arbitrary, and God's laws, I proclaimed, are in need of some serious updates.

Such as?

The forbidding of wine, for instance. Granted, I also hate those pretentious "sophisticated" people and their swirling and sniffing and spitting of wine. Shouldn't there be an amendment of some sort by these deities, an appendix, a second or third edition with an introduction by the translator, explaining the harm, or indeed the benefit, of wine? And how about an apologetic statement in defence of the text's irrelevance in this age of great scientific discoveries. Or a treatise on the importance of free love! Definitely, this archaic lot of religious elders needs to take another look at love . . . What's with your ever-absent patriarchal gods? Their laws are becoming as old as dog's tricks.

But maybe they are absent only to you.

Heureusement, I said, and acted like a Frenchman with champagne and flowers in hand. It would certainly be traumatizing to meet any of them. Just the sight of the blood on their hands would make me want to cuff them to my bed and slap the shit out of them . . .

She smiled and almost laughed.

You are a joker, she said. I have to go.

BRAZIL

THE NEXT NIGHT I picked up four drunk numbskulls. They were all wearing white suits for some inexplicable reason, and they were rowdy. When they had finished barraging each other with *fucks* and *oh yeah, oh yeahs*, one of them, maybe to defuse the inner violence of the group, turned to me, the scapegoat, and asked me where I came from.

I knew perfectly well where that question would lead. I said Brazil, because that would turn the conversation to beaches and thongs and, if I was lucky, football and carnivals. They would find something to agree upon, women on beaches, bikini dances and surfing, and *oh yeah* would become words of agreement and *fuck* would regain its literary sense.

But then one of those smartasses looked at my name on the dashboard and started to shout, What kind of Brazilian name is that? You are a fucking towelhead or one of those things there, from the desert and shit, Brazilian my ass, fuck. You are a camel jockey, liar, and I bet you are taking us the long way.

Yeah, one of them shouted, I don't see our hotel yet, buddy. Are you taking us tourists for a ride? We may be from out of town but we're still in our own country! You can't fool us.

I kept quiet while they shouted at me and jeered and became rowdy again.

And one of them, as I pulled up to the hotel, said, Liar, maybe you should go back to BRAZIL, liar. And they all shouted, Brazil my ass! and slammed the door. They didn't want to pay me. Their alcohol breath said to me: We don't pay liars and cheats.

I followed them into the hotel, my Philips hiding in my sleeve, because I had once promised myself that everyone pays. I told them that I would get paid or I would turn their white suits into splashes of red, I would hunt them in bars and wait for them all night if I had to. I am capable of swiftly pulling the bedsheets out from under their sleeping heads without waking them up, I could make their prostitutes appear in their girlfriends' closets, I could substitute their cocaine lines with fishing ropes that sailed up their nostrils and down their brains, or I could simply juggle bowling pins while standing at their Sunday barbecues in the middle of their lawns...But they all shouted, Liar, liar, and walked towards the elevator, except a short guy who stayed behind.

He came to me smiling, pulled out a ten-dollar bill, and handed it to me. He laughed and said: Brazil, good one. Keep the change, buddy. He clapped me on the shoulder and left.

I went back to my car and tucked my screwdriver away beside me.

That same night, I picked up a man who claimed that he had just run away from the mental hospital. He opened the front door and sat next to me, panting. He had run out through the hospital doors as a stretcher—or was it a wheelchair, he muttered—stood between him and the big nurse who wanted to chain him to his bed, and he laughed for a while and showed me the traces of straps around his wrists. I looked carefully but I didn't see any marks. He claimed to be able to escape every straitjacket, or any underwater tank for that matter, because he possessed the knowledge.

What knowledge? I asked him.

All men are trapped, he said, until they hear the call.

Then I asked him where he wanted to go, but he didn't answer. So I pulled over and said, Listen, pal, if you don't tell me where we are going, you might as well get out, because I am not going any farther. You have to give me some of that knowledge and tell me the way.

He panted and said, Stasis is death.

Fine, but until death arrives we shall be moving. Now where will it be?

To Cyprian's Supper, he said.

Well, you're in luck, I know that joint. You are very lucky indeed, because if I didn't have this knowledge you would be back on the street right now, running from the big nurse.

When I asked him if he had any money, he said that his brother was Cyprian, and that he would pay me.

I drove him to the restaurant.

Listen, I said, as I followed him inside. No offence, but don't you think it's a bit of a pretentious name for such a run-down place?

But the man kept on walking as if he hadn't heard me.

The place was a dive; it was so empty there wasn't even any smoke or music to describe. The madman disappeared, to the bathroom, I guessed, though I couldn't see any stairways or doors other than the one we had come in. So I waited at the bar for a while and then finally asked the bartender if he'd seen a man with long hair go by.

The bartender, for once, and contrary to popular images, was not holding a white cloth between his fingers and polishing a glass and lifting it towards the light. He looked at me and then directed his head towards the glass that he was now in fact holding and twisting a piece of cloth inside, and said,

If Lucian promised you drinks or money, you are not getting them from me.

Who is paying me, then? I asked.

Back table, the bartender said.

I looked around and wondered which table he was talking about.

That way, he pointed, with his cloth and his twitching eye.

When I walked to the back, I realized that the room was bigger than I'd thought. I saw a pool table first, then smoke, and another table farther back with two men at it. One of the men was well-built and had tattoos all over his arms. The other appeared older and wore a hat.

They both looked my way and looked surprised.

I am looking for Lucian, I said. He owes me the taxi fare.

Come and join us, the older man said. I'll cover the fare, but first let me get you a drink. What would you like?

A juice, I said.

Juice! He laughed. He is in a bar and the man orders juice. But he waved away the other guy, who went to fetch my drink.

And how is the taxi business?

It gets better once the Carnival starts, I said.

Everyone in this town waits for the Carnival to make their money, but I say that a man should make his own future. Anyway, he continued, I am Cyprian, Lucian's brother, and I am glad Lucian brought you here, because I was thinking... you see, I have a nephew, a kind of... how should I say this without insulting my sister... he is a bit lost. Not up here, he tapped his head, not like Lucian. My nephew is a good kid, but he can't take orders.

You mean he can't deal with authority, I said.

Yeah, you said it. He can't deal with it. He always ends up making a scene. Once he even beat the shit out of his boss... Last year he worked at the Ferris wheel, but then he fought with an old lady who refused to get off after the last round of the day. She told him she could talk to God better up there. My nephew tried to pull her out, but she screamed. So what did he do but start up the wheel and leave her stranded at the top for the whole night. Lucky for my nephew, it didn't rain and the lady eventually fell asleep praying. But still they fired him. I tried to give him a job at the restaurant but he spent most of his time outside, smoking. He likes the fresh air, what can I say? So I thought he might make a good taxi driver.

Your nephew has to pass the taxi exam first, I said.

I will make him study, Cyprian said.

He has to memorize every road and street name. Or he can simply buy the tests from the Chinese restaurant at the corner and memorize the answers.

Could you write down the name of the restaurant? he asked.

I can't remember the exact name. I believe it has something to do with a lotus, or was it Confucius. I passed my test fair and square. I looked behind me, hoping to see Lucian again.

Lucian will be back. Finish your juice... You know, my brother was a genius as a kid. Sometimes he thinks he's a fortune teller, and sometimes a contortionist. I say it is this town that drives everyone crazy. You're from here?

No. I mean, I've been here long enough.

So you've lived through a few Carnivals.

Yes, many.

It may be good for business but it's bad for my brother's head. When they start setting up for the Carnival, he goes back to his fantasies. The rest of the year he barely speaks. What story did he tell you this time? Was it about his escape from the hospital or the story of fighting the beast? That's his favourite.

The hospital story, I said. I have to go.

Well, thank you for your help, and here is the fare.

Thank you for the juice, I said.

Just then Lucian showed up, elated and restless. He moved back and forth around the pool table. Cyprian took off his jacket and handed it to his brother.

Here, Lucian, show the taxi driver your escape trick.

Lucian took his brother's jacket and wrapped himself inside it. He crossed his arms and moved his upper body from right to left, back and forth, back and forth, exactly as if he were trying to liberate himself from a straitjacket.

It saddened me and I left.

ACT TWO

AISHA

AFTER THE BEARDED lady's death, I left her flat and walked, aimless and alone in this new land. It seemed that nothing chained me to the cages of this world anymore. Even wanderers cease to march one day. I walked towards the carnival tents and passed between their arcades and games. I picked up a gun and I shot the floating wooden ducks, and then I filled the clown's mouth with water from my pistol until the balloons filled and burst with sounds of loss and laughter. I walked with a book in my pocket and a hat on my head, and I won every game and marched with a few stuffed animals who hung from my shoulders and consoled me. I picked up another gun, but before I aimed at the bull's eye, the man inside the booth asked me if I was looking for a job.

Maybe, I said.

I see that you know the game.

Yes, I know.

Grow up around the tents?

I nodded.

You can help me for the season, he said.

I agreed.

No need to pocket anything, he said. I will pay you fairly.

We both nodded because we knew that the games were rigged and that whoever worked inside these cages would steal first and fight or take flight later.

And that is how I met Otto. He was working the cage and he hired me.

At night, we shared a tent. When it got dark, he would dress up, take a pickup truck, and leave for the city. He never asked me to come. And I never asked where he went. I would open the stand and he would sleep until the afternoon.

Once, early in the morning, I stepped out of the tent and walked towards the bonfire to prepare a coffee and salvage a piece of bread. I saw a woman sitting next to the fire with a blanket on her shoulders and her hair filled with beads.

I nodded to her. She nodded back and we both looked in silence at the coals glowing from beneath the ashes.

You must be Fly, she said.

Yes, I replied.

I am Otto's friend Aisha.

A beautiful name, I said.

She smiled. Otto tells me that you are a reader.

Otto noticed.

Otto likes you. You two have more in common than you think. Do you know where he goes every night?

Never asked, I said.

He comes to my place. He sits and he works until early in the morning.

What kind of work?

Activism. She said this and nothing more.

I made coffee and gave her a cup, and before I left, she

said to me, Take good care of yourself, Fly. I am sure we will meet again.

WINTER CAME AND the tents came down and the stuffed animals hibernated and the guns ceased to pop and the water clowns closed their mouths for the season, and as I rolled my last shirt into my bag, Otto asked me, Do you have a place to stay?

I will walk for now and decide later.

Aisha told me to tell you that we could lodge you for a while, he said.

When we arrived in Aisha's neighbourhood, Otto pointed out the apartment building. We carried our bags up the stairs.

Aisha kissed me and said, It is a small place but we will make do. You guys relax and catch me later. Otto, are you helping tonight?

He nodded.

Fly, you are welcome to come and help too, Aisha said. The ladies at the centre would be happy to see you. And she winked at me, smiled, and left.

Otto rolled a joint and passed it to me. Have you smoked before?

Yeah, I said.

Started at an early age?

Yeah, I said, and took a long puff and held the smoke in my chest.

Otto put on a jazz LP, then he opened the cupboard and took out a bottle of vodka. Here, comrade, he said, this glass is for you. Jazz and vodka, the fuel of resistance.

In the evening we walked down the street to a school, and Otto told me that Aisha was a social worker and that, two nights each week, she volunteered in a soup kitchen. In the basement of the school, I saw her in an apron serving food to a line of adults and children. The children were loud and their voices echoed against the low ceiling and the wide floor. Some were running in circles, others were fighting over toys, and the rest sat at little tables and ate in silence and with big appetites. Otto knew many people and he introduced me around. He then took two aprons, hung one around my neck, and tied the other around his waist, and we both stood behind tables and served food.

Aisha kept smiling at me and she passed behind me and touched my back and said that the servers ate last, and then, in a lower voice, she added, It is all you can eat. And the ladies behind us laughed and repeated, All you can eat.

I STAYED WITH Otto and Aisha for a few months. They never complained and never asked me to leave. Otto worked on his causes. I would hear him typing through the night. He alternated between the couch and Aisha's bed, and I would sleep in the small room behind the kitchen. Aisha and I exchanged book titles; she was also a reader, like the rest of us. On my birthday, she bought me a cake and a book of short stories by Langston Hughes, *The Ways of White Folks*. And then I blew out a few candles and she turned up the music and invited me to dance.

Aisha and I did the rub-up dance and she held me from behind and rubbed her thighs against my buttocks, and then we switched and I did the same. And Otto sat at the table with a faint smile on his face and drank vodka and watched us dance, his face full of melancholy.

And Aisha called to Otto, Come on lover, step down, show us your moves.

And Otto stood up and danced and Aisha laughed again.

ONCE WHEN OTTO was away, I lay in bed and lowered my zipper and reached for my erection and started to fantasize and pound, and then the door opened and Aisha came in. She saw me and said, No need to be alone, move over, and she took off her shirt and lay her hand on my chest and kissed my neck. After we were done, a fear came to me and a sense of shame and sadness made me want to cry. I said to Aisha, Otto will be here any minute.

She replied, Otto won't mind. Just lock the door and come back to bed and everything will be fine.

MARY

EVERY DAY, I choose a book or two from the massive collection in my apartment and take them with me in my taxi. I may have neglected to tell you that my apartment is filled with books, towers of books stretching up in all directions. When a woman enters my house, a tunnel of books welcomes her, a carnival of heroes bounces from every corner, and I lead her straight through the welcoming applause of writers and mice.

I sit on books, sleep on them, breathe them. I arrange them by character, the colour of their skies, and the circumference of their authors' heads. For instance, James Joyce, because of the size of his skull, is located at the entrance. As for Rousseau, he comes towards the end, right at the window, and that is for two reasons. First, his slim head size, and yes, that is indeed in accordance with my own empirical measurements (to use the British norms of philosophy), and second, because of his ever-constant need to relieve himself and to be close to nature. There is nothing like the cure of fresh air for cases of bladder infection, paranoia, and Cartesian thinking.

In short, I have a system that defies every methodology of documentation ever made or conceived. A library that contains the world, as the blind Argentinean would say. A true mystery that I keep to myself and share only with the likes of Mary, the lover of books.

One night I met Mary in the utmost embarrassing circumstances. Mary, sweet Mary, innocent Mary, Marrrrry, my Mary... she took a ride with her husband in my taxi.

I was working the university side of town, where young college girls chew gum and hail rides to the dancing clubs. On Thursday nights, they come bouncing out in their tight miniskirts and squeeze themselves into the back seat, all talking at the same time, all sharing the same pack of gum. They block my rearview mirror with the redness of their lips, the magnitude of their ever-expanding tropics of hair. At red lights, they all stop their ruminations and strike seductive poses at the reflections of the store windows along the sides of the streets. And the leader of the pack usually sits next to the driver, calling me Mr. Taxi, inquiring about my wasted life, laughing at the clown figurines that occupy my dashboard like drunk toy soldiers in colourful hats. The irritating popping of their chewing gum, the giggling of the chorus in the back, all this shames my tragic path through the busiest street in town, chanting, You will be stuck on Lenaia Street, Sophocles! You will be stuck with these tarty little monkeys giving oral birth to balloons in the shape of apocalyptic nuclear mushroom clouds.

It makes me want to fly as I sit stranded, wishing for a titanic bubble to lift and raise the car up and take us above this street of loud music, past the parade of teenaged boys driving with hands that dangle in the manner of caged animals, their menacing eyes scouring the long thighs above spiked heels.

Mary had sweet legs and thick glasses and she was crying when her man forced himself into my cab beside her. The first thing I said to her was, Is everything okay, ma'am? And her man looked at me in the mirror and said, Yes, everything is okay. Just drive, driver.

To where? I asked.

Take Highway 18 for now, and then I will show you the way.

When a woman cries in my boat, I turn into a sad infant and then a lover of the high, far seas, a daring buccaneer. On these seas, the lower decks of merchants' ships are filled with slaves and captured women. And I heard the whips from behind me lashing at Mary.

All you care about is your damn books, the man was saying. I need to go out, I need to see people. Books, books, fuck books. You spend all your time reading. And you have nothing to say to my friends, nothing to say to me. You sit there with your passive air of superiority. I am tired of this, do you understand?

I looked in my mirror and saw Mary crying. And when the man started to shout in her face and gesture with ominous hands, I pulled the car over to the side of the road. We had reached the edge of the city and were about to enter the suburbs with their flat houses and little gardens. And that is when I grabbed my thick feathered stick from beneath the seat and opened my door and opened his door and grabbed the hater of books by the sleeve, then by the collar, and I pulled him out of my car and pushed him down onto the pavement. I lifted my stick in the air and it fluttered in my hand and against the wind like a menacing bird quaking warnings not to cross, not to enter my rescuing arc, and I closed the doors and drove Mary away. It was raining that night; for days it hadn't stopped raining. And I looked in my rearview mirror and I saw Mary's husband defeated under the rain. And I thought, not all animals should have been saved from the deluge. Some should have drowned, without a doubt.

Mary, sweet Mary, had no place to go to. So I suggested we go to my house.

I don't know you, she said.

Mary, sweet Mary, I said, you have the same name as my mother the trapeze artist. I'll offer you my bed and my books. The neighbours are all quiet at this hour; you will go to sleep among the pages of history. Have no fear. I'll shelter you and then I'll drive away. I'll leave you with many heroes, I'll tear up the pages with villains' names, I'll let the old Spaniard on the skinny horse protect you from the swirling of menacing windmills and evil knights. I'll send Sancho here for some

Chinese and hot sauce from around the corner. And Mary, sweet Mary, please watch your head as you step in; the bookshelves are low and the spiders' abodes can easily break.

When Mary entered my apartment, she barely made it past the first shelf. She smiled and looked and turned pages of books that sprang from the ceiling of the complaining student beneath me, multiplied and tilted sideways by the eastern wind that blew from the Arabic and Persian section (I put them on the same shelves for the obvious historical reasons). Books fell like rain from above, books opened and closed like butterflies' thighs. Books, she said. Look at all these books! And she laughed and walked among the garden of books, and then we took off our fig leaves and made love in the corner, where verses from heaven touched our bare, cracked asses that hopped and bounced like invading horses in holy lands. We flew out of the city and we landed on the page where Moses split the sea and the Jews marched between those suspended mountains of water, hovering, humming on both sides, and the poor expelled merchants wondered if Moses knew what the fuck he was doing. What if his hand got tired and he accidentally dropped his magic cane, or got distracted by a wet desert ass, or lost his sandals, or what if that lush single malt of a God changed his mind again and the fucking Red Sea closed in on them with its menstrual red liquid? There wouldn't be any of them left. And a goy brother from New York, who was holding a big apple in his hand and who was in it for the ride, was heard saying: I hope the motherfucker, that basket river-floater, fucker of Pharaoh's sisters and butcher of Baal the bull god, doesn't fuck it up. And then, as the sea parted, the man from the hood declared, What happened? Shit, I ain't crossing, fuck. Look how muddy the bottom is, full of crabs going sideways and jelly creatures and shit... our sandals will get tangled in all the algae... this lunatic of a fucker is taking us through a quagmire to claim a few olive trees and a herd of goats. Fuck it, I'll just go back and apply for Egyptian citizenship and become a cosmopolitan landed immigrant, I'll sell papyrus on the sidewalk, drive a chariot for hire, or work on them pyramids, yo.

When I was about to go back to my car beneath the building, Mary asked me to stay.

She cried all night and I read poetry to her from a collection that I swiftly pulled from under my mattress. I climbed the walls and, at the risk of sending everything crumbling down on our heads, reached for funny passages in books. I read to her from Hrabal's *Too Loud a Solitude* and she laughed at the character of the uncle, the drunken train operator who rides his train round and round his garden. But then Mary became sad at the passage where books are pulped and destroyed and, like Hrabal, who failed to save all those characters from the stomping of the pulp machine, we went and opened many cans of beer and drank all night and then we kissed, read, and cried until the Kleenex box next to my bed was nearly empty. So I went down to my car and reached for the box on my dashboard and I noticed that the meter was still running. I stopped it and said to myself, One day, I'll make her husband pay for this.

LINDA

MARY LEFT THE next afternoon, and I got in my car and drove downtown. There was a traffic jam because of a crane blocking the way. A man was tying up a banner that said WELCOME TO THE BEST CARNIVAL IN THE WORLD. It is that time of year, said a taxi driver whose car was stuck next to mine, and then he asked me if he could get through because he was late for a house call. I let him pass, but then I saw him pick up the first customer on the street.

It is that time of the year when everyone in this city becomes covered in slimy greed, and the whole market, where the Carnival takes place, becomes a frenzy for the seasonal sellers, the fishers of coins from kids' pockets, the suppliers of intoxicating barrels. Here come the thieves, the hooligans, the charlatans, the sausage makers, and the walking dolls! Let's not forget the walking dolls . . .

At eight in the evening, I picked up two out-of-towners, typical beer-bingeing sports fans come to watch their team play in a foreign land. These empty-headed chicken-wing eaters are all the same. When they win, they get trashed and celebrate on the streets, shouting with joy, We won! But when their team loses, they need to fuck something, or someone, so they shout, Where are the whores? Take me to the whores!

So I told them I would take them to the Corner, as the red-light district here is called.

I drove to the block where my friend Linda usually stands and I spotted her right away. I rolled down my window and called to her, saying, Ms. Pleasure, please, this way. She recognized me, winked at me, and leaned in to deliver her opening phrase, which included the words *you boys, looking,* and *fun.*

Linda looked appealing in her contained, voluptuous way. She was on the plump side, and her thighs stretched and squeezed within the peripheries of a leopard-print skirt that just managed to contain it all. Her pointy heels made her thighs look longer and her shoulders wider. And with her large cleavage, her wavy black hair, and her Spaniard's eyes, round as two big black olives, she looked like she had burst from a place where gypsies had met Arabs and fucked and done the stomp dance for a few centuries.

She opened the passenger door and sat in the front next to me, talking to the boys behind. One of them asked if she had a friend who could join them. Just around the corner, sweetheart, Linda said and smiled. So I drove there. And we stopped. She called her friend over, and a woman came and leaned in the back window. She was a bit rundown, missing a few teeth from either her pimp's repetitive punches or the toll of heroin use through the years. No good, said the boys in the back. Let's find another one.

So we went around the blocks and up the streets. I stopped alongside a few prospects, but no one was to the boys' taste. It is a busy night, Linda said. Between the game and the Carnival crews, most of our beauties are taken. The guys started getting frustrated and hungry. The one with the baseball cap suggested taking turns with Linda. You wait outside while I finish, he told his friend. No, the other said, I go first, I ain't fucking after you. So we drove a few more hunting rounds but then they got too tired and decided to go and eat and call it a night.

When Linda asked them for her money, the boys in the back of my car refused to pay. There were a few fuck yous and motherfuckers back and forth over the seats. Linda told them that she was like an on-call doctor who gets paid by the hour, and what they did within that hour was not her problem. I stopped the car and told the guys they should pay her something for her time.

The one with the baseball cap told me to shut up and yelled at Linda to leave the car and fuck herself.

Pay me or I'll fuck you up, you two fucking faggots, Linda screamed back.

We ain't paying. I didn't feel anything in my dick, did you, Joe? the guy in the cap asked his steroid companion.

Go fuck each other, you look the type, you fucking faggots, Linda said. One of the guys tried to grab her. Linda pulled her hand from her bag and shot pepper spray right in their faces. I closed my eyes, but one of the guys must have taken a swing at Linda, missed her, and hit me on the side of my head.

Linda disappeared. The two guys were wailing, Bitch, motherfucking bitch, my eyes are burning and I can't fucking breathe!

I jumped out of the car, opened the back door, and tried to calm them down, and I told them not to touch their eyes. They were rubbing their eyes and it was making it worse for them. These two, I thought, are no rebels; it is obvious that they have never been on the barricades of protesters and revolutionaries, they have never waved flags through the tear gas of a nation state. They have never charged with stones and sticks to break down the fences that protect the men in suits, the diggers of gold beneath the indigenous's soil, the oil thieves in boardrooms and the politicians behind citadel walls. The first rule of resistance is to keep your eyes open and protect your nose from the smell of defeat when the waft of power comes to separate you from your brothers-in-arms. In my boat that night, I carried two screaming, defeated cheerleaders. And I started thinking to myself, What's with these crowds inside the Roman circuses and arenas, what's with these pissers of beer, steroid-bloated muscle inflators, these Viking hooligans on the shores of the British Isles?

As they cried and wailed, I caught a breeze that led us straight to a gas station. I pulled them one at a time into the bathroom and pried open their lids and poured water straight into their eyes. They must have pronounced the word *bitch* ten thousand times. So while I helped them, I inquired into the true meaning of the word *bitch*. Do you mean bitch as in dog in heat, bitch as in sexually promiscuous, bitch as in assertive, strong, manipulative, go-getting, competitive, conniving, funny, sweet, or bitch as in someone who fucks with your head and makes you blind to the miseries of the world? Two fucking stooges on a red-eye flight, I thought, as I drove them back to their hotel.

When we arrived, I stopped the car and turned off the meter. Now that their eyes were open, I pointed at the meter and they looked stunned by the amount of money they owed me. Fucking hell, said the ball-capped one, we ain't paying you that. Fucking hell, you took us to the wrong bitches, pimp. You could have taken us to some fucking classy joint. Fucking hell! You should have stopped the meter, because in an emergency you shouldn't charge people. It's the law.

Yeah, besides, the other one said, you took the bitch's side as I remember.

I always get paid, I said, and I always take the bitch's side, bitches.

Maybe that's because you're one of them, fucking faggot. Fuck no, you're trying to rip us off. You played with the meter while we were blind. Fuck, hell no, the muscles said.

So I stepped on the gas and drove into the alley behind the hotel. From below my seat I grabbed my feathered stick. I left it low but made it understood that I held something in my hand. Implicit threats are more effective.

I am getting paid, I said, or I'll close back your eyes. I am no bitch, I said. I am the man who always gets paid.

Fuck that, one said, pulling out some bills and throwing them at me. Fuck you, fuck your team, and fuck your town, asshole! And they opened the doors and stepped out and one of them started kicking my headlight. I performed a trick and made my stick disappear inside the sleeve of my coat and·I swirled the ostrich feathers in the air. I walked along the length of my fender and I strutted like the strong rooster I had grown into. I took their wallets, and after I had wiped their blood from my hands, I went back and looked for Linda.

I found her on the same corner. Fredao, her pimp, was standing on the other side of the street. Linda hopped into my car and said, Fly, drive by Fredao, okay? Let him see you. He'll know it's you and won't think you're a customer and ask me for the money later. I drove by Fredao and then around the block. I gave Linda her share of the money I'd taken from the two boys.

She kissed me and said, Not a word to Fredao. I told him I couldn't get them to pay. If he asks you, back me up. Tammer is getting older, she said, and we need the extra money.

Then she asked about Otto and why he'd stopped passing by. The two of them had become good friends over the years. I told her that I hadn't seen him for a while.

Just in case the police tracked us down, we agreed on some story about how these out-of-towners tried to beat up Linda and take my money, and that is why I had to stop them with my feathered stick.

But I never heard from those two defeated boys again. There was nothing in the news about tourists getting robbed, fucked, or punished. Idiots like that are usually too proud to admit defeat. They just go and get drunk and numb their wounds and the next day go to the gym and pump iron and check their muscles in the mirrors. I must admit, I take pleasure in beating men with big, inflated muscles. One can spot them on the streets by the steroids' effects in their eyes. They always look a bit paranoid, and their whole existence becomes about performing to glass audiences in city windows. There is no mirror that they pass and do not greet with a flex of biceps or the slow landing of a leg. Inflated balloons with broken cords, always walking as if they are taking their first step on the moon.

TAMMER

I HAD MET Linda through Otto and Aisha.

Once, when Linda was in rehab, Aisha brought home Tammer, Linda's son, and looked at Otto and said, The kid is staying with us for a while. Tammer had curly hair and big brown eyes; he held a threadbare quilt in his hands and looked at Otto and said, Food. Otto walked him to the kitchen and made him a sandwich. The kid ate and then stayed quiet.

And that's the way it was for several months. While Aisha went to work, Otto, who was unemployed at the time, stayed home and wrote letters to local newspapers and pamphlets for activist organizations. When the kid came home from school, Otto fed him and helped him with his homework, taught him to wash his hands long enough to finish singing "Happy Birthday" twice, and how to brush his teeth. Before tucking him into bed, Otto would read him a bit of Marx's *The Civil War in France*, adding a twist of Orwellian animal characters. The Assembly and the Paris Commune became the pigs barricaded in a hut made of hay and hats, defending themselves with their tusks and with bombs made of smelly little farts. Otto transformed Monsieur Thiers, a royalist statesman in charge of crushing the uprising, into an evil wolf who wanted to tear down the house and eat the pigs with the help of his foreign army of Prussian bears and the blessing of the pontifical greedy slob Pope Zouaves the lion ...

Then one day Aisha phoned Otto from work and said, Pack the kid's suitcase, his mother is back.

When Linda showed up at the door with Aisha, she was skinny and had only a plastic bag of clothes in her hand. Tammer stood looking at her from a distance, and with a distance in his eyes he watched his mother cry.

Come here, baby, she said. Come, I am taking you home. The kid looked at Otto, then his mother, and stood motionless.

Linda cried and said, You remember Mommy. Come, baby, come, and then she walked towards him and knelt down and hugged him hard, and he looked over her shoulder and out of the little window and into the sky.

Aisha held the kid's suitcase with tears in her eyes. She handed it to Otto and Otto opened the door and followed the family out into the hallway.

Linda, he said, please call us if Tammer needs anything. He is a special kid, and him being in our lives...bring him here anytime, our door is always open.

I might, Linda said, taking the small suitcase. I just might. You are good people.

BOLERO

ON MONDAY, I was outside the man's house by eight. I was tired and my eye was still red from the sports fan's punch in the face, and after ten minutes of waiting I was ready to leave. But at exactly eight fifteen I saw the man swaggering towards me.

You're good with roads? he asked.

I am the best around.

That is what I want to hear, the man said. Take me to the Financial District.

Before each stop he gave me a corner, never an address. He'd ask me to wait, then he'd disappear for a few minutes and come back. Once in a while I saw him shake hands quickly with a bureaucrat in a suit or some other variety of shady character.

Sometimes I took a shortcut and drove through back streets, between buildings, and down alleys, and he was impressed with that. I knew exactly what he was doing. He was collecting money and checking on his dealers and I was driving him around.

At one point he asked my name.

I said, Call me Fly.

He laughed. I like this guy, he is careful. And then he said to me, You are a man of contradictions, Fly. You are sometimes honest and other times not.

I smiled.

Why didn't you keep the bags the other day, man? There was some good, expensive clothing in there.

I have no girlfriend, I said.

He laughed again and handed me a large bill. Yeah, a real fly you are. I'll call you when I need you. You're okay with that?

Yes, I am.

Cool. Now fly, Fly.

I WAS HUNGRY, so I decided to stop at Café Bolero. I sat, ate, and joined the spiders' tables and heard them discussing their rides, their catches in between the swinging of the car doors. I like to listen to them when they are dreaming of houses back in the mountains and overseas. They lace, twist, knit, intertwine schemes; they braid, plait, loop their stories in chains of truth and lies; and then they point, signal, motion, gesticulate, wave, indicate roads, long and short ways, clients who sat, talked, shouted, cried, and escaped.

There was music coming from the ceiling or from somewhere above the tables.

Number 53, the Dancing Spider, as I call him, was standing in the line for food and swaying lightly to the sound of knives and forks. Every year on Carnival nights, the Dancing Spider retires his car around eleven and goes down to Club Ballayou. He dances the balla balla and the bachata and the rumba with contingents of women. These ladies, who live in remote areas of the countryside, have bused in from far and wide to dance at the notorious Ballayou. Married and unmarried, middle-aged, nicely round and voluptuous, they are tired of Sam and Bob on the TV, tired of fantasizing about bubbly virtual heroes on daytime soap operas. These ladies want to dance, they want to get down with the real thing, they want to feel thighs and biceps. There is no substitute for the commotion of the tangible, the smells and secretions of the flesh, the large arms of a worker, the balancing of the heels, and the twisting of the dancing rooms.

The Ballayou is the dark, glittering star of the north, the place where love prevails across the barrier of oceans and the petty divide of culture. It is the opener of eyes and of uptight, reluctant, austere asses. Legend has it that every woman will be invited for a dance or two, and no woman will ever leave alone at the end of the night. The ladies will have the chance to parade their heels on tables surrounded by dark men, with blinking eyes and lips and tongues stretched to scoop every drip of liquid nectar that falls from above. Dogs are women's best friends, and these stray dogs, who have navigated north in the direction of the tail of the Big Bear of the Milky Way, are thirsty African jackals, desert Arabs, stomping gypsies,

and seasoned Latinos howling with anticipation for the luscious, the plump, the healthy, the bumptious, the tubby, the
generous. These dogs wait with the smiles of the hungry
and the jingling hips of dancing warriors, the burned lips
of sweet-talkers with empty, vacant pockets. They gather
at the Ballayou like belugas during a feeding frenzy in the
Arctic. They come with the charm of the poor and a love for
the curvaceous. They come in defiance of the closure of orifices and in celebration of the openness of mouths and ears,
and of radiant pot-bellies under the suns of luminous phal-
luses. These immigrants are fast, young, handsome dancers
by night and slaughterhouse workers, construction workers,
dishwashers, and taxi drivers by day. They are fishers who
grew up in countries of godlike beaches and generous suns.
They know the drill. As kids they watched their cousins and
older brothers courting northern women, sweeping them off
on their small Vespas as soon as the air-conditioned tourist
buses landed on the surface of the southern moon. One small
step for the northern kind, one large step for the hungry dogs.
A woman, these men will tell you, all she needs is a bit of
attention, a lovable smile, and the dance of a lifetime. Inside
the Ballayou, one strolls beneath plastic coconut trees, beside
stools covered in tiger skin, tables laid with Moroccan tin
trays, and a tall lady bartender by the name of Jinna B., with a
big afro and a magnificent bust. And men, gracious men, who
will sweep up a lady's hand in no time and lead her to a dance.

Listen, Number 53 will tell you, with animated hands. It is
like you being the passenger and the beautiful lady being the
night driver. If you're a good night driver, when you see someone hailing a taxi late at night, you never stop right next to the

client. You park a few metres away and let the client come to you. This gives you time to check out his walk, his clothes, even the matter of his breath. No one wants to take drunks in his cab; they will just puke and you will have to spend hours cleaning the car and lose your whole night's earnings. A drunk passenger will pass out on you and you might have to guess where he lives by fumbling in his jacket for a wallet, slapping him in the face to revive him, shaking him by his tie for a confession.

The same thing with the ladies, gentlemen. You have to give them time to observe you, assess your walk... and do not forget to shine a smile on your face... choose a lady, lock your eyes with hers, show your friendly teeth, walk straight, never wobble, never hesitate, and when you are there, slowly and gently pull her by the hand towards the dance floor. Move your hips slowly, hold her waist and then let go, hold her hand and brush her waist again. Be attentive, dance with her in mind. Be as suave as a quiet wave. Do not forget your own hips: shake them sideways and never back and forth. Shine your shoes, clean your ears, always have a nice ironed suit on and no hat, it will cast a shadow on your own beautiful eyes.

THE STAGE

AFTER I'D EATEN I left the Bolero and went back to the streets.

Customers came in and out of my car. Some were silent, some were polite, a few were busy talking to each other about the Carnival and work and life. I encountered the usual old lady with groceries, the lost tourist, the businessman.

Then two guys, a couple, I assumed, got in, softly bickering with each other. It is hard not to listen to others' quarrels. A quarrel imposes itself on your hearing. A quarrel is made of little ultrasonic waves that can be heard and felt through earplugs, dreams of distraction, and even, one might say, the low, ever-present humming of reverberating erections.

In this case, it was a quarrel about money. The older, bald guy seemed to be supporting the younger one, who, from what I gathered, was an opera singer.

You insult me all the time lately, the young man said.

No, you are sensitive, very sensitive lately.

I am poor and my career is going nowhere. Who wants to be an opera singer in these times except crazy romantics like me? So I have a right to be sensitive. I am sensitive.

You are constantly irritated. You have the right to be sensitive in your art, but not with your lover.

My keeper, more like it.

No one is asking you to stay, though I would be sad if you left.

No, you wouldn't, you would just keep some other young man.

I am not keeping you in any way.

Well, you know I will be on the street if I leave you. And you know I have nowhere to go in this city. You are keeping me.

You are keeping yourself.

Well. Then, if I have a choice, I should just take it and make do. Taxi, stop here, please, the young man said.

Taxi driver, go on, do not stop, the older man said.

Stop, please, the younger man said.

Driver, carry on, the older man said.

Stop, please! the young man shouted.

Carry on, I am paying your fare, driver, said the older man firmly.

I have to stop when a passenger asks me to, I said, it is the law. I wasn't actually sure that it was, but I make my own laws to encourage people to flee their confinements and chains. I stopped at the next corner.

Don't go, the older one said, as he held the young man's hand.

The young man started to cry. You know I left everything for you, he said. You made me come here. And live with you. You promised to support me until I got on a roll. You know how important it is for me to sing onstage. And I have the sense that you've lost patience. You want me to leave.

All I want is to make you fly, my love.

Don't call me that. Not now.

My love.

You're making me cry.

My love, my love, my love.

See, now my whole face is full of tears. I hate tears. But you like tears and you never shed any.

The older man started to look for his handkerchief. I turned and offered them my box of Kleenex.

Thank you, driver, the young man said, and they both giggled and then laughed and held each other in the back seat of my car.

The older man paid. And then he took some more money, a large tip, and handed it to me.

This is for your trouble, he said, and I watched them both leave under a full moon and over the wet streets.

TARGET

THE TIP BROUGHT my night's total to about fifty dollars. I had given myself a target: once I reached a hundred, I would call it a night and go back home, check in with the spider on the wall, call Mary, and then read a book and masturbate.

I possess an arsenal of books, a stack of which can be found on the lowest shelf, next to my carpet, within reach to incite my tendencies to sin and to awake my fist into motion. That particular shelf contains a respectable and varied literature that once belonged to the bearded lady. Books such as *L'immoraliste*, *L'histoire de l'oeil*, and *La chatte*, all of them serving me well in times of escape and need. There are also some that I inherited from a professor who left me his vast library. Thus I am able to reach for such studies as *An Unhurried View of Erotica*, by Ralph Ginzburg, *The Housewife's Handbook on Selective Promiscuity*, by Rey Anthony, and Restif de La Bretonne's *Pleasures and Follies of a Good-natured Libertine*. And for a less highbrow selection of work, which I assure you is as effective and as pleasing at times, I help myself to any of the following: *The Adventures of a Nurse Called Lily*, *The Maid with the Golden Whip*, or *A Stroll on Red Boulevard*. Or, to move to a selection of religious and ascetic pleasures, *The Private Diary of a Crusader's Wife* and *The Holy Howl*. But my favourite, as yet, in this area of studies is exemplified by *The Flogging Trilogy*, which can also be found on this most accessible shelf. The trilogy exists in three impeccable first editions: *The Art of Flagellation for the Perverse*, *The Art of Flagellation for the Perverse and Pious*, and, finally, *The Art of Transcendental Flagellation*, which in my opinion would be a masterpiece were it not for the long and unnecessary treatise on how to acquire an oxtail and shape it into a whip.

But before I had the chance to ignite my engine and drive home towards my flamboyant collection and lie down on my father's carpet and "read," a man entered my car. He smelled of expensive cologne and he wore a high white collar, a silk suit, and an eccentric-looking hat that blocked my view of the rear window. What is this, it must be a theatre night, I thought to myself as I drove my car through high and low streets, as I crossed under sporadic city lights and the open, inviting curtains of bedroom windows.

Driver, the man said, in what sounded like a fake British accent, or was it a South African accent, or maybe an Australian accent, who knows and who cares about these subtleties anyway, they are all the product of the same boats and empire—have you ever been in an accident?

Yes indeed, I said. Many, as a matter of fact.

Do tell, driver.

Well, I said, once I was waiting at a red light right next to another taxi. Across the intersection, halfway down the block, there was this lady in a long fur coat and a fur hat. She was in high heels and was waving at us. And when she waved, all her jewels shone and sent us ultraviolet signals. You see, she didn't specify which taxi she wanted. Obviously she didn't care. She would get into the first cab that reached her. She was like evolution: she had no preference besides speed, performance, and availability. I glanced at the taxi driver beside me, and he gave me the finger. Now, the other driver had an advantage: he was on the sidewalk side of the street. But I told myself that I'd rather die than let this fucker, excuse my language, get the fare.

Foul language is fine with me. Just go ahead and *fuck* all you want, the man said.

Indeed, I replied. So when the light turned green, I stepped on the gas. I was ahead but, like I said, he had the advantage, so I swung my car to the side to block my adversary's way. He braked, but he still hit me on the back door, on the side where you are sitting now, in fact. We stopped and got out of our cars. He took a swing at me. It was unexpected. I went back to my car and got a certain feathered stick I carry with me in case of emergencies, but he had already pulled a knife and was coming at me. I swung the stick and hit his shoulder but he was close enough to slice me right here, on my hand; you can't see the scar because of my horse tattoo. I swung my stick and I bashed the shit out of him, sir. You should have seen him drop his knife and start begging. I looked for the lady, but she was hurrying into another car. So I drove straight to the house of a friend of mine who is a nurse. He cleaned the wound and stitched me without anesthesia.

Did that hurt? the man asked.

Yes, it did.

So let me ask you, driver, how do you feel about pain?

You mean, in general?

Let's say in the philosophical sense.

I say the winner gets to see the loser suffer.

Is the suffering of others enjoyable to watch?

It could be, I said.

What do you think of people who get entertained, even excited, by watching others' pain? Do you know what I am getting at?

Like chains, kissing boots, bondage, and so on?

Yes indeed. A very perceptive driver you are.

It is a fact that many cultures turn pain into a legitimate spectacle, I said.

How about voluntary subjugation, he asked. Is that legitimate?

I guess, when you think about it, this is where the so-called sexual liberation movement and the religious self-floggers intersect. The ancient Christians walked happily towards the lions' smiles, and some flogged themselves. And so do some Muslim sects to this day. I am not sure what benefits might come to the man who willingly consents to pain, sir. But there must be some convictions and pleasures involved.

So we shall respect those convictions, driver, are you saying? Let me ask you this. If you were a Roman, would you have attended any of those spectacles?

I would think so, sir. They would have seemed perfectly legitimate to me. We are all the products and the victims of our own upbringing, until we reflect, refuse, and rebel.

Would you attend any similar event in the present, as we speak?

I pulled over and turned to face the man. I smiled and said: If I can leave the meter on and charge for it, yes indeed. And who knows, I might also be rewarded with a large, generous tip.

Why not? Why not, indeed. Smarter than I ever thought, my dear chap. Seek and you shall find.

We drove down to the port. Below the quay there was what looked like a wooden castle, or maybe a mill, or a monster. It was getting late in the morning and I was tired, and when I get tired, I imagine the most spectacular things.

I kept my meter running, shut off the engine, and followed the man.

There was a small window beside the door. The man whispered what must have been a password and, seconds later, a giant in leather opened the door and ushered us in.

It was dark inside, but at the entrance there was a large cage with a few men, half-naked, with collars around their necks. They were all behaving like dogs. One of them was on his knees, sniffing the others and whimpering, one was in the corner howling, another was barking and showing his teeth. They each had long leashes and leather straps crossing their chests.

Gladiators! I declared.

Hardly, the man said. These, my dear, are slaves brought here by their masters. In complete submission. They are here to obey, to be exchanged and swapped. But let's proceed to the darkrooms, and I urge you to listen and not talk.

It was so dark that all I could detect was forms and shades of hands and body parts clinging to each other. If it hadn't been for the little moans of pleasure and the sounds of friction, they all would have seemed like sluggish mermaids, swimming through smells of sweat and cum, swirling around in duality and happiness.

After we left the darkrooms, we arrived at some faintly lit booths occupied by she-males and cat ladies. We watched as a chained middle-aged man with a hairy back was stomped on by a topless lady in tight pants and a face mask. Another man was on his knees and looked like he was simultaneously in pain and ecstasy. He was breathing heavily inside a leather mask. And then we passed a man in a G-string who tried to grab my ankle, but I kicked myself free and walked away. He shouted after me, Fag, fag, come over here, fag, I know you want it. I gave him the finger and puffed myself up like an ant ready to fight.

We began climbing a flight of stairs, and halfway up I saw a giant swing, decorated with flowers that climbed along its ropes. Yes, my dear driver, said the man, when I asked him about it. This is a swing, but use your playfulness and extend your imagination. You call it a swing, but I call it the Beautiful Tide. This world is all about, how should I put it, *Va et vient*, as the French would say . . . And that is when I saw a pinball machine in the corner. A pinball machine! I shouted, in excitement and surprise. Yes, the man said, that is for the bored, the rejected, those who have become immune to life's joys. As we proceeded up the stairs, we passed a few men chained to the railing. One of them was in his underwear, asleep against the metal; another counted, out loud, every step we took. As soon as we reached the top of the stairs, the chained man shouted, Let it roll, Sisyphus!

We entered an open space with many people, drunk, dancing, smoking in each other's laps. In a corner was a large screen with Marlene Dietrich singing in *The Blue Angel*; on a monitor opposite was a loop of two dogs stuck to each other, fucking.

In between, a crowd was gathered around a man getting fist-fucked by a masked woman with long feathers on her head. There was a large bucket of lubrication next to the woman's feet that she frequently dipped her hand into. The man was howling. The man was loud!

My client turned to me and said, How about those Christians, at least they thought that the circus would soon end and they would go straight to heaven, but here, the pain must seem eternal.

It does remind me of passages from the *Inferno*, I said.

Dante never cared about pain, he wanted revenge. Here, there is nothing personal. But let me assure you, many of the ruling elites of our time can be found here. There is nothing like seeing a judge asking for forgiveness, an evangelist screaming OH MERCY, or a doctor opening wide. Everyone loves a comedy, my dear. It is divine.

Dear driver, he said, feel free to indulge yourself in any of the facilities, or, if you choose not to, have no fear, there is no judgment or obligation, you may wait in the guest lounge and order whatever you like. The drinks are on me.

So I went to the lounge and I sat at the bar. There was another man, smoking and keeping to himself. He gave me a quick look and then he leaned towards me. *T'as une tête d'arabe comme moi*, he said, and smiled. Taxi? he asked.

Yes, how did you know?

I saw a taxi outside. And you are sitting in the visitors' quarters and not inside with the animals. Like dogs, they are all on their knees like dogs. *Ils sont pourris, mon ami. Une société de chiens ici. Comme des chiens.*

My name is Cide Hamete Benengeli, he said. You can call me Hamete. No, not Hamlet, it is Hamete. I am a taxi driver too; my car is parked beside yours. I drive a rich person here once or twice a week. Sometimes, when it is cold, I come inside to save on gas, but in the summer I always wait outside. I prefer to be in my car than here in this dirt, but with four kids and a wife it is hard to refuse the money ... I never say a word to my wife about what I see here. I sit, smoke, and think of my kids. I am going to take my daughters back to the old country. This is no place for my children ... The lady pays me very well and that is why I tolerate these scenes of debauchery, why I sit here and wait and let the meter run in my car. *Ça va pas rester comme ça, mon ami. Ça va éclater. L'occident est pourri*, he said.

I offered Hamete a drink. He told me he never touched the stuff here, not because he abstains, but because he was afraid to get a disease from the glasses. After this, he said, I go straight home and clean myself and I throw all my clothes in the laundry and I wash them myself. I don't let my kids touch me before I shower and change my clothes. You might think that the occidentals would have learned how to cleanse themselves after all these centuries of plague and decadence, but if you ask me, they are still dirty.

After a few hours my client came back and said, Let's go. I was never too fond of dogs.

On the way out, my client stopped to recover his coat, and then he chatted with a young man who had a belt of beads on his waist and a diminutive see-through piece of cloth around his genitals. As I waited, I noticed a guest book on a small table. It was opened to a page full of inscriptions; beside it lay a pen shaped like a feather.

I picked up the pen and it was light as a…well…I proceeded to write a long letter in which I thanked the establishment for the moving experience, for the opportunity to witness it through this communal tunnel of the senses, and I mentioned the necessity of the symbolic and, if one so chooses, the experiential as well in the enactment of this lesser existence, the degeneration of all that is tangible, the howl of dogs, the chains of entrapment, the need to personify the fate of men in this inferior world…and as I was about to compose some verses on the subject of the obscurity of entanglement in relation to the scarcity of light, my client tapped me on the shoulder and said, My dear fellow, I am flattered that these dungeons of love have given you some inspiration, but I believe your meter is still running and I do need to get home and release myself from the tight feeling in my chest, literally, that is.

I drove the "British" man back to town. He smoked in my car and I didn't object. There was more than two hundred dollars on the meter, and I was sure the tip would be phenomenal, I mean spectacular, fabulous, darrrling (said with a snap of the fingers), and fantastic. I dropped him downtown. He asked for my number.

I'll call you, he said. You are a smart, hard-working man, perceptive indeed. You have the gift of knowing, and to know is to earn! I shall call you, he said, and he gave me a jolly good tip that doubled the fare.

Ta ta, he said, and calmly walked in front of my car and entered a fancy building with a sentinel in a green suit and top hat who rushed to open the door.

CARPET

I DROVE BACK home. The money was enough to let me retire for two nights. In celebration of my wealth, I parked my car and ran upstairs and lay on my carpet. After I'd battled a few barbaric armies, I declared to the people, *Veni, vidi, vici.* The reception in Rome after our successful military campaign was magnificent. The horses, the slaves, the looting, and my proud soldiers shouting my name brought wind to my chest.

The daughter of the king of the Visigoths was among the captured. I made sure that she walked freely. I didn't want her round ankles to be bruised or ringed with marks of blood. I didn't want her hands to get tired from the weight of metal and chains.

After I rested and visited the public baths, I returned to my quarters and asked for her. She came in, defiant, all washed and covered in a long purple gown, her golden hair combed and long, covering her shoulders. Her beauty made me weep. To tempt her, I left a dagger on the steps. And I saw her eyeing it. Proudly she stood there, oblivious to the marble surroundings and all the gold around us. I ordered my guards and my slaves to leave us alone. I walked around her. She was fearless, just like all of her kind. How many of these Germanic tribes had I slaughtered, how many had I enslaved, yet I had never seen such a beauty. I didn't touch her. I walked farther away from the dagger and a sexual thrill came over me. I wanted her to grab the dagger and stab me. I wanted to see her screaming as she plunged it into my chest calling her father's name. Nothing could move me anymore. After all those campaigns, triumphs, and riches, beauty and violence were the only things that could give me a sense of existence. I wanted to ejaculate while the dagger burned my skin and entered me. I wanted to see her face in the ecstasy of ten consecutive, vengeful orgasms as I covered her with my own blood. A multiple coming in the name of her father, whom I had slain in front of her eyes, in memory of the huts that I had burned, the looting, the rapes, the occupations, the forced transfers. I jerked myself off and I came (*veni*) above my father's carpet as I watched the king's daughter rush towards me with the dagger in her hand.

I took a shower that evening. I rested. After my assassination, a civil war had erupted in my room. Killers surfaced from my library, from the kitchen side, to be precise, where all the history books are kept above the sink and beside the cups of coffee. Men howled and women screamed and the sorrow of wars made me reach for my jacket, grab my hat and spin my keys in my fingers, and go down to my taxi to drive through the streets and look for clients.

I picked up a young woman in a short skirt and high heels. When she asked to be dropped at the corner of John Street and Fleece Market Street, I knew exactly where she wanted to go. So I took the liberty of going a little farther and straight to the alley, stopping at the back door of the strip joint. I stopped my meter and waited for the fare.

She pulled out a handful of change, threw it in my face, and said: You think you're smart, you think you know everything. She left before I could apologize and tell her that, after many years of assessing the weight of people and their lives, I had become a knower. One look in my rearview mirror and I recognized wandering animals and the path of their swinging lives. One look at her gestures on the street, the way she held her bag and rushed into the car, and the way she looked fed up with drunk clients and the herd of bureaucrats who come for Friday happy hours, and I knew.

HAIR

THE NEXT DAY around noon, I received a phone call from the dealer.

In an hour, same place. You're taking my woman shopping. Honk and she will come down.

I picked up a couple of clients and then, at quarter to one, I headed over to the apartment of the dealer. I honked my horn and waited. His woman came rushing towards the car. She had a big leather bag with a substantial amount of fake gold dangling from its sides, very colourful attire, and very high heels. She got in and instructed me to drive straight to the main street. Let's shop! she said.

Then, suddenly, I heard her scream and she asked me to stop.

I asked her if she had forgotten anything.

Well, yes. The money.

I circled the block and reached the front of the building again.

Honk, driver. Honk and he'll come down.

So I did until the dealer came out with a mischievous smile on his face. He leaned inside the window and said to his woman, Forgot something?

Come on, baby, show how generous you are.

In my side mirror, I saw the man digging into his pocket and pulling out a large stack of cash.

The whole thing, sweetheart, she said.

But he gave her about half the bundle.

The whole thing, Zee! Come on, I'll do your favourite thing tonight.

I thought there was a sale on, he said. What happened to the sale?

Come on, baby, the taxi man is looking at you.

He gave her two more bills and turned and went back inside the building.

Cheap motherfucker, she said. Driver, make sure he

always pays you. Don't be fooled and don't be shy. Always ask for more. What's your name?

Fly, I said. And yourself.

Sheila, but you can call me Baby Jane.

Jane? I asked.

No, Baby Jane.

Right.

Once we arrived, she asked me to come in with her. Which I did. She held my hand and said, My man hates shopping. You like trying on clothes?

I am used to it, I said.

Were you a model?

No, I said, I worked as a performer.

Performer, I like that. I was a dancer, until my baby rescued me.

Ballet dancer?

No, lap dancer, she said.

We walked from one store to another. She tried on dresses, shoes, and makeup, and I tried on baggy pants, leather jackets, flashy shirts, shades, and a variety of hats, all on behalf of the dealer.

After a whole afternoon of walking and carrying bags, I drove her to a salon. While she had her hair done, I sat in a café, had a beer, and picked up my book and read for a while. An hour later, I drove back to the salon to pick up Baby Jane, but she was still under the hair dryer, flipping through a fashion magazine.

So I waited outside and smoked. I leaned against an electric pole and watched the city people go by. The sky turned grey and it started to rain. The people of the city took shelter at the sides of the road and under the awnings. My shoes got big and wet and the bottoms of my pants got heavy. So I rolled my pants up, buttoned my collar, walked back to my car and reached for my rainbow umbrella, put a smile on my face, and waited for the lady's hair to roll and turn crispy and dry.

After our escapade of bags, shoes, and hair, I returned Baby Jane to her door. She retrieved the keys from her purse easily, because her hands where utterly empty and I carried the whole lot of shopping bags. I could tell she liked the service by the way she handed me all the cash that was left in her purse. Good help you are, Fly! Just leave everything at the door. My man will come and take it upstairs.

So I took the money and went straight to the Bolero, where it was fish and chips day. My favourite day of all.

DOG

I CAN ALWAYS tell by the strip of cars and lanterns in front of the Bolero who is inside. Some of the spiders always sit together and eat at the same time; they regulate their lives around the filling of their bellies and the smoking of their cigarettes.

Then there is us, the flies, who come and go at all hours.

Sometimes we have to settle for a seat at the counter and endure the wafts of heat that precipitate from the kitchen. And once in a while we have to eat in close proximity to Number 66. He is a fixture in this place. The only words he ever utters are to the owner's daughter behind the counter: Thank you, dear. He breathes the food vapours and orders nothing but coffee. He is neither a spider nor a fly, but a ghost somewhere in between the living and the dead. He is hardly even seen driving. It is said that when he asked for his lantern number at the taxi office, he requested three sixes, but the office refused. They said it would spook the clients. So he settled for two sixes and sits there waiting for the third six to come.

I was lucky that night to find a seat at a table and not have to endure the discomfort of the bar stool and the silence of devils. I joined a few of the spiders and listened to their tales. Number 15 got molested by the taxi inspector the other day, Number 101 was saying. Tell the story, tell them, 101 urged 15.

Number 15 shrugged. I let her do her thing, he said, just like you guys advised me to.

The taxi inspector likes to molest taxi drivers and everyone knows this. At the red lights, she stops and takes a look at you. If she is planning to see you later, she will smile and leave. And then, somehow, she will trace you by your lantern or your friends or, if you are a spider, she will come to the Bolero and ask the waitress the hour of your feeding and the table of your choice. She will come to your car, flash her badge, and sit next to you, and then she will calmly put her hand on your thigh and close to your groin while she busies herself checking your papers and the cleanliness of your vehicle. And then she leaves.

If you push her hand away, you will be fucked with a big fine. If you reciprocate, it might lead to a sexual harassment complaint on her part. If you meet her eyes, she will instruct you to keep your eyes on the road, even though your car is parked and not moving. I suspect that she is conducting a survey, trying to find the relationship between machine operators and the length of their parts. She poses her hand somewhere between your crotch and your knee and she waits until your organ gets longer and wider and then she eyeballs it and notes down your name, permit number, and the length of your shift.

But once, after 66 had finished his coffee and was on his way out of the Bolero, the taxi inspector got in his cab. Two minutes later, she slammed out, her face pale, and she rushed back inside the Bolero, asked for water, and immediately left. It is said that as soon as she got in his car, Number 66 told her the names of her three nieces and nephews and the place where her father was buried. And then he described her child-hood village and the coat she wore as a kid when she tortured the neighbour's cat.

When the inspector sat next to me, Number 15 told us, I stayed still. And when she finished, I pulled out a cigarette, lit it, and then withdrew a Kleenex and offered it to her. She was furious. She made me get out and she searched my car. She reclined every seat. She had a flashlight, she dived under the seats and she looked everywhere. When I asked her what she was searching for, she said drugs. She made me open the trunk. I had a box of groceries in there that I was taking home to my wife. She gave me a fine. She said that the trunk should be empty and available for clients to stow their luggage during airport rides, for their grocery bags if needed, their dead bod-ies and their fucking I don't know what. She was pissed with me and she said that she would find me again to check my trunk and it had better be empty. Sure enough, she stopped me the next day as I was turning onto Horn Street. She opened the trunk and she found two big boxes of Kleenex in there.

She was furious, Number 15 said, and everyone laughed.

She wanted to give me another ticket, but I told her that I was on my way to a big delivery and that I could prove it. That she could come with me to the house and see it with her own eyes, and all the while I kept touching my own thigh, up and down.

Dog, Number 101 said as he laughed, and everyone was laughing.

TURKS

MORNING. I WAITED for Zainab, but she didn't appear. I went up to my place and lay on the bed, but I couldn't sleep and I was horny as a Turk.

So I stretched out on my father's flying carpet and fancied myself a Turkish soldier in the last days before the Battle of Gallipoli. In Istanbul, I went to the café, smoked, and waited for people I knew to arrive. The backgammon dice and the sound of stones slamming against the wooden tables made me wonder if I would ever play the game again. I could see the minarets of the Blue Mosque. My pious mother had asked me to go and pray, but I preferred to spend what might be my last hours walking the neighbourhood and its streets.

I had never met an Australian. I did not even know who they were, what their women were like, but soon I'd go to the battlefield to meet those soldiers who had come from far away to conquer our land. My grandfather had been a Janissary and a mighty warrior. As a child he was kidnapped by the Turks from the lands of the Slavs. He was converted to Islam and turned into an elite fighter in the sultan's army. He was as white-skinned as a Slav might be. And I turned out as blond as him, blue-eyed. Light-skinned, like the Christians are. I regretted that I had not married. Dying young without feeling the body of a woman is a pity. Dying in those awful trenches without experiencing the warmth of a woman even for one night would be my last regret.

So I, the Turkish soldier, walked to the Blue Mosque to see the Sheikh and ask his advice on the matter. Maybe I could hastily get married to someone he might recommend. He said to me: At the rate our soldiers are dying on the battlefield, it would be irresponsible to leave a young girl behind. But calm down, my friend, I know of a widow who might be willing to marry without delay. The *kouttab* could be made in a few minutes. I'll go see her tonight; if she agrees and you can provide a *meher* for her and her children, all should be well. Come tomorrow.

The next morning, I went back to see the Sheikh, and sure enough, there was a woman waiting in the back seats of the mosque, in the women's quarter. We got married and I immediately moved into her house. Her kids were very young; she was still nursing one of them. Her husband had died in battle and now she was in need, she had no one, no family to take care of her. That night she fed me and never looked me in the eyes, but towards the end of the evening, when the kids went to sleep, we both retreated in silence to the bedroom. Her husband's clothing still hung against the wall. I was nervous. I had never touched a woman before. But here she was all naked under the covers of the bed. I decided to get under the sheets with my clothes on. But she stopped me and started to undress me and touch my chest, looking me straight in the eyes. When my organ got strong, she held it in her hand and directed me slowly. She knew that I didn't know how. The Sheikh, I thought, must have briefed her. I ejaculated almost as soon as I penetrated her. She pulled me to her side and said, If you come back alive, this is your home and this is where more pleasure will come your way.

During the battle, I pitied those poor Australians. They threw themselves onto the beaches and under our guns, and we massacred them by the thousands. We were triumphant... Long live Ataturk, everyone shouted, the mighty commander who has saved our land!

As my father's carpet reached the ceiling, I looked at the shores and I ejaculated in between the two colliding histories and felt fortunate to be alive, lucky to have water and to be able to clean myself after these horrific battles that leave you smeared with mud, blood, wire cuts, and bruises.

I finally slept. I woke up in the late afternoon. The sun was already starting to weaken and prepare for an early retirement into the sea, or behind a mountain and a cloud or a silhouette of a couple holding hands and cones of ice cream, or bags of peanuts or bananas to feed the monkey urges inside them and make them hop from one palm tree to the next, until they reached the shore and then held hands again and shared more peanuts. I still had a couple of hours before my shift, and I hesitated between leaving the bed and brushing my teeth, extending my arm to the nearby bookshelf to arbitrarily grab a book and read, or completing the fantasy that I'd started and spreading my semen against the sunset and the crooked, wobbly shore. I read. Then I stood up and brushed my teeth and relieved myself from the burden of liquid I'd amassed during my day's sleep while the kids played and shouted in the neighbourhood's backyards.

Around six in the evening, I poured myself a glass of red juice. All was quiet; the large spider had captured a moth. I turned off the light and decided to leave before the spider struck with its fangs and extracted the liquid from its mummified prey. One big meal is enough for one night of feeding, I thought. Too much food will make you fat as doctors, complacent as accomplished writers, sluggish like Roman orgy-goers, round like dictators' wives, wobbly like elephants, circular like tents, spherical like lanterns, and cylindrical like machine operators.

But I also left because the books were starting to move and the mice in my place were getting restless in between the covers. Before the characters started to leave the pages for fear of their ears being nibbled on or losing their toes to those rodents' teeth, I went down to the basement to prepare my ship for the evening sail.

RAIN

I DROVE MY car through a night that was still and calm. The light rain wet the asphalt and the roads shone with the grey shades of people in long, slippery shadows. I could see the colour of my car moving above the water beside a floating Jesus and a flight of wild geese. I drove. It was a surprisingly quiet night; usually with the rain come the slugs, worms, and monstrous umbrellas, resuscitated from inside women's bags, yawning open above men in hats. With the rain, people surface at the edges of the sidewalk, staring into the puddles like hesitant suicides. What has happened tonight, I thought. Where are those seekers of dryness, those god-fearing souls fleeing the apocalyptic floods, where are the wetted carcasses desperate for shelter and ships? I've been driving for an hour and not one soul has entered my car.

I listened to the soft music on the radio. The Carnival is about to start and people must be sticking the last thread and needle into their costumes or practising their dancing steps, or it might simply be that my lantern has gone out. So I stopped and got out and looked at the top of my car, thinking the light bulb was dead or maybe I'd forgotten to secure the lantern. Because once I picked up a woman with whom I had a fight over the fare. She accused me of taking the longest route; she said that I was driving too slowly and taking her through mazes and labyrinths, and she assured me that she always took the same road and that she'd never had to pay that much. So I responded by accusing her of lying, of giving me a hard time, of being suspicious of hard-working men.

I will pay what I usually pay, she said.

You'll never leave my car until you pay the full fare.

Fine, she said, I'll pay and I'll curse you.

I am already cursed, lady, I said. I am cursed to be a sailor and a wanderer and to be stranded on ships of lunatics and fools down in the London River...

What will it be, the little money or the curse? she asked.

You pay me, I said, and then you can spell and pour and babble whatever you like, I'll just scoop it up into my magic box here that is stacked with layers of soft white sheets. In my youth, lady, I also learned a few tricks. I learned how to make assistants, pigeons, and rabbits disappear. I learned that the universe was created in the void of a hat, that it bloomed from the sleeve of a trickster, and that one day it shall disappear again into the blackness of the pigeon's hole. I know all kinds of tricks, lady. I was once called the Surmise Child, but I am also a thrower of knives, a lover of lions, and an opener of lions' cages, and I can tell from your weight that you have a moonless heart and that your vision is veiled by a fog of superstition and avarice. Curse away, because this is your last stop, and be careful when you get down from the car, because you might fall and lose your bag of tricks.

She took money from her purse and spit on it, she mumbled mumbo-jumbo and she looked at me in the rearview mirror and said: Nothing for you today, nothing for you tonight.

And she left and I watched her carry bags that swung in her hands like chickens about to be slaughtered.

That night I drove for hours and, sure enough, not one customer entered my car. So I drove up the mountain for fresh air and I got out and looked to see if the curse had made my car grow horns, fangs, long claws, and beaming eyes, or if it had just become invisible to the world. I walked from wheel to wheel and looked for bones, chicken feet, or blood that might have smeared the fender or the roof. I lit a cigarette, and that is when I noticed that the light bulb of my lantern was off. That was why no customers had waved to me: they all thought that I was occupied, taken, gone for the day, that I had ceased my shift, filled my trunk with people who wouldn't pay, or that I was dim, gloomy, dead, that my car was drifting with the motions of a lost Portuguese boat around the Horn of Africa and down to the cold abyss of the Antarctic.

So I drove my car to Robe, the night mechanic. All the taxi drivers go to him. He is the only mechanic in the city who stays open all night. Robe is capable of changing bulbs, headlights, horns, handles, and mirrors. He is the master of wires and floating lamps. He hardly talks, he just listens to your problem and tells you to wait in line. There I often meet other drivers complaining of how they've lost their night's fares waiting for Robe to fix this or that.

The bathroom in Robe's place is the filthiest of them all. I relieve myself a great distance from the bowl. I heard a story once of a dictator who, on his trip to his own native village, went to use the bathroom at the town hall and found that it was filthy. He summoned the villagers and fired the mayor. The mayor and the inhabitants of the village were a most fortunate lot, because none of them was hanged. I guess dictators know that the last act a hanged man performs is not saying prayers or eating his last meal but releasing a final drop of urine that slimes down to his ankles and falls at the feet of the crowd.

CAMELS

WHILE I WAITED for my car to be fixed, I saw Number 43 having a soft drink on the sidewalk. When I asked him what was wrong with his car, he said that his horn was broken. I joked, You are lucky you are not a ram or you would never procreate. Then I told him about the lady's curse. He said, If I were you, I wouldn't take the matter lightly. I smiled and said, It was just the bulb that needed to be changed.

Number 43 rushed to his car, retrieved a pen, and said to me, Here, call this lady, she will fix your curse. I folded the paper and stuck it in my vest pocket, still smiling at Number 43. He told me stories about cats that knock on your door at night, spiders that take the form and shape of humans, sorceresses with tails, festivities with masks and chicken feet and chains, and blood, certainly blood, offerings.

What about camels and turbans? I asked.

He laughed and laughed, saying, Camels? No camels, and turbans? No turbans, man. The turban-heads only believe in their book. They can't even dance like we do.

But they are the masters of flying carpets, I said.

He roared and laughed and hugged me. He went to his car and pulled out the floor mat and laid it on the ground. Here, sit on it and fly, show me how!

One day, I said, I'll show you the carpet flight.

And he laughed and laughed and held his stomach and laughed some more. He reached through his car window, blasted the music, and danced a bit around the headlights, and then he picked up his mat and got in his car, shouting, Call the lady, call the lady before you get on your carpet and fly! and laughed again and drove away.

The next day, I called the lady. The first thing she did was ask me how I had gotten her number. I told her that the taxi driver had given it to me. She said that was good, because she only worked on a referral basis. She gave me her address and an appointment for the following week.

The night before my appointment, I drove to her house. The lights were off and I thought she must be sleeping. There was no scent of a dog, but even if there had been, I knew the tricks of animal tamers to make dogs lie down, roll onto their backs, and go to sleep. I jumped into her garden and stole the flowers from her backyard. I opened my trunk and the back door and loaded them all inside, and then I drove with the scent of nature at my back. It was a welcome change from the dampness that people bring with their wet feet. I contemplated having a garden in my car: a few cactuses around the dashboard to protect my belongings from petty thieves, a few roses that could spring from the radio and act as receivers to induce clarity of communication between the passengers and the rest of the world. During the period of festivities, I could allow a climbing plant to grow and cover my car in greenery and so contribute to the saving of the planet and consequently the human race . . . and I could grow fruit . . . yes, fruit and vegetables . . . and trees . . . and if I applied myself, I could one day be looking at meadows in my rearview mirror . . . one day . . .

I got home and went up to Zainab's place, and when she opened her door, I started bringing in the flowers and I filled her living room with pots. She was ecstatic, she was smelling them and laughing, and the more I brought in, the more she found the whole thing funny and amusing. And then, when all was settled and my creation was complete, I stood in the middle of her living room and I asked her if we could both get naked between the branches and play doctor and Bible games.

She said, Absolutely not.

THE FORTUNE TELLER had a big smile and she made her eyes look bigger by staring at me as if she was reading my mind. Amateur charlatan, I thought. The taxi driver must be in on it. He must be fucking her. He must be giving references left and right and getting a cut, or some favour or another. Predictable!

And the first thing the clairvoyant asked me was whether I needed to go to the bathroom. An old trick that I knew from the days when I and Pips the magician cheated people out of their money. Ninety-five percent of the time, people will say yes. And when they say yes, the impostor will let slip a faint smile, implying: *Aha! I knew it.* People, of course, will say yes because they are reminded of all that is held inside, and their first reaction is to want to release it. This response is indeed in the tradition of the Freudian subconscious methods of confession, the Socratic formulas for extracting knowledge and vomiting poison, a liquid *a priori*, the spectacular burst of innate consciousness, a gnosis splash. The last drop might well lead us to the release of a soft determinism, the synthesized potential of porcelain hygiene, the painful path of a kidney stone, the magnificent yellow of sunset horizons...Besides, people will likely have travelled from far away and need to relieve themselves. They calculate that they will be stuck for an hour with the unknown while the lady channels dead souls back to the table. I say pissing would clear the mind to meet the other world, and who doesn't wish to travel light! So I said yes, and I followed with a prophetic gesture of my own by saying, Do not tell me, I believe the bathroom is this way. And I glided gracefully towards the source of water and life.

When I returned, she gave me little stones to hold. Each one cost me a few dollars. Precious, she said, when I complained about the price of the stones. Precious stones, she repeated, and then asked me to be quiet as she started to roll her eyes. She ordered me to hold the stones tight and she proceeded to read my chakra, aura, or some other exotic, hazy package. But when she closed her eyes, my inner voice rose and I started to speak in an old lady's voice: Where are the flowers, Florence? Who stole my vases and my flowers?

She jumped, opened her eyes, and said, What did you say?

I squeaked my voice like Mickey Mouse on helium and said, Flowers, who took my garden away?

The fortune teller stayed silent and then suddenly she burst out, Who are you?

The third ring down... I said in my rodent voice.

The fourth ring down... I continued.

The fifth ring down... but not the begonias... not the lilies, Florence!

I suddenly opened my eyes wide and asked her where I was, and I got up and started to drift around, opening the door to her bedroom and wandering among her furniture and her displays of crystal and china. And then I lay on her bed and started to shiver and rub myself.

She shouted, Come back here. Who are you?

I am Zalou from the outer world, I declared, and started to juggle the stones in my hand, tossing them above my head with my eyes closed. The circus of the afterlife! I cried. The caravan from beyond the dunes, the last act, the wisdom of the joker, the bringer of fire and the eater of hell, the evolution from monkey to devil... Fire of ropes and chariots of fire, and here comes your inner spider to wrap you and sacrifice you upon the tabernacles of the gods... WowooooWOOO!

She was confused. And that is when I lay my hand on her thigh and said, Open the petals and let me breathe the smell of the brown roses.

She screamed and said, Leave or I will call the police. Leave now. Just leave...now. Now! And she started to scream even louder, she was hysterical...

I left and walked down the hallway singing the "Scarlet Begonias" song, which went like this...

SHIP

DURING THE NEXT few days, business improved. Organizers, tourists, and vendors were arriving in town for the Carnival and many of them needed rides to their hotels or around the city. And to participate in the general spirit of entertainment and wonder, I bragged to my customers that my car was protected by stones and good omens, that nothing unfortunate would ever happen to my car, that the stone on my dashboard was spirited, gleaming, and no matter how I sped, sailed, or flew, this ship of mine would never sink, because my car was encircled by a kind of chakra that bounced all the evil eyes away.

I had one woman who thought I was mad. At a red light, she threw a bill at me and left without waiting for her change. I had a man who wanted to hear it all: he giggled and kept on saying, How interesting, and giggled some more.

And then I had a well-travelled man who worked for an NGO, a man who went to poor countries to sprinkle some financial aid and, in the process, I suspect, paid himself handsomely, and he told me about his own private driver, who wore a necklace and slept with prostitutes without using any protection. And when my client warned his driver about the diseases he could collect, the driver would show him the necklace that he wore around his neck and say, This protects me.

Just like your car here, my client said to me. I send money and medicine to him now, he added. I think the necklace must have lost its effect. Once, that is all it takes.

When we arrived, my client tapped me on the shoulder and said, Be safe, don't believe in the stone, and he left.

ZAINAB CAME DOWN the stairs and I told her that I had been waiting for her smile to light my morning. Then I asked if she had her lunch in a box, if she had sharpened her pencils, and if she needed a friend to walk her to school.

Are you being flirtatious and cheeky? she asked me, and smiled.

I could carry your books to the train station!

No need, she said, I will walk alone to the train station.

It is good to be late for the train. It gives us the chance to run after it and wave our scarves like in those old Indian movies. And I suggested we go up to my place so I could show her some books.

I'll borrow your books but I won't enter your home.

Oh, the believer's fears!

Oh, the non-believer's dreams, she said, and she glanced at me in defiance.

Cruel for a believer not to have mercy, I said.

Bumptious for a non-believer to hope for a miracle, she said, and smiled.

Sinful for the pious not to give . . .

Futile for a heathen to hope! Any stories? she added, as we both smiled at each other.

Yes indeed, I said. Talking about lost souls and things, last night I passed by Café Bolero, where all the drivers feed themselves between their shifts and spin boastful tales and stories. Number 55, a pious man who fears God and his many laws, got a call from the dispatcher to pick up a client in front of the supermarket. The old lady asked him to carry her groceries to the car. He lifted the bags but, when it came to the case of beer, he refused to touch it. He said that he didn't touch alcohol, be it open or closed. The lady was upset. She asked him to remove her groceries from the trunk and call her another taxi, but he also refused to do that, just in case one of the bags contained a piece of a swine or something else forbidden. So the old lady tried to pick them up herself and now claims to have hurt her back. Both the taxi owner and the driver are being sued. The old lady is well off and now she is bringing some big-shot lawyer to handle the case. Watch it explode in the news! Watch those journalists salivating over Islam and its values. Terrorism, morning shows, secularism versus religion, stand-up comedians, clowns with paper bags blown out of proportion and popped to laughter and applause!

So, Zainab, I concluded, do tell. What do you think?

I have no problem with booze. I am a Muslim and I drink.

Yes, I gathered that. But what do you think?

Obviously, the man's comprehension of the text is very limited and literal.

And yours is multi-layered, you are saying.

Yes, the text can be read on many levels.

Gnosis for the few, I said.

Not for the few, Zainab said, but for the willing and able.

Exclusivity! Mystery! Interpretation that is changeable and

adaptable, I said. Even the most detrimental of verses should be accepted as an allegory for something wiser and bigger?

Indeed.

But Zainab, my dear neighbour, how about some editing, you know, with a long pen that reaches between the continents and other places. I say! A long pen could be a magnificent invention for lawyers and writers alike.

No, she said. Nothing needs to be changed; the verses should simply be read in their proper context.

So we shift from the literal to the poetic, then to the allegorical, when and if necessary? I asked. Change when it is convenient, stasis when it is not...

Look at it as an intellectual challenge, an exercise in reason and imagination, she replied.

Intellectual masturbation, I mumbled.

What was that?

I said, Then let's treat all these holy texts as stories, fictions, and imperfections that could excite us into tears or erections.

Erections, you said, I heard you well this time?

Of thoughts, that is. Intellectual erections.

I have to go, she said. Your sexual insinuations are becoming childish. I'll leave you with your "intellectual" thoughts... She actually made quotation marks with her fingers. Let me ask you, Fly, have you ever taken responsibility for anything? Have you ever thought about settling down, stopping your drifting existence, maybe having someone in your life...getting a dog...having a child?

No, no. Why have children and leave them in the hands of this laughable world? But, Zainab, now that you are late and the train has surely left, I can see the Bollywood actor waving his scarf in farewell, let me walk with you and tell you about the dancing Shakers who once offered to adopt me, after my mother's death. That order of religious men took a vow never to have children, never to bring another soul into this inferior world. And so their whole community consisted of orphaned children who grew up to become dancers and holy men. Christians they were, but they must have gotten a trace of eastern influence from somewhere... Dionysians, Buddhists, Zoroastrians, Sufis, who knows. Deep, deep inside, I suspect they believed that a lesser god rules this earth and that our bodies are unworthy of our spirits, and the light inside us needs to be released somewhere else, not in this pigsty we live in. Anyhow, some of these Shakers were called the dancing Shakers, because they danced and danced.

The circus used to organize parades whenever we arrived in a small town and the Shakers were invited. The circus was often accused by the Church of being sinful, decadent, and even satanic, and the ringmaster thought the Shakers could give us some legitimacy.

Anyway, the gypsies played and we all danced around the fire. A Shaker with a long coat came to me, and held my small hand, and they tossed me from one to the other. And when the music stopped, the man whispered in my ear, Come with me, child, and you shall be saved. I got scared and ran and took refuge between the monkeys and the dogs until the bearded lady came and said, No one will take you from us, and we both cried as we caressed the dogs and held the baby monkey in our arms.

And what has happened to those Shakers now? Zainab asked.

I am glad that I've got your attention; I didn't know that

you were so fond of dancing people, Zainab. Well, to answer
your question: annihilation, disappearance! The government
regulations changed and the dancing Shakers couldn't adopt
anymore. Their community slowly regressed in numbers until
their wish came true. This lesser world is all about reproduc-
tion, as you might well know. Those who cease to duplicate
simply die.

I could give you a book to read on the subject, I continued.
It might well help in your dissertation. There is no harm link-
ing all these religious beliefs to the same delusional source:
the original fear and disappointment of men...but I know
that a pure, enlightened person like you will resist stepping
into my obscure world.

I have to go, Fly.

Wait, let me walk with you and tell you about another
branch of these heretic extinct Christians. This might interest you. These were called the Cathars, and in some circles
they were referred to as buggers...it was said that they refused to have vaginal intercourse. They only had anal sex and
that was an alternative means of contraception, their way of
undermining the holiness of the body and assuring that no
other souls were brought back to this false, degrading world.
Their orgies must have been loud and magnificent. You see
how all religions undermine our anatomy?

Not all religions. Islam has no problem with the body. As a
matter of fact, the body is cherished, cleaned, loved.

Hidden, I added.

I know what you are referring to, Fly. Maybe we should
draw a veil over this conversation, to make use of your own
insinuation. But then...

Enough, stop it, Fly, Zainab interrupted. I really have to go now. I don't want to miss another train. Please go up and sleep. You must be tired from driving all night. Go get some rest. Your mind is wandering and, if I might say so, you seem a bit delusional.

And so Zainab left and I stood still, watching her rushing in the direction of the train station. Her hair was wet and she held a bag over her shoulder.

MIRROR

MARY CALLED AS I was about to climb into bed. She said that she was moving out of her husband's place and she asked if I could meet her. I put my clothes back on, went down to the garage, and drove the car out.

When I got there, she was waiting outside with only one small bag in her hand. She was crying. She got into the front seat and we looked in the mirrors at her husband, who was standing at the front door smoking and watching his wife leaving him.

I should have sat in the back, she said.

I don't think he would remember me. My place? I asked.

I prefer to get a hotel room, she said. But could you stop by your place first and pick me up a few books for the night?

We drove to my apartment and she waited in the car. I came down with a bag of books and then I drove her to a small hotel downtown. When I asked her why she wouldn't stay the night with me, she said that she had to learn to be alone. We arrived and I took her up to her room. I pulled out a bottle of whisky that I'd brought from home and I left it for her on the table next to the bag of books. Food? I asked her. She shook her head no. Should I call you later? I asked.

If you like, she said, and started to cry.

ON THE WAY back I picked up a passenger in front of a different hotel. The porter waved at me and I was surprised that he did, because all those fancy hotels are rigged. The spider drivers have it all secured in a web of bribes and corruption. The porters and the receptionists are at the heart of it. When a client asks for a taxi to the airport, which is a substantial fare, the receptionist informs the porter, who in turn calls the dispatcher, who is also in on it, and the dispatcher calls one of a few chosen spiders to take the client to the airport. The driver gets the big fare and everyone gets a little something. These few spiders have their rigs set up in most if not all of the big hotels in town, and they all make good money. But once in a while, if the spiders are too busy or too late, the porter is obliged to pick up a taxi on the fly. And this time it was my luck.

I parked and let the porter in his Sherlock Holmes attire open the door for the client. As I was loading the suitcases into the trunk, Sherlock came to my side, blocking the view from the hotel, and stretched out his hand. It remained there, extended, until I took his open palm in my hand and said to him, Elementary, my dear, elementary.

I closed the trunk, got in my seat, and drove the client away.

The passenger was a bit quiet. So I talked about the rain.

Rain doesn't bother me, he said. It is sweat that I fear.

Indeed, I said, I think I know what you mean. Not to be

too philosophical, but I agree with you: it is what surfaces from the inside that counts.

You say philosophical, but I would attribute your comments to religion.

How interesting, I said.

Well, Jesus.

Jesus? I replied.

Matthew 15: *It is not what enters into the mouth that defiles the man, but what proceeds out of the mouth, this defiles the man*, the man in the back seat of my car declared so eloquently.

Well, well, revolutionary, I said. There goes all that meticulously prepared celestial food down the drain. What an anarchist of an anorexic commie that Christ was!

Are you a believer, my friend? Do you believe in the lord Jesus, king and saviour?

To tell you the truth, I am not too keen on kings and royalties...but to come back to your question, I ask, does Jesus believe in himself?

Jesus believes in the Father and the Holy Ghost.

And the Father believes in his own father and so forth, I mumbled, imagining an endless family tree of Godfathers and forefathers and a legion of prophets and holy ghosts moving up and down the branches and clapping their hands between their acrobatic performances that somehow always ended with a fistful of peanuts or a banana peel.

Are you married, brother? the man asked me.

No.

Girlfriend?

Never, I said.

You are not one of those, are you?

Gay, you mean. Not yet, but a fortune teller assured me that I might have a life-changing encounter one of these days.

The fortune teller meant it in the religious sense, I hope. Have you ever considered having a family and kids?

No.

Do you ever think about your old age?

Yes, I said. It is all planned.

I hope not alone?

No, I know exactly how it is going to be, if I am lucky. I'll grow old, I'll sell my books, and give my bed to the Salvation Army. By then, I imagine, I'll already have grown a beer belly and yellow toenails. I shall get a ticket to an old island in the south, live among the locals with the little money that I have saved. Sunbathe and drink rum until the banana regime comes and chases me out, or until the regime chases itself out for lack of any other thing left to chase, whichever comes first.

You should get married and have kids, the man said to me, then you'll know the meaning of life. Who do you think will take care of you and visit you when you are sick and old?

The chambermaid and her mother, I said. The young local girl that I'll marry in the south. Like I said, it is all in the plan. I'll be supporting her and her whole family, her gambler of a brother, and her father, who, incidentally, will also become my future domino game partner and who will make fun of my age every time he wins a game, calling me Papa Turko. I'll be best friends with her mother, with whom I'll see eye to eye on issues of marriage, cooking, and old age. I'll make sure that the fridge is always full, that the white sheets of the bed are run now and again through the washing machine that I'll have bought my young wife for her birthday. My wife, who lost her first husband in an illegal caravan crossing to the north, was in danger of starving with her two kids until I came along from the snowy pole with a dog by the name of Rudolph and offered her a secure life in return for company, good meals, and a tolerant attitude to my sagging old man's breasts, my belly button's disappearance under the flesh of my falling beer belly, and, as I've previously mentioned, my yellow toenails...and that, my friend, would be the sweetest company any chariot driver ever dreamed of in his old age. What a glorious ending, sir! What a reward for a hard life of solitude and wandering. Imagine that I could sit every day on the beach, with the sea in front of my eyes and the white laundered sheets flapping behind my back. I will lie down and watch the passing tourist boats with a drink in my hand, I'll appear before them in my ridiculous swimsuit that covers the tumbling parts of my decaying body. And, if I am lucky, I'll die watching the ocean against the backdrop of a white movie screen with memory fragments and episodic replays of my life bouncing on the washed bedsheets as they dance through the turbulent blows of life.

I still think that you should get married and settle down before it is too late, the passenger behind me said, as I drove and watched the road and the rain, as I listened to the sound of the wipers' monotonous swings. The same rhythm, the same dance, the same swing of the pelvis after dinner and between the news breaks and the sway of the nocturnal toothbrush, the same keys, same breakfast, and same *The doorbell is ringing, darrrrling*, the same dog with its monotonous tail swings to welcome you after your car engine has stopped above the same spot of oil on the ground of the same garage. We arrived at the airport. The rain had stopped and the wipers rested.

I unloaded the man's luggage from the trunk. He paid me and we shook hands, and as he was about to turn and depart he said to me, Good luck with your solitary existence. But remember, my son, the Lord's path is always open.

So long, I replied, may we all have one good flight before we rest among flowers and the orbits of hungry worms.

He left and I turned back towards the city and drove through the empty roads, and I rejoiced at the privilege of a ride through the falling rains.

THE DEALER CALLED my apartment. When I answered, all he said was, Tonight we are on.

So I waited for him once more. He came down wearing shades though it was late in the evening. He got in and sat in the back seat, quiet. I watched him in the mirror and waited for instructions. He waved his hand and I drove straight ahead, and when we reached the end of the street he said, Left and right and straight to the port area. He wasn't talkative at all. But then he said, You can go home early tonight. It is just a meeting.

We arrived.

Good, he said. Park behind the container here. Then we waited and we both watched in the rearview mirror.

A big car came from behind and pulled up next to us. There were two men inside. I tried not to look. The less I know, the safer I'll be, I thought.

Stay here, the dealer said. I'll be back.

So I turned off the engine and opened a book to read, but the light was dim and I didn't want to turn on the interior light. Carefulness and survival instincts made me welcome the dark. I will give it fifteen minutes, I thought, and then I will leave. It was an overcast night, there was no moon to be seen, and there was a fence between my car and the river. I don't often listen to the radio, besides it drains the battery when the engine is not running, but some of those spiders pass their lives driving and listening to talk-show programs. With time, if they spend enough years in this land, they start complaining about foreigners just like themselves and lazy people and the government's waste of money. And though none of these drivers pays any taxes, they start walking like big taxpayers and old men with large umbrellas who feel justified in their sense of entitlement because they fought old wars and gave half their money to the nation state. Buffoons, some of these drivers are. They like to have those voices in their heads.

Once, in Café Bolero, Number 115 stood up and grabbed the public phone in the hallway next to the bathroom and he kept dialling until he got on. The waitress turned up the volume and everyone in the café got quiet, and then the right-wing anchor, with his little-girl voice, interrupted 115, first corrected his English, and then asked him, Where you are calling from? And he followed that with: I thought you were calling from India, pal. How did we let you in here? Everyone laughed and thought it was a good joke, but I left the restaurant, sat in my car, and cried.

A light beamed from behind me. I thought it was the dealer come back to interrupt my thoughts, but then a man in a guard's uniform knocked on my window. I could see the silhouette of his partner in my mirror, standing behind my car on the other side. I slowly rolled down the glass and made sure he could see that both my hands were on the wheel.

What are you doing here? This is private property.

Whose property? I inquired, for no reason.

It is the port authority's property. There is a sign back there. No one is allowed in after 8 p.m.

Well, the sign must not be lit, or I would have seen it.

You are trespassing. Licence and registration, please.

I had just handed him my licence when another car pulled up. The dealer stepped out, walked towards us, and said, He is with me.

The security guard immediately handed me back my papers and the dealer got into the car. As I was about to drive away, the dealer asked me to wait. He lowered the window and called the man back. Thursday, he said. The guard nodded and turned away.

FREDAO

IN THE DAYS when I lived with Otto and Aisha, Linda would come around. And often she would bring Tammer and leave him for the night. Other times, a week or more. Tammer was a quiet boy; he accepted things and hardly complained. He seemed not to object to being around new people. When his mother left, he would just stare after her and then look away. Once I made him laugh by turning myself into a clown. I juggled a few balls and I balanced on the edge of the sofa with an umbrella in my hand. I pulled coins from his ear and sang with water in my mouth. The kid laughed and said, More.

One day Otto went looking for Linda on the streets because Tammer had a fever and was asking for his bed and for his mother. That was how Otto met Linda's pimp, Fredao, who was from Angola and claimed to have been a child soldier with UNITA, and to have participated in the liberation of Angola from the Portuguese.

Soon after, Otto decided to talk to Fredao about helping Tammer with his school fees and books and clothes. Otto, man, Fredao said, when they were both drunk, sitting under a bridge on the banks of the town's river, listen, the worst kind of colonization was us poor niggers who were colonized by the Portuguese. The French gave us some culture, the British some laws, but those Portuguese gave us nothing. And when the filth left our lands, they dismantled everything down to the last light bulb in the factories and the last neon light in our stores. But then the Cubans came and they were not colonizers... I started my career, Fredao smiled, by providing women to the Cuban soldiers, and that is how I learned the pimping business. He laughed. A soldier needs guns, food, and sex no matter what, and our women were willing to give their bodies to those fighters because the Cubans installed schools for our kids, provided us with doctors for our sick, clean water, medicine. What did the European colonizers leave behind after hundreds of years of ravaging our continent and our bones? Nothing!

After Fredao was done with his rant, Otto looked him straight in the eye and calmly said, The kid is asking for his mother and he needs to be in school again.

The kid's mother is working hard. She is working for the cause, the pimp said, and laughed.

ONE DAY, AISHA came home and asked Otto, What are you going to be, Otto? Where are we going with this?

I am going to take care of you, he said, and held her in his arms.

Otto took on many jobs after that. He was a shoe salesman and a warehouse clerk. He delivered Chinese food, and sold shirts on the street, and he always organized at night. He wrote ferociously, demanding public housing and protesting against greedy developers. He wrote some fiction, but Aisha read a few of his stories and then one day she told him: Otto dear, you are no Baldwin, I say you should stick to propaganda. And she passed her fingers through his hair. Some of Otto's articles were published in fringe newspapers and activist pamphlets; others were read aloud at demonstrations.

Late at night Otto and I would listen to old speeches by Stokely Carmichael and play Black Panthers cassettes and sit at the window and smoke. Before demonstrations or meetings, we would fill buckets with warm water, gradually pour in starch, and mix it to make wheat paste. We'd carry the pamphlets in our backpacks and walk the neighbourhood with our buckets and brushes, pasting electric poles with our homemade glue and covering walls and blocks in calls for justice and revolt.

One night a police car pulled up quietly behind us. Only when they were nearly touching us did they switch on their beams. I, Fly, who was accustomed to the glaring floodlights of circus spectacles and the harshness of stage lights, jumped over a fence and fled into the neighbouring backyards. But Otto, nocturnal creature that he was, froze like a deer in the road. Two officers began pulling down the posters. Instead of running away, Otto protested and kicked one of the buckets. It hit the police car, covering the hood with glue. They pulled Otto into the shadows and beat him with sticks and left him half-conscious on the road. That was for dirtying my shoes, one of the officers said on his way back to the car.

When I realized that Otto had stayed behind, I ran back. I saw him lying on the ground. I went to him and tried to pull him up. His shirt was bloodied, his eyes rolled in horror, he hissed, spat red colours, and cursed, Fucking cops, fucking pigs. He wiped blood from his face and said, It is not over between us...

Aisha kept up her work with battered women, neglected children, and evicted tenants until one day, not long after Otto's beating, she collapsed. We are both burned out, she said, crying. It is time to rest. We decided to split up. Otto and Aisha left the house and the neighbourhood, and I went my own way. They put the struggle on hold because they had watched each other getting older and poorer and seen their comrades leaving the cause and getting married, holding jobs, and raising children. Aisha said to me that now they wanted to take care of each other, and I understood. And she wept and told me how much they both loved me.

For years afterwards, I wandered alone, though I stayed in contact with Otto and Aisha. Once in a while they would come and live with me for a week or so, and we would talk about books, music, and the old days. Once or twice they mentioned Tammer and his troubled mother. Then they would leave and I wouldn't hear from them. Until one day Otto called me and asked me to meet him at the hospital. Aisha was in a single bed and looked much older and very frail. She hardly recognized me, and I held her hand and wept. I looked at Otto and I said, Forgive me, I am crying, and Otto said, We are all crying.

AFTER AISHA'S DEATH Otto withdrew for a while and no one saw him. I would call him but he would never call me back. And then, suddenly, he showed up at my door with a beard and a six-pack of beer and he said, For a short while. He slept in my bed at night while I went to work. In the morning I would wake him up and take the bed and sleep while he sat in the kitchen and smoked and drank coffee until the afternoon. Then he would eat a piece of bread and leave, and the apartment would be empty for a few hours.

Otto stacked the kitchen table with files and literature. He would sit there and write, copy, and take notes. He borrowed books from the library and read and bent pages and underlined paragraphs. When I asked him what he was working on, he said he was gathering a list of important people.

For donations? I asked.

He laughed, puffed a few rings of smoke, looked at me with a half-smile, and said, Yeah, donations. You are a joker, Fly.

Once I tried to bring up Aisha, but he looked at me and said, She is dead. They killed her.

Who killed her?

This world killed her.

One night I came home and found the kitchen table cleared and a note telling me he was moving on and that he would be in touch.

A few weeks later, Otto joined a large march organized by community groups, unions, leftist intellectuals, anarchists, and activists. They had mobilized to protest a three-day summit held by the leaders of the region, who planned to impose a series of neoliberal economic policies.

The march was attended by thousands. The police erected fences and closed a part of the downtown and forbade all access to it. Speeches were made by various workers and leaders, flags of resistance waved, banners flown, and songs sung. One evening a few hundred activists camped out around a big fire in the park. They drummed and danced all night.

Otto was there. All of a sudden he heard the sound of activists yelling. A voice from the police megaphone ordered them to put out the fire and vacate the park. The activists started to boo and shout and the police, in full riot gear, banged their sticks against their shields and marched, pushing the crowd back, and then another platoon approached in the same slow and relentless manner from the opposite side. Otto shouted, It is a sweep! and he raised the beer bottle in his hand, ran towards the line of police, and threw the bottle against the shield of an officer. The bottle fell and shattered. Many were arrested, but Otto was singled out.

I hadn't heard from Otto for many months. One morning, as I was about to park my car in the garage, I saw him standing on the sidewalk in front of the building. He was smoking and had a foam cup of coffee in his hand. I parked my car and went to him. I stood there and tried to engage him a bit longer, thinking I might catch Zainab on her way down, but he walked towards the entrance and took the stairs up and I followed. He breathed heavily, he looked hunched and fatter, and his leather jacket moved in gigantic forms against the light of the stair's windows as we moved between the floors. A faint smell of food rose from a neighbour's apartment. I immediately thought of hunger, it must have been hunger that was causing Otto's slowness, because when Otto was down before, he would go through weeks of drinking hard liquor and eating one meal a day, or sometimes only peanuts in the morning.

He sat at the kitchen table, and when I offered him food, he asked for a glass of water. He pulled out some pills and swallowed them.

Talk, I said, and he told me the story of his incarceration.

BARREL

I AM BLEEDING, Otto said, as he sat on a chair in the police station.

Name?

Langston.

Real name.

Stokely.

Real name.

Carmichael.

Real name, one of the officers said, and he pushed a paper and a pen towards Otto.

I can't write.

Real name, he repeated. Write down your fucking real name, because I know who you are. So just write down your fucking name. I have your file. It's been a while, but I see you are making a comeback. Kind of like those Motown singers, and the officer looked at his partner and they both smiled. Now write down your name.

Otto wrote down *Stokely Carmichael*.

Your real name.

Black.

Look, Bob, he wrote "Black," but he looks a little pale to me. I wonder how that happened. It must have been his great-great-grandmother holding on to that white boy's ass in the barn and not letting him pull out in time. Now, real name, motherfucker...

Panther Fist, Otto wrote.

I'll ask you again, write down your real name.

God.

One more chance, chocolate-milk boy, the officer said.

A *Fuck you* appeared on the paper.

Otto was pushed out of his chair. One police officer watched while the other beat him with his stick. After a while the second officer came over and started kicking Otto and stomping on him.

Otto started to shout, I am God, motherfuckers! *That* is my real name. My name is fucking God.

The first officer smiled and said, The man needs help. He thinks he is God.

They left the room and Otto was left on the cold floor, his head hurting, his body still. He closed his eyes and lost track of time.

LATER, TWO MEN in green aprons came to see Otto in the interrogation room. They said they were there to accompany him. When he asked where they were taking him, one of the men spoke to him softly and sounded very professional.

Sir, I have to inform you that you are now in our custody and that your safety and well-being have been assigned to us and are out of police hands. We ask you to cooperate and make it easy for everyone. You will be driven to a psychiatric ward for assessment. In the event of non-compliance on your part, we might have to employ restraining measures. Now I want you to answer me with a simple yes or no. Sir, do you understand what I've just told you?

Otto laughed and didn't answer.

Sir, the man said, you have to answer me, because if you refuse to cooperate, we might just have to restrain you.

Otto looked across the room and saw one of the officers who had beaten him standing in the back with a file folder in his hand. The officer looked indifferent and kept his eyes on the table pretending not to hear, but Otto knew that the officer was listening and Otto felt alone.

Are you seriously taking me to a mental hospital? he said.

Sir, do you understand what I just told you, yes or no.

Otto nodded and the officer approached the orderly and gave him the file.

IN THE BACK seat of the car Otto was squeezed between the two men. He was silent and never said a word.

When they arrived he was led down a hallway and into a room. The room had no windows; it had a metal bed and a chair in the corner and nothing else.

A nurse came to Otto and handed him a hospital gown.

Take off your clothes and put on the gown. The doctor will come for you.

I don't need a doctor, he said, but before he had a chance to say anything more, the woman left and locked the door behind her.

Otto refused to stretch himself out on the bed. That, he thought, would constitute an admission of a pathological state. So he went to the chair in the corner and sat. Then he realized that he was thirsty. He banged on the door and a few seconds later the same nurse opened it and said, You better keep it down.

I need water, I am thirsty.

She closed the door and a few seconds later opened it again, and Otto stood there with a paper cup in his hand and drank. When he was done, the nurse took the paper cup away.

In the room Otto's mind wandered. He talked to Aisha and offered her a larger pillow, he asked her if he should bring the bed up or call the nurse, he told her to be patient until the doctor came back, he promised to smuggle hash into the hospital, he thought it might relieve her nausea. And then he felt like weeping, but that might also be an indictment of madness, he thought.

He had been stripped of everything, but it was the metal bed that he loathed and feared the most. He wished he had some alcohol, or company, or a book. Most of all he longed for Aisha, to see her lying on her favourite couch reading with the sun on her back, her round exposed thighs, her glances at him between pages, her grimaces of endearment and disapproval: at his singing, his loudness in the kitchen, his long rants about jazz and politics, his cursing in the mornings. Her childlike obsession with pages and words.

He thought about Aisha's life, her childhood after the exodus of the white people to the suburbs for fear of property value depreciation when the blacks moved in. The only white person who stayed behind was Mrs. Rooney, a retired librarian and an avid reader. She decided to stay because, as she liked to say, she had enough love for everyone. I will die here, among the good people of this land, she'd say. All races are good by me. I don't see why everyone is in such a rush to leave. With time, Mrs. Rooney started to lose her eyesight, and she relied on her good neighbours to bring her food and medicine.

One day, while Aisha was reciting her homework in the hallway, Mrs. Rooney invited her in. Sit down, child, and read to me, she said. You read so well. So every day Aisha would go to Mrs. Rooney and read to her and indulge in her cookies and sweets. And every once in a while Mrs. Rooney would hand Aisha some coins, which Aisha would keep hidden in her winter shoes in the summer and then switch to her summer shoes in the winter. A few seasons passed and then Mrs. Rooney's nephew came and took the old lady to a nursing home; her sight had gotten worse and she'd almost burned down the building. The night before her departure, Mrs. Rooney called Aisha and said, Choose any book from my library and I will recite it to you. And Aisha chose a book and Mrs. Rooney started reciting it all by heart. Aisha was bewildered and sad. If you have them all in your head, she asked, why did you make me feel needed?

I just wanted you to read and cultivate a love for books, my child, the old lady said, and asked Aisha to come closer. I am giving away all my books to the library, Mrs. Rooney told her, all of them. I won't give you any of my books, because now that you are a reader, you have to read your people's books.

And then she gave Aisha a card and told her, When you reach the age of twenty-one, you call this number. My girl, I did leave something for you after all.

Aisha passed the age of twenty-one and never called. She'd misplaced the card, and Mrs. Rooney seemed a thing of the past. One day, though, the lawyer for Mrs. Rooney's estate telephoned and asked Aisha to come and visit him at his office. Mrs. Rooney had left her a humble cottage with a piece of land around it, and a modest amount of money.

When Aisha and Otto and I went our separate ways, they decided it was time to leave the neighbourhood. They moved to the cottage and stayed there for a few years. Aisha loved it. Seclusion suited her, and the cottage was distant from everything. They took long walks to the nearest village and carried the food home on their backs. In the summer, they sat under the large tree that shaded the cottage and cooled the breezes that passed by. Aisha would read and Otto would smoke pensively and curse the flies. In the winter, they used the metal stove that was in the middle of the room. They lived frugally on the little inheritance. The cottage was equipped with an axe and a shovel and all that was needed to survive a winter.

But after a while Otto got restless. They would go for days without encountering another person, and for weeks without receiving a single visitor. The ascetic life was too much for him to bear. Otto got a part-time job at the quarry. He would hitchhike with the lumber trucks and the few locals who by now knew of the black couple's existence in the village.

Then Aisha got sick and they had to go back to the city for treatment.

After months of agony, sickness, and the hospital's miseries, Aisha whispered to Otto, It is over. Take me back to the cottage and bury me under that tree, away from these metal beds and crosses.

And that is what Otto did. When she died, he left her body lying in a makeshift bed for two nights and on the third day, he took the shovel and dug a hole under the tree and buried her. And then for the next seven days, he polished a large stone until it turned smooth and glossy. He set it at her grave and wrote on it: Here lies a reader and a fighter. He read her favourite poem and then he turned away from the grave. He closed the door of the cottage and walked back towards the city.

In his room in the psychiatric ward he tried to remember that poem. He remembered the original name of the poet but couldn't remember the name he'd chosen later in his life. Everett LeRoi Jones, he repeated, yes, but what was the new name? An African name, yes, an African name. Maybe I should have changed my name, he thought. But I tried that, and those brutes didn't believe me. Instead they put me in here. The poem, he thought. The poem, Aisha's favourite poem:

> Dull unwashed windows of eyes
> and buildings of industry...

And then what, Otto said to himself, trying to remember. And then what...He fixed his eyes on the metal bed. Say it for me, darling, one more time...He was talking out loud, and he stopped himself. But then what, my love. Say it again, he whispered, turning his back to the door. Could someone read that poem to me? And again he heard his own voice and he hushed himself and moved the metal chair to muffle the spoken words.

After a few hours, Otto was still in the room in a hospital gown, and he was starting to feel the cold on his exposed legs and bare back. The woman had taken his clothes away. He thought about covering himself with the bedsheet, but to take the cover off the bed and wrap it around himself would only make him look like one of those hobos with no teeth, shivering around the barrel's fire.

Finally, after many hours of solitude and sporadic monologues, the door opened and the nurse asked him to follow her.

He was led to another room, even more confining than the one he'd just left. The walls were utterly empty, but he did find some comfort in the wooden chair, which was warmer than the metal one in the previous room. He thought about the physics classes he'd taken as a teenager. Metal is a conductor, wood is a receptor. And for a moment he felt like assuming the theatricality of madness. To climb up onto the table and conduct an orchestra, singing, Metal is a conductor, wood is a receptor, metal is a conductor...

He stayed on the chair and extended his legs in the direction of the door. Cigarettes, he mumbled. His mind tried to trace the path of his belongings. Where might his plastic lighter and his pack of cigarettes be now? Had his things been transferred from the police station to the hospital? Small details such as these made him feel normal.

He tried to imagine what the assessment would be like. They'd be sure to ask about his childhood...yes, that predictable Freudian trick again. The death of his father and then the death of his mother. His white-trash suburban aunt, his mother's sister, who'd hated his black father and wondered why her sister had married one of *them,* as she put it. And her slob of a husband, who'd sit there watching the game and make Otto and his younger brother Martin go to the store to fetch the beer...images of he and Martin with their suitcases, shuttled from one foster home to the next. And then Martin's death. He'd joined the army and was killed in the line of duty, in what Otto called a useless death for the hegemony of an empire. His body was never found.

This interrogation, he thought, would be much like the last, in the police station, without the muscles this time, maybe, but with psychological arrogance and threats. His body was bruised but somehow he felt energized by it all. A good fight was always welcome. That was what he missed most after he and Aisha left the struggle and retreated into nature. But then he remembered what Aisha had told him before they quit: We can always come back. The world doesn't change much. There will always be a just fight and a cause to die for.

And that is when the door opened and two people entered the room. Otto looked at their white teeth and wanted to burst out laughing, saying to himself, Shit, the non-smokers are here. He looked closely at their faces and saw a man in his late forties and a young blond, attractive woman. Judging by the way she held a pencil between her fingers and a pad close to her chest, she seemed all ready to take notes.

Hello, said the man. I am Dr. Wu, and this is Genevieve, an intern with us here. She will be joining us, if you don't mind.

Otto didn't respond.

So, how do you feel?

I would like a cigarette.

I don't smoke. Ms. Genevieve, do you smoke?

The intern shook her head.

So I was looking at your file . . . but let me start by asking you some questions. These are standard questions that we ask all our patients. He glanced at the intern and she lowered her chin in agreement and paused her pencil.

Do you ever hear voices? Dr. Wu asked.

No, I don't, Otto replied categorically.

Do you experience episodes? Let me explain: do you sometimes feel as if there is a separation between yourself and your environment?

No, I don't.

Good. Do you at times think you belong to the realm of certain deities?

No.

Do you believe in God or in gods?

No, as a matter of fact, I am an atheist.

Interesting. Mr. . . . . Blake, was it?

Otto.

Then do you think that you are God?

I just told you that I am an atheist: why would I believe that I don't exist?

So how can you be sure that you do exist?

I could only be sure if I lit a cigarette between my lips and blew.

Mr. Blake, let's discuss, chronologically, the series of events that brought you here.

I really would like a cigarette: it might hold off my hunger. I haven't been offered any food since this morning. And I believe that might well constitute an infringement of a prisoner's rights. How about that for a chronological event.

So you think you are a prisoner here?

I think you consider me as one, and you have certainly been treating me as one.

Not at all, Mr.... Otto. We are here to help. But to go back to our previous discussion, you did, at the police station, write on a piece of paper that your name was God. I have the paper with me right here. It is your handwriting, I believe?

I was being ironic.

Yes, I see. I believe you, but my concern now is the self-infliction situation.

You mean the beating.

The police report stated that when you were left on your own, you managed to hurt yourself.

I was *beaten*, man. I was beaten. I want to see a lawyer and I demand that my injuries be examined and matched to the pig's stick. Do you hear me, Doctor? I was abused. Police brutality. Yet another case of police brutality. Now I won't go on with this nonsense before I get a lawyer.

Well, Mr. Otto. I am sorry to hear that you won't cooperate. You see, under the circumstances, we have to make sure of your mental well-being before we proceed to the judicial side of things.

Listen, you motherfucker, get me a lawyer now.

Okay, Mr. Otto. I think our session is done here. I will make sure you get your assigned meals and the needed sustenance.

And my cigarettes, Otto said, as the intern rushed to open the door and the doctor passed through.

A HUGE GIANT of a warden appeared and escorted Otto back to his room. A few minutes later, the nurse came with a small plastic cup in her hand. In the presence of the giant, she approached Otto. Suddenly, like a genie engulfed in smoke, the giant began to talk: This is your medicine. The doctor has prescribed it. You must take it three times a day. There is no compromise here. The medicine will be completely swallowed as instructed. I advise you not to try to avoid taking the medicine. The medicine should be fully swallowed in my presence. There is no margin for manoeuvring, sir. After the medicine has entered your mouth, I will ask you not to swallow it but to hold it on your tongue and open your mouth and stretch your tongue out so I can see the pill there. After you have done that, you are expected to immediately swallow it. Once the designated pills are swallowed, I will ask you again to open your mouth in order for me to examine it and be certain that the medicine was fully ingested. Please do not try to dodge or avoid taking the medicine because let me assure you, sir, we do have other means to ensure that the medicine's benefits are fully exercised.

The medicine made Otto drowsy and brought him a sense of detachment. He finally gave up resisting and mounted the bed. For months he was confined there in the state of a sleeping vampire, an in-between zone of consciousness and unconsciousness. He was finally released when the bruises on his body had faded. For months afterward, he experienced withdrawal and a sense of unbearable numbness. From the police beating he had suffered some kind of concussion, but he hadn't felt its effects until he stopped taking the medication the doctor had forced on him.

Slowly the withdrawal symptoms wore off and he went back to looking for various odd jobs. But the periodic fits of rage and depression never stopped coming. The experience had changed him. He couldn't listen to his favourite records. He had trouble concentrating. Loud noises hurt his ears; he went through abrupt phases of fatigue and erratic sleep. One night, some kids were blasting music under his window and drinking beer and smoking on the sidewalk. He stormed out and asked them to move. There was a lot of posturing and shoving. And in the middle of the commotion, Otto felt something that he had never experienced before in his whole life. It was a short, passing moment where he knew that he could have badly hurt one of the kids. He grabbed the boy by the throat and closed his fingers around his neck. The boy started to turn blue. A neighbour intervened and liberated the kid from Otto's hands. Otto turned and walked away.

His finances were depleted. After moving from one cheap hostel to another and enduring the fights of drunks and the attacks of bedbugs and the smells of mould and hobos, he found himself a room in the basement of a house that he shared with an alcoholic older woman on welfare.

Otto never got along with her. A good-for-nothing religious nutter, was how Otto referred to her. Later on, she would tell anyone who asked that he was a godless, angry man and a loner. They avoided each other.

WHEN OTTO HAD finished talking, I dug my hand into my pocket and pulled out the money I had made that day. I ignored the change and gave him all the bills. He hesitated, looked me in the eye, took it, and said, Brother Fly. He hugged me and he left.

MANUSCRIPT

THIS TIME, IT wasn't too long before Otto got back in touch. He called me at home. It was early in the morning and he knew that I had just finished my shift. He said he wanted to meet in the afternoon when I woke up.

Around four o'clock, I changed my clothes and brushed my teeth and went to meet Otto. He looked even older now. His cheeks, which had once squeezed his eyes and given him a look of cleverness and experience, had fallen in wrinkles and defeat. His hair had turned white at the sides and he looked even heavier than he had the last time.

It's the effect of those asylum drugs, he said. They make you put on weight.

I turned off my lantern to indicate to the passengers of the city that I was off-duty and I drove with Otto to the shore. The rain had ceased, but the water from the river still reached the pathway under the viaduct and kept the ground moist. I parked but left the headlights on, and the light skimmed the surface of the river. Through and beneath the car's rays, gentle waves took on the arched shapes of dolphins inhaling the wet air that crossed between the two shores of the American north.

Here, Otto said, and pulled a bottle from inside his coat.

We stood for a while in silence, drinking and smoking and staring at the water and the sky.

They tried to kill my spirit in that place, Otto said. If you resist and get vocal they try to pacify you. They do it to the masses through all those corrupt, complacent journalists, but people like us, who see through power and greed and protest its savagery, we risk being crushed. It is still a fight. It is still a fight for me, Fly. It will always be, Otto said, and then took a long puff from his cigarette.

I watched a small boat pass under the bridge. It had a torn flag hanging from the back of its deck. The flag, with its fading colours, had turned into a neglected cloth. With my eyes I followed the boat and its white trail of parted water that eventually merged and collapsed onto itself to become waves and a river again. Smoke rose from Otto's mouth as he spoke.

I say they should feel fear, he said. That is the only way for them to realize what the dispossessed go through. I say we need to show them a different face. They are no longer afraid or embarrassed by the faces of the disfranchised. So we need to show them a mask: a mask of horror...I say they should tremble and be forced to stand at the cliff of death and hunger.

They are everywhere, Fly.

Who is everywhere? I asked.

Otto threw his cigarette on the ground, stepped on it, extinguished it, and said, Listen, Fly, I've been collecting notes and gathering data on some more people.

What for?

Just notes, observations, records. Fly, man, I called you because I need a favour from you. You have to help me here.

The pyschiatrist, the one who so-called treated me, Dr. Wu, hails a taxi from his private clinic every Tuesday and Thursday around eight in the evening. I've been watching him. He is at the hospital most of the week and those are the only two nights he can be counted on to be there. I have a list of people, Fly. I document their lives and their habits. The hours they leave, the places they eat, their licence plate numbers...documentation, Fly. We have to gather information, that is how power rules. Knowledge, Fly. Knowledge and organization.

You just park in front of his clinic and bring that monster to me, Otto said, and I will only ask him to read. That is all I want him to do.

Reading is good, I said, but no one should be led to reading by force.

They should be forced to know the other side of the story, Fly.

They do know it, but they don't...

Yes, Otto said. But even if they don't care, they should read back to us, out loud, what we've written. And when they do, we should be right there beside them. Maybe their voices will tremble, maybe they will express fear. And that should be enough for us to start fighting back. You and I go back a long way, Fly. And I know that you will help me in this.

What would Aisha think?

Aisha would have asked you to. She loved you and she loved me and she never backed down from a fight. She fought to the last drop of her life...she belonged to both of us. I shared and I never judged because I loved you both.

ACT THREE

CLOWN

ON MONDAY EVENING, I took my car and drove through the downtown, where the Carnival and its people filled the streets with songs and beer mugs and decorations and costumes. I picked up half-naked men and women in masks. I had dressed up as a magician that night to amuse myself.

I drove around the periphery of the grand square where most people gather. I laughed when a woman in fishnet stockings ripped them and asked me if I liked them better that way or before . . . Before, I said, and pulled some flowers out of my sleeve for her. A cat-girl asked me if she could rest her paw on my shoulder while I drove her to the big outdoor theatre, and when she paid me in bills, I asked her to open her paw and help herself to the change I owed her. A man who tried to practise a few magic tricks on me lost a ten-dollar bet when I turned his pigeon into a book and his hat into a box of Kleenex.

But the next evening, I left my gas tank almost empty. I combed my hair back and put on fake glasses, a wig, and a top hat in the manner of those Irish elves. The wig reached my shoulders and some of its hair covered the side of my face. I removed my taxi permit, which had my photo and my name on it, and I stuck it in the glove compartment.

I waited in front of the psychiatrist's clinic. Otto had mentioned that he was short and wore black glasses and that he walked with his eyes towards the ground. He was easy to recognize. At ten past eight, he came towards my car, got in, and gave me an address. I nodded and started to drive. I looked at him in the mirror but he was busy examining a folder, and before he had a chance to look up at the road and protest, I took the ramp that led below the bridge. And I stopped the car.

Finally, he looked up. What is going on? he said calmly.

It is an emergency, I said. I must be out of gas.

Where are we? he said, looking out the side and rear windows.

My apologies for the inconvenience. I'll be right back, sir. There is a pay phone right here. I'll be right back, I repeated, not to worry, be right back, and I affected a heavy foreign accent to throw him off.

I saw Otto. He had a purple clown's wig on his head and a red plastic ball on his nose. A sloppy lipstick job was broadly pasted around his lips and white paint covered his face and neck all the way to his ears. He wore his old leather jacket over his clown suit and he looked cold.

I walked towards the river. I glanced behind me and saw Otto getting into the back seat of the car. And then, after the elephant had balanced on its hind legs and lifted the dog with the curve of its trunk and all the animals had waited through the applause, the clown pulled out a gun, stuck it against the psychiatrist's ribs, and said: Give me your wallet. Listen, fucker, no one will hurt you here. I just want you to sit still and concentrate. He pulled some pages from his leather jacket, poked the man with his gun, and said, Read from the top down. And the psychiatrist started to read. But the clown interrupted: Read from the *top*. State the name of the poet and the title. From the top, and he poked Dr. Wu once more.

And so the doctor read:

> A Poem Some People Will Have to Understand
> by Amiri Baraka,
> formerly known as LeRoi Jones.
> Dull unwashed windows of eyes...

I went down to the river's edge. I threw a few rocks at the devils in the water and I smoked and looked at the bridge going across, then I lit a second cigarette into the fog. In cities it is useless to look at the stars or to describe them, worship them, or seek direction from them. When lost, one should follow the tracks of the camels. I watched the car lights passing and vanishing overhead, and I imagined my mother swinging off the bridge and my father, the camel lover, going in circles, throwing rocks, and reciting prayers beneath the fullness of the moon.

I walked back. I didn't see the psychiatrist, but Otto was leaning against the door smoking.

Where is he? I asked.

He's gone, Otto said. He took a walk. Here, I got you the fare, I made him pay. And don't worry, I stood in front of the licence plate when he got out and he didn't see a thing.

We drove towards the city. Otto pulled out a bottle of bourbon and drank from it. He offered it to me and I took a short sip.

Fly, my man, Otto said, as he smoked and drank, let's call this night "The Revenge of the Fool." He trembled, Doctor Evil trembled...I made him read and he was stuttering, there was fear in his eyes. I made him repeat it all about six times... I made him read about the lives of prostitutes, the religious right's policies and their effects on poor neighbourhoods... the guy started to beg me not to kill him...shoved the gun in his mouth and I thought, Now, Doctor, how does it feel? For months you shoved all kinds of pills into me...When I pulled the gun out of his mouth, he asked me if he should say his prayers...I said no, not yet; read...He was uncomfortable reading about prostitutes...There is a war out there, and believe me, Fly, it was never really between Jews, Muslims, Hindus, Crusaders, and Confucius. The final battle is between those who love, respect, and liberate the body and those who hate it, Fly. Pull up here. I am due for a drink. Do you want to come and check out the Carnival crowd? I say let's celebrate a small victory for the oppressed, the clown said, and looked euphoric and already drunk.

Not tonight, I said. I need to cover the day's rental and fill up the car. It is the season to make good in this town.

Sure, Fly, making a living is all right, Otto said, as he slowly got out of the car.

Otto, I called to him, it might be a good idea to rest for a while. You always have a place. Just come by, or stay.

It is a fight, Fly, it will always be, but remember that you are my brother and I love you.

MIME

AFTER MY SHIFT I waited for Zainab, but she didn't come down. I hadn't seen her for a few days. I knocked at her door. She opened it halfway and said, Not now, Fly. I have somebody here. Just go. Go drive or something.

But wait, Zainab said. A woman knocked on your door last night. She was crying and she looked pretty upset. She mentioned something about a delivery or a necklace.

Mary, I said. It must have been Mary.

Okay, so go to Mary, said Zainab, and she shut the door in my face.

I drove to Mary's new place; she had moved into an apartment next to the market. She wasn't home. I waited for a few hours but she still didn't arrive.

In front of her place was a bar with its door open. I sat in my car and watched the back of a man hunched towards a poker machine. He smoked against a screen of vanishing hearts, passing spades, rolling fruit. The neighbourhood was infested with gambling dens, pawnshops, rundown laundromats, and vicious dogs. But the Carnival also reaches that dodgy side of the downtown, and in the afternoons, the neighbourhood people start to play music on the street, and they come out to drink and dance. Carnivals also belong to the marketplaces and the poor.

After a while I went to a pay phone and called Otto, but no one answered.

I went back to my car and waited for Mary. Two customers asked to hire my services. The first was a mime who pointed at the passenger seat next to me. I shook my head and, with my hands, I signalled to him that I was off-duty. When he still insisted, I locked the passenger door and frowned at him. He gave me the finger. I was speechless.

But the second customer got right into the back seat. I told him that I was not in service. Your top light is on, he said, so that means you must be working. I hit the button and turned off my lantern and said, Okay, not anymore. But the law dictates that you should take me, the man said. You can't refuse a customer once he is inside your car.

Well, yes, I can refuse a customer. As a matter of fact, I do it all the time.

I'll take down your licence number, he said.

Fine. Do whatever you like, but leave my car.

Sure enough, a few days later the taxi inspector came looking for me. She found me at Café Bolero: she had spotted my cab in the parking lot. Some of the drivers covered their thighs with their napkins and plates when she came in. There was an atmosphere of embarrassment and panic. She asked for me by name and then walked towards me.

Do you have your licence on you? she asked.

Can't this pleasurable encounter wait? I said. I am eating.

There is a complaint against you.

What is it about?

Refusal to take a customer while your dome light was on. The man you refused to take the other day was an employee of the transit authority, and he filed a complaint against you at the taxi commission.

Okay, so now I have to spread my thighs and let him molest me?

Everyone in the café started to laugh in disbelief. All those numbers went under the table, spitting food and hiding their faces. Some ran to the bathroom and some closed their eyes and shook their heads.

I can revoke your licence right now.

Without a hearing? I said.

Yes.

Based on what, sweetheart?

Don't call me sweetheart.

Officer?

Let's go to your car.

What a femme fatale, I whispered to myself.

You said something.

No, I was just remembering the time when I was a child in the circus and the lady with the whip told the monkey man to jump but then...

She made me open the trunk and the glove compartment. Checked the lights and did the rest of her little routine.

Now drive.

Where to?

Drive. I just want to see if your car is making any noises.

I drove straight to a back alley and parked there and opened my thighs wide and leaned my head back and closed my eyes in submission. Here, I thought, I am being a good citizen and participating in the government census. Indeed, information and the gathering of information are essential to every state before they fuck over another nation or drive their own citizens into poverty and despair. The measure and length and diameter of every organism should be assessed before one exercises indulgence, war, or occupation.

She molested me, touching my thighs, and then she called me a faggot for no reason, or for a reason, and told me to drive her back to her car.

She left and I entered the restaurant, walking with the bowed legs of a cowboy just off his horse. The piano started to play, the chariot drivers started shooting their guns into the air, and all the dancers danced and the crowd laughed and the cowboy bought drinks for everyone and shot more bullets into the sky in celebration of the loss of his virginity to an officer of the state.

HUSBAND

A few days later I went back to Mary's new neighbourhood and I saw her just as she was about to enter her building. I ran across the street. I grabbed her hand and she embraced me and started to laugh. She seemed unusually euphoric and talkative. And then her mood changed and she said, I keep crying all night. And the books you gave me were all so harsh and sad. I called my husband. Then I told him that I slept with you. He called me a slut. I am not going back, Fly. I asked him to pack some of my books and leave them at the door. I need you to pick them up from the house. He'll be there. Could you do that for me? I can't go there…I haven't stopped crying. Do you remember where the house is? It's a bit far. I'm sorry but I think of you as a friend…I tried to go for a walk today but all those Carnival people in their masks and disguises made me scared. I had to run home. I locked the door. I keep imagining them here in my room. Could you please do me this favour? Please. And I promised to give him back a necklace. It was his grandmother's. He wants it back. Could you take it to him? Here. I trust you with it. Sorry, I'm crying... I can't stop crying... He would have brought the books himself, but his car is in the shop, he said. I think he's lying. He is leaving the country, he said. He quit his job, he's selling the house... I urge you to do this for me, Fly... I am not well. And she started to cry again.

I took the necklace and put it in the glove compartment of my taxi, and then I drove to Mary's husband's place. It took me about half an hour to get there. I drove through the suburbs, where all the houses looked identical, one variation or another of the same thing. I said to myself, I'd rather fire myself from a cannon, pick up the shit of elephants and eat it, suffocate inside Houdini's water tank, lie beneath the running horses, or sodomize a big cat in a cage and pay the consequences than get trapped in these suburbs of cardboard, gossip, and conformity.

I parked at a gas station and called Otto. This time he was home. Otto, my man, I said. Could a harmless, farcical clown be ready in about forty-five minutes?

Who is the guest reader this time? he asked.

A hater of books, I said.

I'll make him excel in his recitals, he answered.

Gently, I said. Very gently.

Can do. What do you suggest for reading material?

How about *The Clown*, by Böll? I said. That would be an appropriate joke of a title...

Yes, but Fly, man, I don't have that book. Where am I supposed to get it?

Just go to my place, I said. You still have the keys. By the way, the extra key to the taxi is on the same ring. Don't lose it. People are more interested in stealing cars than books. Choose a passage from any novel you find.

Fiction is overrated, Fly. We've discussed this. In the time it takes those novelist fuckers to contemplate a few poetic passages, a thousand kids die from malnutrition. Immediacy, man, that's what counts. What do you say, Fly?

Fiction would still be my first choice. Let's not underestimate the power of imagination.

Suit yourself. I'll see what I can find.

Meet me at the bar, in the back alley. Be there in an hour, I said.

I arrived at the house and knocked on the husband's door. The man answered and he looked me up and down, frowning, and before I could say that I was there to pick up things for Mary, he pointed at some boxes in the corner.

Could you take off your shoes? he said.

That would make it difficult to go back and forth to the car, I said.

Well, the rule here is that no one enters with shoes on.

Well, the rules have to be broken today, I said.

Do you have the necklace?

Actually, Mary decided she would like to give it to you in person, since it is valuable and all, and asked if I would drive you to where she is.

I thought she trusted you, at least well enough to fuck you.

Listen, man, I am just in transit here. I take what comes. Are you coming?

Fine. But you should have taken off your shoes.

We began to drive back to the city and he lit a cigarette in my car.

There is no smoking inside the car, I said.

He looked at me and said, I thought the rules were to be broken today.

Right, you got me, Mister....?

Are you asking for my name?

Nothing is mandatory here.

My name is Chad. You could have simply asked my wife.

Too painful, I said.

I like you, Mister.... and where is your name? I see nothing on the dashboard.

You don't have to bother with my licence at the moment; I am off-duty. Just call me Fly.

Right.

I drove with the window down. Rain, wind, and the night entered the taxi. I asked him for a cigarette and the white of our smoke crossed, mingled, and disappeared.

We both stayed silent. He would look at me sideways once in a while; I was sure he was picturing me above his wife. A filthy low-life, a loser of a driver. He was probably thinking that she'd grabbed the first thing available just to hurt him. Anything to stick it to him: it was all about him. This arrogant bastard, I thought, this uncultured mechanic capable of reading only manuals and sports sections! Who the fuck does he think he is. At least I'd made sure he sat in the front, next to me. I ain't his bloody driver, I said to myself. I am his equal. I am the new victorious general that is taking over and entering, triumphant, through the city arches...

So you are fucking my wife, he finally said, to break the silence.

Among other things we do together.

Let me guess: you cook.

No, not much of a cook. I am afraid my kitchen is very flammable. So I avoid cooking.

Flammable? What, do you have bombs in your cupboards?

Worse: books. My cupboards, my stove, the top of my fridge... all filled with books.

Right, that would please Mary. Listen, man, taxi driver, or whatever you think you are. You want to take care of this woman, go ahead. But make sure she keeps taking her mental pills. Which reminds me... here... and he slammed a bottle of medicine onto the dashboard. Now she is your responsibility. Enjoy.

We arrived and I parked in the back alley behind the bar.

I'll be right back, I said. I'll go and buzz her.

I left and I entered the bar.

A clown went straight to the alley. Opened the passenger door and sat next to the hater of books and laid his hand on his own waist.

I have a gun, the clown said. I strongly suggest that you read this passage I am giving you. Do not leave the car and do not resist the book in your hand.

The husband looked surprised. He opened the book and stared at the first page.

Out loud. Read out loud, the clown said with authority.

And the hater of books started to read, but before he'd finished the first sentence, he looked up and said, What is this, some kind of a joke? Did my wife put you up to this?

Just read, asshole.

He resumed reading but again he stopped. There's not enough light, he said. And I don't have my glasses. And I don't have to read anything.

Then you keep the book, Otto said, and again I strongly suggest that you read, and that is for your own welfare. You are to write a summary of it: that will be your assignment. I will find you again and assess your progress. Never underestimate a clown with a book. Now get out.

Mary's husband walked away shouting, Is this some kind of a joke? Is this some kind of fucking joke?

Otto left the car, making sure his clown hat didn't fall and that the gun was well secured in his bag, and disappeared.

And when I went back, the husband and Otto were gone.

That night I met Otto and I asked him, How did the book-hunting go?

Fly, man, your library is big but disorganized. Nothing is in alphabetical order, or in any order, for that matter.

Yes, but do tell, what book did you finally assign him to read?

On my way out of your place, I grabbed *Finnegan's Wake* from the shelf at the entrance.

Good. Let the fucker suffer, I said.

GIRAFFES

LAST NIGHT I picked up two women in love. They talked and kissed in the back seat of my car. They didn't mind my seeing them kissing each other, but they didn't want me to hear a word they said. They kissed and whispered and stroked each other's hair, and I watched the road in front of me and peeked at Ecstasy and Ecstasy in the mirror. I drove across the bridge and above the water and down to the other side of town. It was a clear and spectacular night that these two butterflies were missing. Had they been paying attention to the world, they would have seen a low moon, bright and big, suspended above the swinging bridge. I went underneath it and drove south. I like going south; I like the idea of going towards the warmth. I was thinking this just as one of the girls' heads disappeared, and the eyes of the other closed, and her chest heaved. I took Exit 64 and waited at the ramp for the green light to come. I kept my silence; a faint red reflection from the traffic light bounced off the dashboard and shone on the back seat. I watched the upper body of one of the women extend and contract. Little, quiet moans that sounded like the faint squeaks of small animals rushing up the trees...

When the traffic light turned green and replaced the red reflection, I accelerated slowly, not wanting to deprive anyone of a romantic touch under a spectrum of colours and the delight of the full moon. The moon should be colonized, I thought. Mankind should seek a happier beginning, and humans should be free to stroll hand in hand regardless of their weight and orientation. The ultimate weightless existence of a species, effortless in an environment where everything floats. Floating lips, floating sighs, floating shoes, and knees and stockings floating above the dashboard, around the mirror and the seats. Life in space, I thought, should be modelled on the current situation inside my car as we speak, what a great model, what a great premise with which to experiment with the loss of gravity: the elevation of the superwoman. And as I drove with all the windows shut, everything started to levitate: I witnessed the rising of toes, the upward flowing of hair, the inflation of chests. And I heard a howl rise towards the moon.

We reached the address they'd given me and I announced our arrival at the requested destination. Immediately two heads reappeared above the back seat. They stopped, took deep breaths, fastened their clothes, looked at each other, and giggled. And then Ecstasy opened her purse while Ecstasy fixed her hair. Ten dollars and sixty-five cents, I said. The first woman gave me the exact change and said, You got your tip, didn't you? And she winked at me.

Now, as I get older, I prefer money to watching other people's flights and pleasures. I would like to amass enough to one day play dead, or clown around on a beach full of ballplayers, divers, and bouncers, a beach of women happily and horizontally suspended under large umbrellas, in strings parting their luscious moons, a bit of sand on both sides of the shore, with topless skies above and the cheers of the waves and the clapping of clams.

Once I picked up a professional clown dressed as a giraffe. He told me he was late for a kids' show, where by now, we both laughed and assumed, the audience would be filled with sweets and drinks, awaiting the performance. His face came out of the middle of the giraffe's long neck. He opened the window and stretched the giraffe's head outside. I drove him fast and he held the animal's head steady and it stretched above my car roof and towards the sky.

We laughed, but I knew how sad a kept creature could be. A giraffe is a sad thing, I said. Yes, I know, he said, it doesn't fit into low-ceilinged houses or basements. Always bowing its head, always feeling big and small.

You should live on the roof if your basement is getting too small, I told him. You should eat meat if leaves are scarce. You should be fighting for those kids instead of trying to heal them with balloons and laughter. You've wasted your life, and you could have been tall and above everything, I said.

Drive, the giraffe said to me, drive. Look ahead and not at the car's roof. You are a lousy traveller. All you do is think, talk, and go around and around in circles. You are as poor and as miserable as any of us kept animals. You are a prisoner of your own windows and point of view.

I was raised by clowns, buffoons, comedians, and cannon fodder and they are the saddest creatures I've ever met, I said to him.

Don't forget the sons of freaks like you, he added, and held his head more tightly against the wind. If your father had loved you, you wouldn't have felt sadness around laughter and the wonder of kids' joy.

Here, he said, as we arrived, here is your fare and a lollipop, which will keep your mouth shut. He yanked his long neck inside and opened the door and bounced down the sidewalk and towards the house, where a few kids with painted cats' moustaches and dogs' ears waited for him to blow balloons and shape them into birds and mice and little kangaroos.

SALLY

THE DRUG DEALER left a message on my phone. The fucker never says anything but Yeah, we are on tonight, same, same, and he hangs up.

I waited for him at eight at the usual place. We drove around and checked on a few dealers of his. He shook and slapped a few hands, and then he wanted to stop at a strip club for some business, as he put it. Wait here, I'll be back in an hour, he said. Park in the back alley, I'll tell the bouncer that you're with me. Just keep cool, I'll be back.

I waited and watched as the dancing girls arrived. They carried their bags on their shoulders and waited for the bouncer to open the door and let them in. Neither acknowledged the other.

I knew a dancer named Sally once; I used to wait for her every Thursday and drive her home late, after her shift was over. She was smart, well-read, she was studying French literature at the local university, and we hit it off. First we talked about books, because she saw a book lying on the dashboard of my car. I believe I was reading Jean Genet at the time, *Our Lady of the Flowers*. And when she saw it her eyes brightened. A reader, she said, and smiled.

Sally grabbed the book, flipped through it, and said, Listen, I have nothing against masturbation, but don't you think the act is a bit overdone in this novel?

What else is there to do when you have a free spirit and you are confined to a small world of jailers and walls? I said. What else is there to do but to summon the world and lament and masturbate beneath your jailer's nose, and break his keys and his chains?

Sure, I guess, whatever keeps you sane, said Sally. It's a masterpiece in its lyricism, but it gets suffocating, claustrophobic. I can't imagine being kept in a cell, I'd die.

And then she asked me about my working hours. I said, I have no particular shift. My hours are flexible. I work here and there for as long as necessary to cover the car rent and the gas, and so that I will be left with a little change.

Are you hungry? she asked.

A little, but I would love to see your bookshelf first, I said. Unless you prefer to see mine.

I have a feeling that your collection would be a bit intense for me tonight. The last thing I need is another image of a metal bar. I danced around one all night. Is pasta okay?

Yes, I said, and we talked about our lives some more. She wanted to be a professor of literature. She'd never believed in loans and debt, so to support herself and pay her tuition, she worked Thursdays as a dancer and a couple of nights a week as an escort. She was strong and had rules: she never kissed her clients on the mouth, she made it clear that they should not touch her neck or her face, and she always made sure they took a shower before her eyes, even if they assured her they'd already had one.

In time we became good friends. And every Thursday I would wait for her in my car. We occasionally slept together. There was friendship between us and no love in the romantic sense; well, at least that was what we agreed upon. She would tell me what had happened that night, her meetings with her clients, like the story about the man dressed as a clown who ejaculated as soon as she came through the door. Once, a friend of her father's turned out to be the client. She promised not to tell his wife, he promised not to tell her father, and that settled it. But as she was leaving, he stood at the door and tried to touch her face. Listen, she said, I haven't talked to my father in years. I can afford that, but can you afford your wife's alimony?

At the end of every month, Sally would take a car with two work colleagues and drive to the south shore, to a meat-packing town where men worked in slaughterhouses for low wages. She and two prostitute friends would rent a couple of rooms in a cheap motel and host these workers, charging less than half the usual price. Charity work, Sally called it, and she explained it as a religious gesture, pointing out that Mary Magdalene had been a prostitute before and after meeting Jesus. Certainly after, she said, and giggled. The girl who'd initiated the project was named Maggie, short for Magdalena, and that is why they called themselves the Magdalena girls and were known by the slaughterhouse workers as the Magdalenas.

Most of these workers, Sally told me, are away from home. They have no one, and they can't even afford to leave the meat-packing town with the little money they earn. Some of them are highly educated, some are just poor villagers. All kinds. I even met a doctor once, she said. He was an eastern European. He spoke English with a very strong accent but with eloquence nonetheless. He came to my room; he was very nice, I'd say graceful, in his manners. He came cleaned up, shaved; they all mostly do, they treat it like a date. They take us very seriously, they groom themselves and some even wear cologne; you would never know that they take apart animals and bathe in blood all day. The first time, this doctor brought a bottle of wine and some flowers, and he tuned the

radio to a classical music station. He brought out his own con-
doms, then he washed his palms, his thumbs, and his wrists
and he let the water rinse over him while he sang opera, and
he walked out of the bathroom with his hands up in the air
like a surgeon. He opened the wine and served me. He even
brought two glasses. He was gallant.

When he went to the bathroom, I checked his bag. I often
check their clothes after they strip and, if they carry a bag,
I open it and quickly peek inside it. We take no chances. He
had a book in there, and I took it out and saw that he was
reading Hašek, *The Good Soldier Švejk*. I laughed, thinking,
What is this doctor in the middle of nowhere doing reading
Hašek? I keep on meeting these well-read men in all these
odd places. Anyway, I didn't want him to know that I had
opened his bag. But I did ask him if he was Czech. At first,
he said no. But I was sure that he was. He asked me why I
asked. I told him that he reminded me of my uncle. Is your
uncle Czech? he asked. Yes, I said, his name was Jaroslav. The
doctor was all confused. What was his last name? he asked.
Hašek, I said. He laughed and poured me wine, saying, You
are one careful woman, and he lifted his glass and we drank.
He sang some more opera in German and drank so much
that he fell asleep, but I had to take him out of my bed because there were other workers waiting. So I called these two
Albanian brothers who come at the end of every month and
try to get us girls to have them both at the same time. But we
girls have rules and everyone knows them very well. No anal
penetration, no more than one man at a time, and of course a
compulsory shower... I called these two Turks, well, Alban-
ians or whatever. Every time they come, they bring us blocks

of olive-oil soap and figs and other sorts of food that their mother sends them; they are funny and harmless, villagers with big, rough hands, loyal and grateful. Anyway, they carried the doctor down the stairs and shoved him into their car and took him away.

I tell you, though, we had to train these workers. Like I said, some of them are nice, but some are angry and disappointed with life. They come to this land thinking that they have made it, escaped the misery of their homes, but then they get stuck in awful jobs. I mean, my job is hard too, but I try to keep it clean and interesting, as much as I can. But these men, they are immersed in blood all day and it is cold in those factories, with hard conditions and long hours. After they finish their shifts, they go back to their complexes and shower and sleep; that is all they do, that is all there is. Some have been doing it for years. Once they threw a party at the dormitory and they invited us. The food was amazing. Some of them were very good cooks. They all dressed up and, when we entered, they came one by one and kneeled and kissed our hands and offered us flowers and wine in plastic cups and they treated us like queens. When we first started the project, some of them were aggressive. Their lives had gone from one humiliation to the next. But later, they learned to respect us and love us. The smart ones among them try to save a bit of money or send it back home, and they do better because they have some sense of accomplishment, the small reward of knowing that their relatives or family are better off. But others, at the end of the month they get drunk and blow it all on poker machines, booze, or drugs. At first we refused many of them. Drunk, rowdy, we would just say no. Maggie, my partner in this, whom I adore, knows the working class. She grew up in a destitute small town. She watched her father and uncles lose their jobs. She taught me a great deal about how to handle these guys. She is so impressive. She shouts at them and they become like little boys.

Once, a Moroccan guy entered Maggie's room. All macho, sure of himself, well-built, and dismissive. He acted boastful and condescending. He barely said a word to her, and then he took off his clothes and pointed to the bed.

Maggie said, We are going to talk first.

Okay, he said.

Good, I see you understand English. So here it is: I am not going to sleep with you because you have no respect for women.

He was very surprised, maybe because no woman had ever talked to him that way.

In Morocco, you guys treat your women like dogs, Maggie said to him. Here, even a prostitute like me has to be respected.

Une putain de raciste, he called her.

Well, okay, I am a fucking racist and that is how it is, she said. Now you pick up your clothes and leave or I'll let someone come and kick you out. We are charging you close to nothing out of the goodness of our hearts. If I was a racist, I wouldn't come all the way here to make your miserable life a bit more bearable. We girls could be somewhere else, in fancy hotels with champagne, charging five times more for this. It is out of the goodness of our hearts that we come here every month. And all your friends know it and they are appreciative. Now pick up your clothes and get out.

Now this tall Arab stood up and looked at the ground, and tears started to run from his eyes. He tried to apologize. But

Maggie grabbed his arm and said, That still won't save you. Come next month with a better attitude and we'll see. I tell you, the Arab left like a little baby who misses his mother.

We do it as an offering to the poor, Sally said. There is something grand about degrading one's body for a higher purpose. I've grown to love these workers. They come, happy to see us. Their smiles are wide open. It is the highlight of their month. I have one Mexican, he kneels on the bed every time and prays before he takes off his clothes, and again after we are done. And then he kisses my hand and crosses himself and leaves. He doesn't speak a word of English. But I understand what he does. He and I are the same. I do it out of humanity and he sleeps with me so he's able to carry on with his life, so he can support his family back home. But when I do my escort shifts, things are different. The moment my phone rings, I become a different person. I am not me, I become, how can I put it...temporary, oblivious, separate...my body has no importance, it's only a passageway, I say to myself. The car from the agency comes, I go to the meeting place and face those customers. I have more problems with those bureaucrats and rich men than I've ever had with the factory workers. But if I have any trouble, I press a single button on the phone and the giant driver from the agency is at the door, breaking it down in a second.

As time went by, I got to see what a lovable, intelligent, and ordinary person Sally was. I slowly started to get attached to her and she knew it. And then one night, while working as an escort, she met a handsome young lawyer. After they were done, he paid her and she went back to the limousine trembling and crying. She assured the giant driver that she was fine. She arrived home and she called me. She was scared. I don't know what got into me, Fly. I did a stupid thing. Here is this intelligent, rich, young, beautiful lawyer. We talked and I slept with him without any protection. I don't know what got into me, she said again. I've never been so reckless. I called the driver to tell him that I was extending the hours, I even covered them myself. I didn't want to leave. I think I am in love with this man. He refused to give me his number. I guess he is married, like so many of them, or maybe just judgmental. I don't know what's gotten into me, Fly, she said.

The next Thursday, I waited for Sally outside the club but she didn't show up. I asked the bouncers, who knew me by then, and they said that she'd quit. I called her phone and it was disconnected. I went by her place and asked around. The caretaker told me she was gone. She had paid her last month's rent and left, he said.

I never saw Sally again. For months, I looked all over for her. I even went to the meat-packing town and found the motel at the end of the road. I bribed the receptionist. He was a big, unshaven Turk. I bribed him because I know the histories of empires and their subjects; the Ottoman Empire was notorious for a system based on bribery, I read all about it in a book written by a British traveller and I still have the book in my library: to be precise, on the second shelf from the bottom at the entrance to the bathroom, with the rest of the orientalists' literature.

When I asked the Turk about the Magdalena girls, he said that the fiesta had ceased. The three girls didn't book the rooms anymore, and the workers had stopped showing up. Except for a tall Arab, he said, who comes at the end of the month, rents a room for the night, and sits on the ledge of the window and smokes.

THE BEARDED LADY

WHEN MY MOTHER woke up, that day my father left, and didn't see the camel and its saddles, she fell to the floor and pulled her hair and screamed. The dog, the chimp, and the horse circled around her and scooped up her tears, patted her arms, and licked her face into consciousness. The strongman carried her to bed, and I watched as the bearded lady caressed my mother's face and covered her forehead with wet towels. My mother became so weak that I started to eat my meals, take my naps, and do my homework in the bearded lady's tent. And when I asked about my mother at night, before my bedtime, La Dame, as the bearded lady called herself onstage, would say, Your mother is in a parallel world. Eat and let me tell you a story.

She began reading to me from French classics. We wept for Cosette in *Les misérables*, we laughed at *Le malade imaginaire* of Molière, we read *Les fables de La Fontaine* to the monkey.

Once I saw the bearded lady taking a shower and I asked her why she had a penis like mine and breasts like my mother's. She came close to me and said, Because I am everything. Men want to be men and women want to be women, but there are those who are both and neither at the same time. One day when you grow up, the world will tell you that there is only this or that. When you leave and live among those people who applaud and cheer your mother and me on the stage, you

will notice how different we are, and what a magical childhood you had. Here in these circuses and carnivals we all love
each other with our oddities and queernesses. People leave us
alone because we mesmerize them with tricks, tickle them
with feathers, tie them up in wonder and hope. We never let
them know that we read books, that we love everyone and
accept everything, that our bodies are free, that we travel,
resist, and fight and that we give refuge to convicts and revolutionaries, that we have saved gypsies and Jews. We never
let them know that we untie ropes, that we train horses to
dance without the weight of armour or swords, and we keep
it a secret that the strongman loves the cannon man, that
they cook dinner for one another, that they share the same
bed, and that every time the cannon man is up in the air with
smoke trailing from his feet, the strongman waits on the
other side to catch him if he falls. And, my little child, do not
tell a soul that we are knowers and non-believers. We know
that after this grand act of life nothing is left but the dust
beneath the elephants' feet and the sound of the monkeys'
clapping. When they come to you with prophets and prom-
ises of heavens of honey and milk, remember that we are no
more than flowers having our last glance at the world before
we die, with grace and with gratitude for the wonders we
witnessed, for the magic box we built, the animals we loved,
the carpets we flew, the stars that we encountered after the
spectacle ended and the spectators were left to lament and to
wait for the coming of their phantom trains to take them to
their imaginary heavens...

Then, late one night, my mother wailed and shouted and
ran between the tents. She tried to open the locks of the cage

and throw herself to the lions, but the lion tamer came to her rescue and covered her naked body with a quilt. And again I stayed with the bearded lady, whom I loved and whose beard I kissed every morning before she offered me bread, butter, and milk.

One day, my mother gained back her strength and went up on the ropes and hanged herself. She was discovered because of the dogs' howls, and because the chimp pointed to the sky and the elephant walked in circles around the large tent, trumpeting an end.

I know that my mother was buried somewhere between the Danube River and the heel of the Italian peninsula. I remember holding the hand of the bearded lady and marching behind the band of gypsies, the elephants and the horses in coloured feathers above dancing hooves. Her coffin was carried by the clown, the strongman, the cannon man, and her favourite white horse. We walked in silence, and then the music began and got loud and we all danced with umbrellas in our hands.

Wanderers, tent makers, and animal herders have the privilege of dying anywhere, the bearded lady said as she gave her eulogy. The earth is their land and all the roads are their burial ground.

Above the open grave, my little left hand was squeezed in the bearded lady's palm, and my right grasped a handful of dust. I threw it over my mother's remains and the gypsies played again.

The next day, the circus packed up and moved on. On the way, we were stopped by border guards who blocked our roads and mocked our ways. The officers tried to steal the horses but the clown distracted them and the magician made all the animals disappear. And then food became scarce and the animals' bones bulged against their sides. They all slept in hunger, they all whimpered, and our money ran out. Finally, we came together and the owner of the circus gathered some sticks and threw them into the bottom of the magician's long hat. One by one we drew them out. I was handed a gun and five bullets. I walked to the stable and I shot the biggest horse.

After six days of horsemeat and feeble fires, the mime drew sad faces and the strongman gathered everyone and said: We all must depart upon our different paths. We'll take the horses to Ireland and set them free, the dogs to Spain, and the elephant and the chimps to Africa. The rest of you should go wherever you see fit. The world has gone mad and our way of life was bound to change.

The bearded lady packed our bags and told me: I'll write to my distant cousin in the Americas. He lives in a city where a carnival takes place.

HAT

AFTER WE HAD all wept, sung, and danced our goodbyes, the bearded lady wrapped me in new clothes, a hat, and new shoes. We took a boat from Marseilles and sailed through the Mediterranean and then into and across the Atlantic.

On the boat, we encountered a magician who was doing all the tricks we knew so well. The bearded lady and I stood there and smiled as he performed: the Floating Wand, the Protocol of Knots, the Lantern of Diogenes, the Frame of

Cards. And when he was done, the two of us went to him and asked if he could perform for us, in private, the Enchanted Bank Bill, or the Wreath of Flowers in the Hat, or the Magical Bell and the Butterfly.

The magician laughed and introduced himself as Mr. W. Frinkell. And when the bearded lady asked his real name and offered to feed the birds in his hat, he said, Call me Pips, and we all shook hands and I, who was rehearsed in the art of illusions and sleeves, offered to assist him with his next show. I picked up his tall hat and collected the riches while the handkerchief turned into birds and the stick turned into flowers and the horizon into a sun and the hat into the world. At night, as we walked along the deck, he told the bearded lady, I've been around the world, and the sweetest people I've ever met are dwarfs and misfits.

During the rest of the crossing, I would wake up in the middle of the night and see that the bed I shared with the bearded lady was empty except for me, but I was happy because I knew that Pips would take care of La Dame. He would love having her in his bed as the sea rocked the boat and splashed the deck and the little round windows with water and fish and every other kind of creature that originated from the sea.

Pips decided to travel with us the rest of the way, and when we arrived in the Carnival city the three of us shared small rooms with a communal bathroom. Pips found a few birthday gigs and a restaurant where we performed some nights, but then, suddenly, poverty hit us and hunger surfaced again from beneath our clothing and hats, it settled in our mattresses and covered the tablecloth, and we all went looking for jobs.

I wore a turban on my head and a long robe that reached past my feet. I stood on corners while Pips shouted, The Surmise Boy, ladies and gentlemen! He will guess your age and weight and the remaining number of your living years...

The bearded lady couldn't find a job because people here want everything to be clear: men are men and women are women and those who are in between are left to the vultures and the crocodiles. We were barely surviving, and one day Pips held me and said, Listen, kid, I have another trick up my sleeve, but you have to help me without our lady knowing. He showed me a book on "spiritism," as he called it. He flashed the book in front of my eyes. I read the title, *The Book of Mediums and the Secret World of Beyond and After.* When I tried to grab it, Pips pulled it back and said, You will read it someday.

With the little money we made on the street, Pips rented a room and proclaimed himself a spirit medium. We fed on old ladies who had lost their husbands, mothers who talked to their missing sons in the jungles of war or the sunken ships below the seas, and we summoned lost lovers, wives, dogs, sons, and daughters from the beyond. When new clients called for an appointment, Pips, to look important and sincere, would ask for a reference, and then he would ask for their names and the year of their birth and tell them that he would be in touch soon. And I would go to the library and research past addresses, occupations, and lives. Then, in the afternoons, Pips and I would stroll to our clients' childhood places: we would note trees and watch kids play, we would observe the colours of window frames, the meadows, or the electric poles nearby. We went to the local bars and coffee shops and made conversation. It was easy to evoke the dead, because their traces are everywhere. Their past lives stretched and covered candy stores, benches, water fountains, dirt roads, and dusty graves. The dead, Pips would say, are what we make of them.

Pips and I dimmed the lights in the rented room, hung velvet drapes, and skilfully positioned the dancing tables and talking chairs. We bought a cheap skull and passed thin ropes through it. And I let my own dark spirit hide behind the wardrobe door to pull the rope and make the skull talk and shiver. We built a wooden box, placed a bell inside it, and positioned the box under the table. Whenever the box was kicked or nudged, the bell would ring. Just when the spirit was about to respond, Pips would hold the client's arm and ask everyone to move back from the table, hold hands, close their eyes, and let their bodies fall forward. From there he would faintly jiggle the table with his head, making it shift and squeak, and kick the box.

Later we oiled the wardrobe's door so that when it opened, no sound could be heard. Before the client came into the room, I would slip inside the wardrobe with a few sealed envelopes. During the session, Pips would ask the client, let's say it was a lady, to write a question to the deceased. She would insert it into an envelope, seal it, and Pips would take it from her and ask her to close her eyes and concentrate. From inside the wardrobe, I would exchange envelopes with Pips, right under the lady's nose. Then Pips would ask the lady to open her eyes and read the answer of the spirits. The messages we wrote were always vague, a reference to a place that we, Pips and I, eerie humans that we were, had visited the day before.

Pips even made deals with the undertaker. He promised him that, once in a while, a client would come to him wanting to upgrade a loved one's headstone to something more expensive. And Pips would take a cut. The contents of some envelopes read *The white stone, change the white stone*, or simply *the fountain, I am happy here*, or *Grandpa*. From inside the wardrobe, I tried not to breathe heavily, not to sneeze, not to laugh or feel sorry.

For a while business thrived and we ate well. Pips walked around in a new suit and bought the bearded lady flowers from the shop. And then, one day, the bearded lady cornered me with a stick and a rope, and I confessed that the money had come from the wishes of old ladies and the desperation of orphans. That it was collected from mothers in tears and extracted from old husbands who had no one left to talk to. The bearded lady cried and said only clergy and charlatans would promise to secure the welfare of the dead. She told me that we might be jokers, tricksters, rope walkers, and buffoons, but we had never been the kind to swindle desperate believers with falsehoods. And she held my hand and said, The best of them fall when they are in despair; they spend the rest of their lives and their fortunes on seances and dark chambers, waiting for the table to rattle, for the glass to speak. Listen, my son, all we're allowed to sell is the wonders that we see, the acts that we witness, and the plays that we perform. Now close the curtains and go to your room before the door opens and hell breaks loose.

Late that night Pips appeared and the bearded lady grabbed him by the skull and pounded him to a pulp. She called him a swine and packed his clothes and threw him into the street.

She cried all night, she climbed into my bed, and I swept away her tears and kissed her beard.

HUNGER

THE DRUG DEALER came out of the strip bar, sat in the back of my car, and said, Okay, let's call it a night. Drop me at the next bridge, the blue one. I'll show you once we get there.

But then he became friendly and talkative and I wondered if he'd had a few drinks and a lap dance or two. Hey, Fly, where you from, he asked from behind his shady cool glasses.

From everywhere, I said.

Yeah, like you're from China or Timbuktu. But really, are you from here?

I grew up among the animals, I said.

So you are one of those farmer boys; we do business there too, he said. My grandfather was a farmer, but his kind, the God-fearing, churchgoing farmers are all gone. Now they all have TVs on their roofs and orgies in their barns. The flux, Fly, man, the flux of time. If everything goes tits up, there's always the farm and the cows... speaking of which, are you on for long drives outside of town?

Anywhere the wind brings the barley and the dough, I said.

That is my man, Fly is the man. Fly, are you gay?

No, I said.

No offence, but I am asking because the other day you said you had no girlfriend, so I didn't know if you meant, like, no girlfriend but a boyfriend or if you're just into ascetic living, deprivation, or masturbation. You know these things can be tricky.

No, no girlfriend.

But you do get laid, don't you? Not with animals, I hope. Are you into kink, chains and shit, classy whores, white pussy, pink pussy, Chinese pussy, black pussy? Because I could set you up. Just say the word.

Much appreciated, I said. But you know how it is with mixing business and pleasure.

It can be pleasurable, the dealer said. My girl is my accountant, manager, fashion consultant, and my whore, if you know what I mean. Hey, we were never properly introduced. You are Fly, I know. Call me Zee. Zee as in "zee one, zee only Zee," and he laughed...And thank you for asking me my name, Fly, now that we are friends. That was very polite of you, Fly. Very polite, Fly.

I looked in the mirror and smiled. He smiled back.

You do high, Fly?

Not on the job, I said.

I'll leave you something for tonight. You know, something nice for your long-looking nose. Turn left here, we are close...

Before he left my car, Zee handed me a capsule with a bit of cocaine inside. I immediately went home for fear that the taxi inspector would be feeling sentimental. I knocked on the Romanian's door. She opened and said, Yes?

I have something I thought the doctor might be interested in, I said.

Like what?

Pharmaceuticals.

You're selling pharmaceuticals to a doctor? she said.

Yes, you know, I've noticed that he has this habit of passing the back of his hand below his nose, and I happened to have something for this medical condition.

What condition, she asked.

You know: the itchy-nose, bug-eyed, permanent sniffle condition. I noticed it as he was giving me a lecture on the benefits of good consumption. Of food, that is.

Okay, cut the joking, what do you have?

Nice white snow.

How much.

A cup of coffee. Inside, I added.

She let me in.

I gave her the capsule.

She went straight to a table in the middle of the room.

We both sat on the edge of the bed and she spread out some cocaine and lined it into a few rows.

Do you have a bill on you? she asked.

I handed her one. She rolled it and immediately went down on it. Then she swept her nose and said, What do you want for this?

I have a good friend who is like a brother to me. I want him to be able to consult a doctor. And I also want to talk, if you have a minute.

She picked up the capsule, put it in a side drawer, and said, The leftovers I am saving for the doctor. Now what do you want to talk about?

History.

I don't know anything about history, she said.

Your history, I said.

What am I, a tree? Do you think I am so old that you can ask me about my history?

Life, I said. Your life.

My life? What for? Why do you want to ask me about my life if you can have something else?

I can't.

You mean you can't do it?

Well, no, yes, I can, but I prefer to be alone.

So what do you want to know?

Tell me about your house.

You are in my house. Look at this tiny dump. You have the same size house as me.

What was your childhood house like?

Oh, that house. I don't know. Nothing special. You know how it was in those communist places.

Where was it?

Why? If I told you the place, would you know it?

Well, I might. I grew up in the circus and we crossed many lands.

Well, that's funny, she said. The place I grew up in, everybody called the Circus.

Oh, I knew we had something in common! I rejoiced. What colours were your tents?

Well, no, not that kind of circus. Actually it was called the Famine Circus.

Yes indeed, I heard about it from a Romanian magician who also played Dracula now and then.

Dracula is from Transylvania, she said. I come from Bucharest. What did you hear about it?

I heard that a dictator built a large complex and a large palace, which caused the nation to starve.

Yes, that's it. Now what do you want?

I just wanted to make sure that the doctor gets his gift. And that you are happy.

What is it to you, my happiness?

Does he pay you?

Pay me for what? she shouted.

Does it cover the food and the rent? I asked.

Get out, you crazy man. Get out now before I call the police. Crazy man. Crazy! she shouted, and she pushed me out of her apartment and slammed the door in my face.

Expelled, offended, hungry, I left.

TEMPLES

I ENTERED MY apartment and squeezed myself through the history section at the entrance to the kitchen. I made myself a small sandwich with a bit of olive oil and goat cheese. I ate it and then moved towards the carpet on the ground. Transylvania seemed too bloody, too morbid and full of fangs for me at the moment. Besides, it was daytime and the vampires were still asleep. So I wondered which event in history I should recall. From all the filth and violence that we talking apes have caused since our descent from the branches and our expulsion from the banana paradise, which seance of lust, horror, and blood should I choose to rectify today? Which plain, mountain, or river should be my battlefield, and what history should I exorcise to further the evolution of bacteria into a gentler, dancing ape? As I lay down, an image of red rivers of clay passing between the cedars took me back to the ancient Levant, where, for every virgin who left the temple of Baal after offering her lips, breasts, and collection of orifices to the gods, thousands more would be born to walk across the Canaanite's land and fill her place. I, handsome, half-naked Adonis, lying on the carpet, I am no Greek, as those Europeans mistake me for, and the wild boar that killed me had no land but that demarcated by his piss on tree trunks and stones. And the Greeks were not Europeans, because they never gave a fuck about Günter and his pale-skinned tribe. The Greeks always looked and marched towards the east, through the olive trees of the Assyrians, down to the Egyptian deltas, and towards the boastful Persians, their arch-enemies. So here I was, fancying myself on a carpet below a vineyard, drinking wine and waiting for the Greek diner-owner Bacchus to accompany me on my long trip to the temple. Before the Mongols, the Arabs, the Hebrews, or the Hellenics; before Telly Savalas, that bald-headed actor, I, Adonis, walked these lands in peace. Our temples were filled with our obedient daughters, who waited to be deflowered by a stranger. Those were our customs. Only afterward would they be permitted to marry and to begin a family. Those were the Cannanites' norms, I repeat. Some parents even bribed strangers and priests because no man came forward. Offerings always involve blood, and ours came from between the thighs of our women, where everything started, where all originated. It was the blood of a virgin that coloured my thighs and the river beneath my feet.

After I left the temple, I walked out to the high valley and up the Kadisha mountains of the Lebanon range. A wild boar smelled the blood on my thighs and charged at me with his tusks. I bled and watched the river turning red all the way through the valley and down to the Mediterranean Sea. There was an instant bloom all over the land: cedars sprung like uncircumcised male genitals, and water gushed like springs between the Nile and the Euphrates. Everything seemed to thrust and climax with the beat of howlers and ejaculators who covered the land with white semen, evermore to be mistaken for sacred snow.

MARY (AGAIN)

I WASHED MYSELF and called Mary. She sounded a bit incoherent on the phone. She talked about her husband, who had threatened that if the necklace was not returned...and she was crying, telling me I'd stolen from her and betrayed her. I assured her that I still had the necklace and would bring it back to her. I asked her to wait for me.

I took my rescue plane and flew towards her place. She hadn't eaten in a few days, she said. And her hair was not washed; it looked lumpy. She was skinny, with bags under her eyes. I gave her the necklace and the medicine. She threw the medicine against the wall and said, This is shit. It doesn't work. I am not crazy, I don't need any pills for my head.

I held her, she seemed frail. I opened the fridge and took out a container of yogurt. I smelled it and tasted it and spooned some into a glass bowl and gave it to her.

I can't leave the house, she said. I am afraid of all those creatures in their masks and their masquerades, smiling. They creep me out.

It is the Carnival, I reminded her.

No, it is hell. They are all demons underneath. I pray that they go away. I pray all the time. The virgin will help me. I will pray to her.

I asked Mary if she had someone, a friend, I could call. Parents, anyone.

No, she said. They are all gone. Dead. I'll pray, she kept on saying. I'll pray, because Jesus loves me.

There must be someone I can call besides Jesus, I said. Jesus hardly ever replies to calls, not for the past two thousand years.

Father Smiley. Call Father Smiley.

What is his number? I asked.

I don't know.

Where can I find him?

In the church, she whispered.

Which one?

St. Mary's Church.

I'll find it, I told her.

THE CHURCH WAS closed. I went around to the little house beside it and knocked on the door. An old woman answered. I guessed that she was the secretary, judging from her glasses and her busy desk. She made me wait and then, eventually, she showed me into the priest's office.

Mister Priest, I said.

Call me Father John.

Mister John, I said. It's Mary. She is not well. She sent me here to see you.

Which Mary?

Not that one, I said, pointing at the icon on the wall. The angelic Mary with black hair, I said.

Her family name?

I'm not sure, I never asked, but we are friends and she is not well.

Yes, but like I said, my son, there are many Marys. I myself know several.

What if I called her Reading Mary? She always has a book in her hands. Glasses, nice...well, nice smile, I guess.

Yes indeed, said the priest, and lifted his index finger towards the ceiling. I know who you are talking about now.

She is not well, I repeated.

I'll come with you. Are you driving?

I am in a taxi.

Right. Let's hurry up then, we wouldn't want the driver to hike the fare.

WHEN WE GOT to Mary's, the priest sat down next to her, held her hand, and said, How are you, my child?

Father, she said, make them go away. They are all devils. They are everywhere, Father. They are all talking and moving around me at the same time. The voices...

The priest took me aside and whispered: She needs to be taken to the psychiatric hospital. I know someone I can rely on there.

When the priest asked her to come with him, though, Mary refused to leave the apartment. They are out there, Father, she kept saying.

Have no fear, I told her. Just hold on to the Father's cross and zap them away.

The priest frowned at me, but my advice worked. Mary hugged the old priest with one hand and held the cross with the other and pointed it towards the neighbours' doors and at every corner of the stairs and in the lobby. We managed to walk down the street and get in the car and drive.

At the hospital, Mary was helped out of the car by an attendant and she was taken away through a glass door.

The priest followed behind her, but I was not allowed to go in. I watched my Mary disappear.

BURIAL

EARLY THE NEXT morning, I picked up a clown from the street. Or at least I thought he was a clown, walking with a wobble and a smile. He was drunk but I didn't notice: even I, a guesser who had grown up among performers and impersonators, failed to see the tragedy beneath the disguise. The clown entered my car and collapsed on the back seat. I tried to wake him but he chuckled and cried and then passed out. I feared that he had died, until I finally heard him puff and snore. I was happy he was alive, so I took off my jacket and covered him.

I drove aimlessly until I arrived at the city shore. I left the clown sleeping in the car and walked towards the river and lit a cigarette. When the bearded lady died, after a long and painful illness, I kissed her beard and left her in her bed, then I bought a shovel and returned in the middle of the night. I wrapped her in a quilt, carried her small body on my shoulders, and laid her in the back seat of my delivery car. I drove outside of town. I passed the cemeteries and all I saw was rows of marble and a legacy of stones. The herd always lies together but the Jinn passes through the night alone, the Arabs would say. I stayed in my car and waited for the dawn. I made a hole in the ground. I climbed a nearby tree and swung like a monkey; I hoofed the ground like a horse, sprinkled dust like an elephant, and mourned like an owl. I dropped the quilt like falling curtains, I applauded for the final act, I turned off the sign on the top of my roof, I covered the rearview mirror with a little piece of cloth, and I drove back to the city alone.

When I went back to my car, I saw the clown walking towards the water. He dropped his pants in an attempt to merge his body fluids with that of the river's moving current. I waited until he was done, then I whistled.

He walked back to the car and got in.

Where you are going? I asked.

He could barely mumble "the Dream Inn" before he passed out again. I drove him to the Dream Inn Hotel. I gently woke him, took him to reception, and left.

I WENT STRAIGHT home and lay on the carpet. The phone rang.

Yes, I said, bitter at the interruption of my brewing fantasy. I was about to join the Red Brigades in Italy. The Italian minister was in the back of the van, all tied up and about to die. The woman beside me, driving, had pulled over and handed me a number. I'd stepped out of the van and into a phone booth and, just as I imagined the police sirens were coming towards me, I realized that it was the phone in my house ringing.

I answered as I buckled up.

Hello, a voice said, this is Miss Such-and-such (I didn't catch her name) from the diocese. I am calling you on behalf of Father Smiley at St. Mary's Church.

Is Mary okay? I said.

Well, I believe so. But it is the Father who wants to speak with you.

Let him come then and speak, I said.

Well, he is in the hospital.

With Mary?

No, I believe Mary has left the hospital.

To go where? I asked.

I think the Father needs to talk to you concerning a few matters, she said, ignoring my question.

Fine, I said. Which hospital?

He is in St. Mary's Hospital.

Not the church of St. Mary but the hospital of St. Mary. Am I correct?

Yes, Miss so-and-so said.

Okay, should I meet him at the St. Mary's Restaurant inside St. Mary's Hospital?

No, you can go straight to the room.

The number of the room?

It is 107.

Perfect.

Thank you. God bless you, she said.

I hung up the phone and went back to the van and discussed it all with the Red Brigades girl.

Plan B? I said.

She nodded and looked seductive in her assertive way.

I'll show you how to get to St. Mary's Hospital, I said. We could always drop the minister there.

And the manifesto, the ransom? she asked.

I'll see if the Church will pay it, I told her. The Vatican's citizens are wealthy.

I took my car and flew below the clouds. When I spotted the hospital, I locked my wheels and took a kamikaze dive towards the lot. I walked inside nonchalantly and took the stairs and entered the room.

I hardly recognized the priest. He looked as if he had been kidnapped by aliens and tied up in plastic wires, and he also looked frailer and older than he had the last time I'd seen him. Behind him sprouted a jungle of flowers and a row of get-well cards picturing bowed heads, a collection of Marys, and crosses and little houses. I went straight to the window and checked on my car. I had left it parked in the Doctors Only lot as a protest against favouritism and privilege. So far, the car was still there, safe. I stretched my neck and looked out the window, but I didn't see any tow trucks coming my way. Nothing alarming, only an ambulance siren rushing towards the emergency doors.

There were two nuns in the back of the room whom, at first, I didn't notice, or smell, for that matter. When do you think the priest will regain consciousness? I asked them.

We don't know, they replied in a synchronized chorus.

Is he asleep? I asked.

Yes, he is, they said.

Should I come back later?

If you like, sang the duet.

I'll go down for a cigarette, I said, and return in an hour. By the way, have you seen Mary?

Sister Mary?

No, that Mary is Caucasian, I said. Mary the reader, the one who reads all the time. She always has a book in her hand.

The nuns looked at each other and said, You'd better speak to the Father.

I went down to the cafeteria, bought a coffee, and looked at the slim rows of books in the gift shop. There was nothing I could read there, inferiorities to numb the mind from the pains of the world.

I went outside and joined the company of the shivering expelled smokers. Hospitals are a carnival of death. A masquerade of haggard eyes gazing at the white, purgatorial walls, a faint chaos of hunchbacked mothers chasing orderlies, of doctors disguised in aprons, pointing magic wands at nurses in angelic uniforms and muffled tap shoes, waving bandages mistaken for egg rolls. Hospitals are asylums with flying ambulances, bed bells to summon the physician's spirits, sponge baths above white linen, janitors swinging mops over hazy floors, evening moans at the last sunset, and fridges full of ice for arrested hearts.

Sir, I said, are you up yet?

Ah, you've come, the priest said with difficulty.

Yes, I am here. Now what?

I wanted to ask you, son. Do you think of God, life, and death?

Yes indeed, all the time. I think that your god doesn't exist, but death does; so does life.

Then the priest started to cry. Son, something very meaningful has happened to me.

I nodded.

I died and I came back.

Like Jesus, I said.

Well, yes and no. I wouldn't put myself in the same category. I am not worthy. Something miraculous happened to me the other night. I had a severe heart attack and my heart stopped. I went through a tunnel and I saw a lake, and my father, and my uncle. It was peaceful and serene. But then something pulled me back. I went through the tunnel in reverse, I could feel someone dragging me and I turned my head and I saw you, and it was you who was bringing me back here, to this life. It was you whom I saw, son.

Well, I don't know what to say, I told him. Sorry I interrupted your dream.

It was not a dream, it was very real.

Well then, I have many people who could testify that I was here on this planet. I stopped and ate at Café Bolero, but otherwise I was working, driving my cab to keep my life in order. I picked up many clients who are here for the Carnival. All kinds of lost souls, Father.

Yes, yes... but, son, do you believe in the other side?

I believe in others, and in humans, and in a world of wandering and of constant change. And I believe that I am here now, and that one day I'll leave just like the butterfly leaves, never demanding anything more than the air it has touched with its own wings.

I believe that you are more than that, the priest said, breathing noisily through his tubes. I believe you are a force. I believe you rule this world but not the next. And you brought me back. I believe you are some kind of demiurge, and, I suspect, a lost one. Maybe even an evil one.

Well, Father, I think the only evil is you and your lot of delusional believers who make women suffer, who tell Africans to abstain from sex and not to protect themselves. I believe you are a hater of misfits, a suppressor of clowns' laughs, scissors to the ropes of mountain climbers, chains to the wanderer, and a blindfold to the knower: a hater of men. But you are also a lover yourself, a lover of power and buffoon dictators, a protector of arms dealers and thieves, pardoner of hypocrites with pious tongues and dirty hands...

May God forgive you, my son.

May your god, if there truly is one, forgive himself for these inferior creations. I am leaving, but I need to know where Mary is.

Mary is gone, he said.

Gone where?

We arranged to send her to a convent overseas.

Where overseas?

I won't tell you. Your company is not good for her. She is in good hands, with people of faith. Good people. Her people now.

I want to know where she is. I want to send her a few books.

There is only one book that matters in her life now: the one that saves us.

There is no one single book that could possibly save us.

You can leave now. I need to call the nurse. Maybe we'll meet again.

And this time I'll make sure not to pull you back, I said, and left him there and walked back through the long hallway and down the stairs, outside the building and to my car.

I took the wheel and my car flew towards the marketplace and the Carnival, and I fancied myself a bird, then a tightrope walker in a clown's attire, singing and testing the rope with my empirical feet. Now the clown becomes a Joker, then a prophet chanting to the festive masses: I shall chase the clouds and stop the rain and save your lives from this endless charade of puppets and strings! Ladies and gentlemen, the Temple of Wonder is yours to enter, watch your head as you enter the tent, and kindly take off your shoes, a new life is waiting for you just inside. Here is your chance, ladies, to come back as a tiger, a lion, or a mockingbird, here is your chance, gentlemen, to see the eternal light and be saved from the burden of daily life. Just sit tight in your seat, clap when you are told to, and leave when you hear the buzz of the Joker, or when the light above the door goes long and horizontal. Hurry, the show is about to start! Step inside and all your troubles will be forgotten. But do not eat from any of the forbidden foods, the big cat might get excited. And kids, do not sneeze when the man reaches with his bare hands for the lion's throat. Do as the others do and you will see miracles and the illusion of flying horses, the revival of the old and the greatness of the divine! Come into the temple of bliss and joy and you will be given a new mask, a new life for eternity ever after.

GUNTHER

THE MAN WITH the British accent called.
Are you ready for another adventure, my good man? he said.
Always ready for good clients like yourself, sir.
Half an hour later I was at the door of the building.

Okay, old chap, let's do this. My dear Fly, we are about to meet an unusual writer, a rather, how would I put it, cultish figure, maybe.

A novelist, I hope, I said with barely contained enthusiasm.

Yes, a novelist.

Brilliant, I said. What would be this novelist's name?

My dear, names are names and just names.

No need for names, I said, but what kind of literature does he or she write?

It is a she. And to satisfy your inquisitive mind, I would say the writing is rough and dirty. But now even leather-boot literature, as we call it, is a bit passé. No longer shocking—even a bit laughable. Well, in any event, she is expecting me today. I have the privilege of meeting her alone. And at one point in the evening, I would like you to meet her as well.

Sure, I said. It is always a pleasure to meet dirty novelists. I once contemplated becoming one myself...but instead I stopped typing and picked up another creative habit that has kept my fingers busy ever since.

Yes, yes, I am sure, and what reader or dreamer doesn't imagine the romantic life of a writer, who lingers between the desk and the fridge in the morning and in the evening attends cocktail parties thrown by the nouveaux riches and society ladies who hardly ever have the time to read? Everyone craves fame, sex, and an eternity of acknowledgement, and so on. But, believe me, your life could have been worse. You could have experienced paradise and then suddenly been expelled for no valid reason. I mean, imagine having fame and accolades and then one day, *poufff*, as the French would say, losing it all, your name obscure, your books pulped and recycled into toilet paper. Then your only consolation in life would be a few old photos and your daily drinks over the kitchen counter. Which brings me to the person we are meeting today. Here is the address, he said, handing me a scrap of paper, where we will encounter that once-famous writer.

Yes, I know that hotel. Rather expensive, I said, trying to imitate that ever-intimidating language of spies and skinny punk singers.

Tell me about it. I am paying the bill. So, my dear friend, do you have a name?

My name is Fly.

Fly as in flight? Or as in insect?

Not sure.

Right, we never choose our own names, et cetera, et cetera. But, since you recognized my voice on the phone, I do not think it necessary for you to be acquainted with mine.

No names is good, I said.

Excellent: let's buzz.

To save time, I avoided the middle of the city and its numerous traffic lights and I took an exit that led us straight to the highway. As I accelerated, the man opened the window and leaned his face into the oncoming air.

Go on, my good man, take off and soar, he screamed. In my rearview mirror, I saw his hair quiver and his vibrant silky scarf flutter, flap, and leap against the winds.

Now. We have arrived, I believe. So, Mister Fly. Listen to me. I want you to go up to the room in forty-five minutes exactly. Not one minute later or in advance. Here is the room number. You knock three times and you enter. After you enter, you must make sure that I am released from my obligations. Understood?

Yes.

You must release me immediately, without any delay, I repeat.

Sure.

Good, Fly. I see you have a clock on the dashboard. Let us adjust the time so that we are in sync. I would estimate that you should leave seven minutes before the appointed time, and do take the stairs for the purpose of accuracy.

Sure, I said again.

Understood?

Understood, I said.

Here also is a Swiss knife, a present from me to you. Bring it along and keep it in your pocket. You will know what to do with it when the time comes.

THIRTY-EIGHT MINUTES LATER, I went into the hotel, took the stairs, and found the room. I stood at the door and knocked three times.

The person I assumed was the novelist in question opened the door, dressed all in leather, with a long bullwhip in her hand.

You are early, she said with an authoritative voice and the upright posture of a gypsy dancer.

No, I am on time. Where is he? I said.

I am not done with the program yet.

I pushed her aside and entered the room. My client was tied up on the floor, buck naked, with his own socks sticking out of his mouth. When I tried to release him, the once-famous writer cracked her whip behind me and said, Do not dare to touch him before I finish my drink.

I have my orders, I said.

I have mine too, she said.

We both looked at the man, and he was shaking his head ferociously and drooling from the side of his mouth.

Look at your watch, you little shit, she said, addressing me and reaching for a pair of handcuffs.

I stepped on her whip and, before she had the chance to pull it back, I punched her in the face. She swung at me, but I saw the punch coming, so I did a backward flip and, by accident or not by accident, I kicked her in the chin.

She fell back against the dresser, hit the TV, and then pulled herself up and ran, wailing, to the bathroom and locked herself inside. Sobbing and shouting, He hit me, he hit me! I'm bleeding...

I searched my pockets for the stupid little red knife with the cross. It took me a while to open it. I hesitated between the big blade or the nail scissors attached to it. The man was turning blue: I thought he might be suffocating. I immediately pulled the sock out of his mouth and he took a big gobble of air and started to cough and spit.

I cut the ropes with my Swiss knife (I'd settled on the largest blade). The man immediately freed himself and rushed, barefooted, and on his knees, to the bathroom and begged the dominatrix to open the door.

I am sorry, Master, I am so sorry, he said, coughing. Next time I'll take all the punishment. Fly here is just a taxi driver. He is a bit slow. Good help is hard to find! It is entirely my fault.

She opened the door and said, Look what your beast did to me. I'll never see you again. You are a stupid man, Gunther.

And now I have a black eye, she shouted, and I have a book signing coming up! And she slammed the bathroom door.

Let's go, the man said to me. He put on his trousers, quickly gathered his clothes, grabbed his shoes and slimy socks, and we rushed out of the room and into the hallway, where he started to laugh and put his shoes on. That was magnificent, he said, when we were once more in the car. Good job, indeed, Fly. Magnificent! It was just like a scene from a Godard movie: absurd and philosophical. You, my man, you do not blink. You are physical and visceral. You act without hesitating or thinking about your act. It is funny, we were discussing this the other night. I was in that novelist's presence, in fact, along with some other friends. We were discussing writers, writing, and the act of writing. I was reminded of a scene from the Godard film *Vivre sa vie*. Have you seen it?

I do not have a television.

Pompous rubbish, you should have a TV. The visual and the popular are essential. Anyway, in this film, there is a beautiful, young, intelligent woman who is seduced by a pimp and turned into a prostitute...but the particular scene I am referring to is when she meets a philosopher in a Parisian café. The old philosopher tells her the story of a gangster who put a bomb in a car, then turned to flee. But then he began to think about the act of walking, imagining the act and trying to understand the motion or the force that makes one's legs move forward. And the mere act of thinking about the mechanics of walking crippled him and he became paralyzed.

And the bomb? I asked.

We don't care at this point whether he is dead or not. He is a gangster, why should we care? Not to be judgmental. But all this is to say, Fly, that I think you could still be a writer. I might be wrong but I believe that, contrary to the fighting instincts you displayed here today, while you were writing you might have thought too much about the act of writing. And that is precisely what has happened to our novelist. And lately she has been on a crusade to glorify French culture. Ha! I assume it is to compensate for her provincial, parochial background. We recently had a heated argument about the complicity of culture and cultural figures in the project of imperialism. She went on a tangent about the greatness of Henry Miller, but if you ask me Miller is overrated. Ninety percent of his writing is incomprehensible, and incantation of the word *cunt* does not make you a sexual liberator. She wouldn't hear it, she banged her fist on the table and almost spilled the wine. You see, she thinks that she and Miller have contributed to the American sexual revolution. Rubbish. I believe the only revolution that matters in that country was, and still is, the black revolution: anything else is a residue of European enlightenment. Anyway, let's not get too philosophical here. Just to say that I think her reluctance to untie me today might have had something to do with our argument. Of course, it could well have been unconscious, the unconscious is full of murderous impulses, after all. She is back to her excessive drinking and she's picked up born-again Christianity on the way, as well as bondage, not that there are any contradictions there, watch me roll my eyes... I am glad you came on time, anyway. Well, now that you are driving, I trust you won't think about the act of driving or we will never get home, will we, my saviour? You look pensive, my dear Fly.

Well, I am thinking of the leather lady, I said. You know, the writer we left in the bathroom, spitting blood.

She will be fine. Do not worry. I'll call her tonight and we will laugh about it. Some excitement might be good for her creativity. For the past ten or fifteen years or so she's been struggling to produce something substantial. Now, do drive me back home. There is only so much excitement a man can take in one day.

May I ask you something? I said.

Do.

The lady called you by a name. Is that your real name: Gunther?

Here we are. I leave you. Ta ta!

DUEL

I TOO DECIDED to call it a night. I wanted to go home, put on the light, have a drink, and watch the battles of life unfold. On the way there, I encountered many young men and women in costume: cross-dressers, Einsteins, masked animals and half-naked beasts, and other undefined creatures. Many waved to me, some even banged on my car. I turned off my lantern and waved from inside the glass, informing them, in mime, that I was off to partake in the glorious intoxication of man's history. My mind was made up; I was heading back to my rug to invoke the sun, the blood of martyrs and insects, the fermenting of liquids, and the flying carpets of old palaces. I would lie on the floor and think of President Lincoln and his almost fatal duel with a foe. It was stopped just in time, and who knows what would have happened if...

As I drove back, I remembered a true story I had heard at Café Bolero. The story involved Number 72, otherwise known as Mani (or, in my lexicon, the Sex Spider), and Number 89, whom I recently dubbed the Tight-ass Spider. Gathering at the taxi stand one day were many numbers, a whole collection of bored spiders. Business was slow; the taxi commission had just hiked the fares. People, in protest or frugality, preferred other means of transportation that particular week, though they would eventually accept, forget, and go back to taking taxis. Anyway, a well-dressed woman passed by Numbers 72 and 89, and she did a back-and-forth, at times stopping, at times smiling, looking indecisive and even a bit confused. Number 89 said that she was a hesitant customer, perhaps one of those boycotting the taxis. Number 72, the Sex Spider, replied that she wanted it.

Number 89 mocked the Sex Spider, who then made a bet in front of everyone who was present that day: If I manage to pick her up and take her to a room today, he said to Number 89, I'll get to fuck you. If I don't, you are free to fuck me.

I am not into fucking men, the Tight-ass Spider replied.

Well then, the Sex Spider proclaimed, if I win, I fuck you, and if you win, I will pay you one thousand dollars. The bet was on, and the Sex Spider went on the trail of the woman. He smiled, dropped his chin, and lifted his eyes. He spoke, and smiled some more, and then pointed to his car and ushered the lady to the front seat. He waved to the bystanders, whose eyes were all wide with disbelief. The Tight-ass Spider said, That does not mean he has won. The bet is for him to actually get her into bed.

Two hours later, the Sex Spider managed to convince the dispatcher to state the following on air: Witnesses needed for an historical event involving the initiation of Number 89 into a new world of adventure and happiness. All those involved please be at Motel 9, on Vignard Street, in fifteen minutes.

Twenty cars showed up in the lot of the motel as the Sex Spider walked out, hand in hand with the woman. It was said that Number 89 had been in denial, and a burst of sweat broke out all over him. All the taxis honked and proclaimed Mani, Number 72, the winner and the groom.

Two weeks later it was discovered that the woman in question was a prostitute.

There is no one to match the Sex Spider in his appetite for love and adventure. The Sex Spider is a talker and a lover of bouncing thighs, long and short thighs, shiny thighs, shaved thighs, and hairy thighs. The Sex Spider is an equal-opportunity lover. He loves all the world and its inhabitants, as he often proclaims, people in all their colours, shapes, and forms.

Once, in Café Bolero, we were sitting side by side, and we got into a conversation about the state of affairs in the world.

I said to him, This world is an inferior place.

Not at all, he said. God created each one of us with a light inside. I've had sex with all kinds of people; every single person has a kind of beam inside that shines once they are touched properly.

You've seen that beam? I asked.

Of course. I see it all the time. Why do you think people prefer to have sex at night? The beam is there.

You don't say, I said.

Listen, the Sex Spider said. Do you know why I ask everyone to call me Mani now?

Do tell, I said, as I ate my salad and fish.

Well, once I picked up a customer, a beautiful older woman. She was a professor of history or religion or maybe both. We had a bit of polite chit-chat and then we talked about philosophy and life and she asked me where I came from. The moment she knew that I was Persian, she started talking about Mani, the prophet Mani. I said, Of course I know of him. Well, she said, then you know the myth of the two worlds. Well, of course, I said, I know it, but tell me again.

So she said that in the beginning there were two worlds: the world of the dark and the world of the light. And they both existed without knowing of one another. But when one day the dark world saw the light world shining in all its beauty, the dark world decided to attack the light world and make it his own. But the light world knew that if the dark world touched him he would cease to be pure. So the god of the light world sent his son to fight the dark world in the dark world's territory, in order to save the pure world from being touched... The son was shining with light and he flew away with his arms and swords. But once he reached the dark world, his ass was kicked. The dark took the son inside his world and broke him into a million tiny pieces of light, and those pieces of light were spread all over the dark world.

And then what, I said.

And then, said the Sex Spider, I looked at the professor lady in the mirror and I said to her, Every time I see a beautiful lady like you, I see light and I know that there is a wonderful other world out there. I drove her home and she asked me inside for a coffee. A beautiful lady, long thighs, loud screams, and a big light that shone from inside...

ONCE, AS I was driving along the highway back into town, I saw a taxi with a flat tire at the side of the road. I recognized the Sex Spider's car and I stopped to give him a hand. But before I got out of my car, he rushed to my window and gave me an address and asked me to go and pick up "Larry" from a restaurant downtown. It is urgent, he said.

I drove fast, because it seemed so important to the Sex Spider. I arrived at the restaurant and parked in front. The valet came and asked me if I was waiting for someone in particular. Larry, I said. The valet smirked and went inside.

From outside, the restaurant looked fancy. Two big guys in shades and dark suits were standing in the manner of bodyguards at the front door. I waited and then I saw a large woman with extraordinarily long legs swinging her hips towards my car. She was stunning.

She arrived and waited for the valet to open the door and she got in the back seat.

I said, Excuse me, but this taxi is reserved for Larry. Are you Larry?

She looked me straight in the mirror and said, in a thick, manly voice: At the base, yes.

I smiled and told her that Mani couldn't make it. He had a flat tire.

Perfect, she replied, it sure is my day. He is always late, but now today, just when I need him most... I've had a horrible evening. Are you a friend of Mani's?

Yes, I said.

Well, I hope you are having a good day. But before I could reply, she said again, I had a horrible evening. I thought I was going to die. Those men in there are total pigs. They have no culture. It is hard to be taken seriously in this world of vultures and pests. I am about to cry, excuse me.

So I immediately pulled down my box and offered it to Larry.

Thank you, she said. Finally, someone who has some manners and respect. What is your name, driver?

I am Fly.

My friends also call me Limo.

Nemo? I asked.

No, Limo, as in liminal, in between. But oh, Fly, what a horrible evening that was.

Tell me what happened in there, and why you seem so upset, I said, as I started to drive.

Oh well... why not, since you are a friend of Mani's. I guess I can talk to you. Okay. I received a call for a performance. They said it was in an Italian restaurant. I asked them how they got my number and they said it was through the friend of a friend. Usually I prefer to stick to my show at the Piccadilly. I perform there three times a week with other trannies, transvestites to you, from all over the world. We have a fantastic show, it's a first-class cabaret. We have the twins who do their double act, and then the muscle boy comes and lifts the two girls up into the air at the same time, with their skirts blowing up and all. I do three songs, a monologue, and the finale, in a long blue dress and feathers. Anyway, when I received the call, I refused at first, but then they offered good money so I said okay, one private party. The restaurant seemed like a high-class place.

So I arrived and was led to a back room. There were five very handsome men, wearing expensive Italian suits. They welcomed me and offered me drinks and spoke to me nicely. They asked me if it was really true that I was a man, because I looked like a beautiful woman and so on. The usual. They offered me drinks. And then the waiter rushed in and said the birthday boy had arrived. They dimmed the lights and as soon as he stepped into the room they all shouted Surprise! and the waiter put the music on and I went towards the birthday boy dancing and singing "Happy Birthday." I was dressed as Marilyn Monroe. All the boys were whistling and cheering. Then the birthday boy squeezed me and started to kiss me . . . and it got very rowdy . . . they all started to scream and throw their drinks on the floor and take off their jackets and swing them over their heads. I danced with him for a while and then one of the other boys, while we were dancing, came over and said to him, Hey, Frank, grab it . . . and before I had the chance to pull back, this Frank had stuck his hand under my dress and grabbed me down there. Then he quickly let go as if he had touched the devil himself, and started to curse, and he pushed me away. I tripped and fell on the floor, on my back . . . with my high heels . . . you can picture it, I'm sure. All his friends started to laugh. I felt so humiliated. Here I was on the floor, soaking in drinks and dirt, and I was afraid to cut myself on all the broken glass around me. Then the birthday guy went crazy, *he* was insulted. He came at me and kicked me and tried to stomp on my head . . . if it wasn't for his friends pulling him back . . .

And then, listen to this, Fly, then this monster reached inside his jacket and pulled out a gun. He was going to shoot me. I was so afraid. But his friends stood in front of him and tried to calm him down, saying, Frankie, Frankie, take it easy, it was just a joke. I was on the floor shaking and crying, thinking, I am not a joke, I am not a joke! Then one of the men gave me his hand and pulled me off the floor and apologized. He pulled out a big stack of money and handed it to me. He called the waiter and the waiter escorted me to the bathroom to wash, and that is when I called Mani. I was crying, but his tire...

Anyway, I'm glad he sent you. Before I left, I told the man who paid me that I am a respected artist and not a joke. And that next time he shouldn't treat people as jokes, because we are all human beings, that's what I said to him. There is still beer and whisky all over my clothes and I smell like cigars, it's disgusting. I am still shaking. I should have known from their big gold rings, but you know, I am glad Mani didn't come, because if he saw me like this...he is short-tempered and those guys could really hurt him. I know the type; they are criminals, they own many of those high-class restaurants. Money laundering, that's what those places are for. Which reminds me, I definitely have to send my dress to the cleaners, I have a show the day after tomorrow. Long live the Piccadilly! Here, we've arrived. How much do I owe you, Fly?

Nothing, I said. It is on the house.

Take something. Please, those monsters paid me a lot of money tonight. Here, take it and call it a night...take it and turn off your light and go home and sleep. Here, Larry said, and pushed two large bills into my hand.

Thank you ... and good night, I said.

Good night, Limo said, and she left.

STEEL

THE NIGHT AFTER my adventure with the no-name once-famous writer, I went to the Bolero. I arrived, secured a table, lifted a tray, and went up to the counter to order food. The Greek owner was in the kitchen. I could see his stained white apron and I imagined he was sweating under the blue and white scarf he always wears tightly around his neck. Light blue and white, like the rest of this place. It is said that, after consultation with the oracles, the owner planted a ceremonial Greek flag and some postcards next to the cash register so that Hellenic supremacy could reign over the Latin name, Bolero, which he had retained for pragmatic reasons.

The owner's wife always looks tired, bitter, and dissatisfied, her glasses about to sink down her ancient Hittite nose. It is the daughter, that little goddess who appears and disappears from behind the brume of food offerings, who saves us all from starvation. Her long, curly hair constantly hovers over the stainless-steel warming trays. Not once since she began her work here, has she ever dipped her hair into the food. Her hair is measured and trimmed with admirable precision, but I am sure no driver would mind that salty addition of flavour, that extra Homeric tang, that divine transgression. Besides, I've heard that a mixture of yogurt and olive oil brings a shine to one's hair.

Soon enough, two spiders came to join me at the table. They set their trays across from mine and we formed a trinity.

I wanted to make an observation about the number three and its fundamental role in Hellenic culture, but Number 76, whom I wavered between calling the Spider of Interruption or the Spider of Destruction (I settled on the Samson Spider in the end), was agitated and had already started telling us about his encounter with two rich boys.

The other day, he said, I picked up these two brats. Right away, they started acting funny in the back seat. When they asked me how the night was going, I told them I'd just started and they were my first customers. I'd done about ten hours of work by then, but the moment you tell them that, those bandits start to imagine the piles of money you're carrying. But one of the kids said to me, I bet you have it under the seat. I said, Have what?

You know, the money.

And what is it to you?

It is everything, motherfucker, the kid said.

I looked in the mirror and didn't see a weapon. Two little fuckers dressed in expensive clothing, trying to scare me, I thought.

You motherfuckers better hold on tight, I said, because you've got the craziest driver in town. You think I give a fuck about this, you little assholes?

And I stepped on it. I was doing one-eighty or two hundred on the highway, the car was shaking! To freak them out I started to sing opera and conduct an imaginary orchestra. I am Samson! I shouted. Let this temple fall on me and my enemies, o Lord, for my hair has grown back! I have no fear and my people have risen...or some shit like that. Then I started to invent songs about the Lord and the second coming and I said to them, Get on your knees, because soon the temple will be restored and we shall all be saved...Hallelujah!

One of them pissed in his pants, and the other started to beg. The kid confessed they were only playing and trying to scare me. They were not planning to rob me, they were from a rich family and they'd give me money if I would just stop the car...The next thing I knew, there was a policeman chasing me with his lights and sirens. I pulled over and they slapped me with a big fine and a warning.

And now, said the Samson Spider, those two punks turn out to be the sons of a wealthy businessman who finances the mayor's campaign. The man is suing me for reckless driving and endangering his kids. Their lawyer wants a psychological assessment. He asked the taxi commission to revoke my licence. How much can a man take? I want to defend myself but I don't have the money for a lawyer. I'm willing to stand in front of the judge and tell him what happened, but my wife is worried and fed up. I never see my kids. I'm always working...She says if I lose my licence she will leave me, take the kids and go back to her parents...

Then I, Fly, who is not a Spider but a wanderer, stopped my food consumption, looked up at the spider, and said, What company does the man work for and what is the man's name?

His name is Mr. Sarnath Patel. He is the CEO of Dovlin Steel. A man who pillages the world and pollutes six villages and won't give a damn about a taxi driver like me. I am ruined!

I stood up and returned my tray. The owner was outside the kitchen now. He was pouring coffee into a paper cup decorated with stripes of Greek temple columns, matching the colour of the walls and his own white apron and blue hat.

The next day, early in the morning, I went home, took a shower and shaved, and then I immediately drove to the Dovlin building. At the reception desk, I asked for Mr. Patel, the CEO. They told me to wait and then a man in a uniform came down and called me to the security desk.

What is the nature of your business? he asked.

I am a taxi driver and I am here on behalf of another taxi driver. It is the matter concerning Mr. Patel's sons.

The uniformed man asked me to stay put. Then he stood up and left.

Half an hour later, a woman, accompanied by a bodyguard, came down and took me up to the twenty-fourth floor. At the elevator doors, I was met by two other security guards or maybe bodyguards, who showed me to a table and searched my bag. There was a book I'd picked out from my library at home, *Invisible Man*. For the longest time, when I was arranging my books, I had assumed the book to be a manual on magic and the art of disappearing. But the story, of a man who lives in a hole full of light, turned out to be more magical than any manual. The guard looked at the book and mumbled, Here everything and everyone is visible, and he shoved the book inside the bag with such disrespect that I had to stop myself from throwing bolts of lightning to bring the building crumbling down.

Next, I was offered coffee or water. I chose coffee but it didn't appear. I waited for another hour. At intervals, the woman came out with faint apologies and requests for my patience. Mr. Patel is a very busy man, she didn't cease to remind me.

Finally, Mr. Patel arrived with the woman, his secretary, trailing behind him. I immediately assessed his weight by the heaviness of his steps on the carpeted floor and I knew that the coffee would never come.

He humbly shook my hand and said: I apologize for the wait, but I have only a few minutes to spare before I leave for the airport. I was informed that you are a taxi driver, and a friend of the driver who took my two sons on a dangerous ride.

Mr. Patel, I said, I shall be brief. My friend did what he did because he was scared. We taxi drivers are under threat all the time. In our profession, we are vulnerable. I am here to ask you to reconsider and to drop the lawsuit. The truth is, your kids misbehaved, and my friend did what he did to protect himself, out of fear for his life...

The man interrupted me. Your friend broke the law, he said calmly.

And who doesn't break the laws? Does your grand enterprise always obey the laws when it ravages these lands from above and below? When it pollutes villages and rivers with poisonous liquids? And how many deformed faces and crippled kids should sue you back? I hissed in his face.

Without a word he was gone. His secretary ran after him in a panic. Seconds later, the two security men were beside me. They asked me to face the wall.

When I protested, one of the gorillas put his mouth next to my ear and whispered, I will only ask you once.

I walked towards the wall. He told me to lift my arms and spread my legs.

He searched my waist and passed his hand between my thighs, over my torso, and under my armpits, then he asked me to remove my shoes and socks. When they were done searching me, they told me to put my shoes back on, and both men stood very close to me and escorted me to the elevator and down to the lobby and out of the building.

I went out and cursed everything around me. I walked across the lawn. The stretch of green was wide enough to hold a chopper; long enough to watch enemies approaching, exposed; vast enough to give defenders time to sound the alarm and prepare. Lawns are the most cunning short stretches of land. Behind that innocent, well-maintained, pleasing greenery there are ruthless gates, conniving rulers, extractors of gold, and drivers of slaves. In those glass citadels and towering dungeons, I see meek creatures, hunchbacked servants, and diabolic yes-men conspiring around water coolers, stirring storms in coffee cups, carrying out orders to steal the sugar cane from the land and the water from the underground, a murderous waltz that will never stop until they dig out the last meal from the bellies of the poor.

I cursed and cursed my way off the lawn and I spat and walked out of those mirages and oases of death to reach the concrete side of things.

JESUS

THE NEXT DAY I waited for Zainab at the entrance of the building. She appeared and said, I am starting to think that you time it.

I never hide the fact that I wait for you, I told her.

Listen, Fly. I am seeing someone. And I think the person will be coming here more often. So, you know...

Yes, I know ... is that person from here?

Yes, from here.

What is his name?

None of your business, Fly.

Circumcised?

Fly, don't start with your childish jokes.

Just asking.

Stop it, I mean it. Besides, it is none of your business.

Ah! So you know!

Leave me alone, it is too early for your offensive obsessions.

I just want to know and then I will leave you alone, I promise.

No, not circumcised.

Ah. I am all for interfaith intercourses. They can only result in a sublime secular experience. What does this intact
and complete person do?

An academic. I have to go.

Farewell, my dearest Lady Zainab, and do be safe, I said to
her as I dropped my cabbie hat with the reverence of a Spanish knight in the presence of an enchanting moor.

You too, drive safe, Zainab said, with grace and chivalry.

I slept for a few hours, and then some construction started up outside. I woke up and I thought of Mary. Poor Mary.
They married her to Jesus, and Jesus is an asexual circumcised revolutionary. What future is there to be had in that
scenario? I wondered.

I took a shower and combed to the side what was left of
my hair. I tucked my shirt under my belly, recalling all the
food I had eaten the previous day. Nothing to be proud of,
nothing to regret. All the advice that the doctor had given me
was forgotten.

BILL

THE DEALER CALLED and so I went to pick him up at his place. His woman waved from the window and screamed: I am waiting for you, Zee baby! And she waved at me and said: Good luck to you, good man!

We drove downtown, made a few straightforward rounds. Are you up for it next week? he asked.

Yes.

Good. I'll call you. Do you know the industrial area?

Yes, very well, I assured him.

Good. You want cash or some blow as payment for tonight?

Cash.

Right. Fly the cash man. He tapped me on the shoulder and opened the door and I watched him walking away from the car.

I had dropped him at a nightclub. He passed the long line of people waiting to go inside. A few bouncers immediately surrounded him and they opened the door wide, ushering him in as if he were the king of the street.

I drove a few metres and a large man stopped me. He had a thick neck and tottered like a wrestler.

Up Main Street, he said, barely fitting through the door.

Right, I said, looking at him in the mirror. I thought, if my neck got caught between his steroid-inflated elbows, I'd hear my pipes crack before the light changed.

By the friction of the wheels against the city's asphalt, I felt the heaviness in his mind, and so, to make things lighter, I talked about the weather. Damp today, I said.

He nodded.

I asked him if he was a wrestler, and he smiled and said, No, man, all wrestlers are faggots. I am not into grabbing other guys' asses and sniffing the sweat between their balls. I am no dog.

I interjected with a comment about wrestling and how it still survives in the Persian peninsula to this day. It must have thrived during the Macedonian occupation. Cultural influences, I continued, and traces of the past can well be found in the most everyday things. Alexander the Great, upon his conquest, ordered his army officers to marry Persian women... but then I looked in my rearview mirror and realized how all this history talk must have sounded pedantic to the muscles in my cab, so I stopped myself and, to bring things back to the present, I asked, What do you do, then?

I work as a bouncer, man.

At the club behind us?

Yeah.

I just dropped a friend there, I said.

The whole world is there tonight, he said, but I've got some business to do in the next neighbourhood. Can you get me to Main Street fast, before the waitress I'm meeting goes home?

I'll do my best. We drove in silence for a while.

Stop here, he said, handing me a hundred-dollar bill. Could you make it quick with the change?

I pulled out a stack of money from under the seat and gave him ninety-two dollars. He left in a hurry without leaving me a tip.

I drove for a few metres, stopped at a red light, and looked at the bill he had given me. It was as fake as Monopoly money.

I did a U-turn and went back to where I had left him, but he was gone. I drove around the neighbourhood and said to myself, Think, Fly. The muscleman wasn't going home. I parked my car and walked. The first thing I did was look for a dive with a waitress inside and also, judging by the neighbourhood, a poker machine, a couple of old-timers behind pints of beer, and a cigarette machine. I found one. The place was empty except for the staff and, sure enough, the muscleman. He was talking to a woman in a very short skirt and flimsy high heels. He saw me and turned away, but I tapped him on the shoulder.

What?

The bill you gave me is no good.

That isn't my problem anymore.

I think you gave me a counterfeit bill and you should take it back.

I think you should leave, he said. He pointed his finger in my face, but his eyes focused on a point somewhere between my chin and my belly button. I could feel the threat of his biceps.

Does the name Zee mean anything to you? I asked.

The man's finger wavered. The woman turned and left. Then he stepped back slightly and said, What about Zee?

I am what you would call his private driver. I could call him right now and he could straighten things out between us. Or I could just give you back your hundred and you could give me back the money I gave you, and your next ride would be on the house.

He nodded. Pulled the cash from his pocket and handed it to me.

Could you wait outside for a moment, he said politely. I have to finish some business with the lady here.

After a few minutes he joined me in the car and said, Okay, back to the club. He sat next to me this time, not behind, and he kept looking at me. Finally he said, Don't I know you?

Don't know.

Yes, fuck, you are that cabbie who used to wait for the blond every Thursday at the strip bar.

Yes, I said. That is me.

Sure it is, I recognize you. Small world, he said. I quit over there. This place I'm working at now is happening, I'm much better off. I get one of them clubbing bitches every night. They stick their number in my jacket and I bring them to the front of the line. Too bad about your girl, man, what was her name, Sally?

Yes. What about her?

You should know, man.

I should know what? I said.

I thought you were banging her.

No. We were friends. Do tell me what you know.

It seems to me that you were more than friends. Look at you sad and all. Anyway, man, all I know is that one night, she locked herself in the bathroom and she wouldn't open up or go onstage. She cried and cried and I had to break down the bathroom door. I found her lying on the floor naked, crying in her high heels and bikini. She wouldn't say anything. She just cried. I called another girl and we brought her clothes. She said that her best friend Maggie, another dancer, had died in a motorcycle accident that night. I gave your friend some water and she took her bag and left. And that was it. Your girlfriend never came back to work.

Do you know where she went?

No, man, those girls come, and go. I don't get involved in their personal lives. But, I tell you, your girl needed help. Whatever she lost must have been hard on her.

Here's the door, he said. I'll get out. Drop by one night and I'll buy you a drink.

And he walked towards a long line of women who stood, half-naked, shivering and waiting in the cold.

ACT FOUR

THE KILL

I CHECKED MY mailbox and found junk mail, some bills, and a few letters for Otto. Traces from the time he lived with me.

So that evening I decided to look for Otto to give him his mail. I went to the bar where he liked to hang out but couldn't find him. I asked the bartender, who told me Otto usually showed up a little later. I drove to his apartment, the one he shared with the old lady. He often complained about how she was always smoking and getting drunk on rum and Cokes. Her room was stuffed with empty Coke cans, hundreds of them arranged in rows covering the bedroom walls. The biggest existential question in her case was whether she would die from diabetes or liver failure. Otto thought it would be obesity. Just like the rest of this nation, he said. Communists and Muslims are not the enemies to fear in this land, Fly. It is the food consumption that will eventually blow up in everyone's face.

But Otto wasn't home, so I went back to the bar and, this time, I saw him sitting on a stool talking animatedly to a well-dressed man.

I approached them and found myself in the middle of a heated argument. The man had a thick French accent that reminded me of the bearded lady. Otto was telling him that the French empire and its culture were dead, and rightly so.

The man said something about a lasting contribution to world culture.

Otto looked revolted and said, Culture? Let me tell you about culture. I walk through the museums and I look at the monuments, those celebrations of theft and oppression, and all I can think of is the suffering of the slaves and the starving workers who shaped those massive stones and carried them on their backs. You know what culture I believe in? I believe in the slave revolt of Eunus against the savagery of the Roman Empire; I believe in Haiti's emancipation from the colonial French, and when they gave it to Napoleon the Third up the ass. Violence and resistance are the only answer. Empire has to feel pain or it will never stop devouring you. It is only when a gun is put in a person's face that anything changes. All empires are hungry cannibals…

Let's go for a stroll down to the river, I said.

No rivers, Fly. The only liquid I need to see right now is in a glass in my hand. You go ahead to your river. How many chances do we get to speak to a journalist and a colonizer?

I beg your pardon, sir, said the Frenchman. I am not a colonizer.

Well, let's talk Algeria then. Let's talk about your culture and your celebrated writers.

At this point I told Otto I was leaving. I offered to give him a ride back to his place. But Otto stayed, drinking and talking to the French journalist.

I drove to the nearest station and filled my car with gas. I picked up a bag of peanuts. I ate it and went looking for work.

ONCE LINDA DISAPPEARED for days and she left her son alone. She was getting high in a crack house. Luckily, Otto had decided to visit Tammer that week. Aisha was in the hospital and had been asking for him. But when Otto entered the apartment he saw the boy hungry and dirty, his face full of snot and drenched in tears. The neighbour woman, hearing Otto arrive, opened her door and said, That kid has been whimpering like a puppy. He's been asking for food. The woman stood there frowning. She looked Otto in the eye and said, I was about to call the cops. If the kid's mother can't take care of the child, someone should. The city has got to know about this.

Otto assured her that all was well and immediately closed the door and took Tammer in his arms. He opened a can of Chef Boyardee spaghetti that he found on an upper shelf and heated it.

Soon Tammer was shoving the food inside his mouth and looking at Otto with droopy eyes of disbelief and sadness. Otto called Fredao, shouted, and ordered him to come at once. After Tammer finished eating, Otto took him to the bathroom and gave him a bath, and then he combed his hair, put him into his pyjamas, fixed his bed, told him a story, and tucked him in to sleep. He washed the dishes and tidied the house. He picked up the clothing that was lying all over the floor and lit a cigarette and waited for Fredao.

When Fredao got there, Otto opened the door and grabbed him by the collar. He pushed him against the wall and said, You fix this mess.

Fredao pushed Otto away and went over to the neighbour's apartment. Fredao smiled and introduced himself as the father of the child, saying that the boy's mother had been in an accident and had been taken to the hospital, and that he had been coming to look after Tammer but got held up in a long traffic jam and his car broke down. He'd had to wait for the tow truck... You know, Fredao said, when it rains, it pours.

The woman didn't buy a word of it. She looked at Fredao's flamboyant hat and flashy suit and said, The kid is skinny: he has always been skinny, ever since I've known him. He comes here and begs for food. I give him candy, but I ain't his mother, I shouldn't be giving him food. I think somebody else should take care of him. You people are not doing a good job.

Fredao smiled and said, We appreciate your concerns, ma'am. Here is something for your trouble.

Are you trying to bribe me, mister? The woman filled the hallway with her shouts. This kid is about to starve to death. Do you think I will watch a child suffering and be quiet?

Well, ma'am, like I said, it is for your trouble. You gave the kid some candy and in return I am giving you something sweet. There are two ways to taste things in life: the sweet way and the bitter way. I didn't offer you the bitter because I like to start with the sweet, but if people don't want my sweets I have no choice but to offer the bitter way. Now, what is it going to be, lady, this or that?

I ain't calling this time. You can keep your stuff to yourself. And the neighbour slowly and reluctantly closed her door.

AND NOW, YEARS later, here was Tammer knocking at my door. It was morning and I had just fallen asleep after a long shift. I heard banging, and then a voice calling: It's Tammer. Open up!

I let him in. He looked much older and skinnier than I remembered. When I asked him about his mother, he asked me if I had any coffee and doughnuts.

I can boil some coffee, but no doughnuts, I said. What's up?

Otto wants to see you, Tammer said. It's urgent. He said to bring him some booze, cash, and food.

Where is he?

He's staying with us.

Your mother's place?

No, under the bridge.

Let's go, I said.

When we arrived, I looked at the traces of campfires and the pigeon bones, the empty booze bottles, and the hobo clothing scattered around on the ground. Otto emerged from behind a cement column that was spotted with bird droppings. He looked hungover and cold. I handed him a bag with the food and alcohol, and an envelope with a bit of cash. He broke off a piece of bread and opened the screw-top of the wine and started to gulp it down. Tammer had stayed in the taxi and I could see him fiddling with the radio dial.

You know what our problem is, Fly? Otto said. No matter how much we try, the rituals and the symbolism beat us. You've brought me bread and wine. He started to laugh. It must be my last supper. He laughed again and then he said, They're coming to get me.

Who is coming to get you? I asked.

I killed a man last night, Fly.

You killed a man.

Yes. I killed that journalist.

He moved away from the dark and into an open space. The cars above us rattled and shook the metal beams of the bridge. I stood there not knowing why I was paying attention to the sounds that shook and rattled above us. And suddenly I repeated, You killed a man.

It just happened, Fly. I don't know how. It felt feverish, I felt as if I was under a blasting sun. We were talking about Camus and I thought of Algeria and its million dead. I can't remember pulling the trigger. I remember telling the journalist that Camus was an asshole. The journalist answered, Yes, but he was a great thinker nevertheless. I insisted: An asshole, you hear me? Anyone who supports the colonial power to deprive the indigenous of their rights and their land is an asshole. And people like you supported the *Pieds-Noirs*, you and your republic are assholes. And then the Frenchman turned his back on me and left to sit at another table...

I left, Fly, and I was going to go home, but I kept on thinking of Algeria...I waited in the alley until he came out and then I followed him to his hotel. I think I put the clown nose on my face. It was in my pocket. And I had my gun. After that I don't remember. It was dark. We were in an alley. I made him repeat the names of places, Napoleon's Spain, Haiti, Vietnam, Algeria. The man started to cry. My gun was up against his head, Fly. I remember him telling me, You don't need to wear a mask. You don't need a gun. I know who you are. We can talk like two civilized people. But then I made him repeat: *My country is not civilized, my country is not civilized, I am not civilized, I am not civilized, Camus was not civilized*...and I felt something rush to my head, almost like a heat wave, and the gun went off and the man was on the ground. I don't remember what happened next. I must have been drunk. The gun just went off, Fly. I don't remember. Fly, I can't remember.

And Otto ran his hand through his hair, which looked clumped and greasy. I offered him another cigarette and I pulled out my lighter, and he sheltered my hands with his hands to protect the fire.

I told him I would help him and I asked him what he wanted to do.

I will be moving around for a while, he said. I won't let them catch me, Fly. I am not going back to that asylum.

The gun? I asked.

I am keeping it as a last resort.

Throw it in the river, I said.

I told you, Fly, I am keeping it as a last resort. Capture and submission are no longer options. But I can't stay here. This play is almost over. And we should know when to bow and when to leave.

Wait, I said.

And Otto held my head and kissed my forehead goodbye.

THE NEXT DAY, two officers knocked at my door. I let them in. Ironically, they stood between the crime section and the culinary section, both situated next to the window as a precautionary measure against arson, grease fires, and food poisoning, among other methods of murder.

Are you an acquaintance of Mr. Otto Blake? they asked.

Yes, he is a friend.

How long have you known Mr. Blake?

Twenty years, maybe more.

Did Mr. Blake ever reside here?

He has crashed here occasionally.

But some of his mail is sent to this address?

Yes, he moves around. He must have given this as a permanent address.

Did he ever mention a Mr. Bouchard to you?

No. I don't know who that is.

He is the French journalist who was killed two nights ago. Shot in the face. With a nine-millimetre gun.

I shook my head.

Mr. Blake was seen having an argument with him at the Irish Pub on Curtis Street. Do you know anything about that?

No, I don't, I said.

Were you at that pub on the night of the seventh? That was Friday.

Yes, briefly.

Was Mr. Bouchard present?

I wouldn't know. There were too many people.

Here is a photo of Mr. Bouchard. That is before the damage.

I can't recall, with the Carnival and all. It was chaotic. I only talked to Otto.

Was Mr. Blake talking to Mr. Bouchard?

Like I said, it was crowded.

Do you know if Mr. Blake had a gun in his possession?

No, I have no idea.

Where did you go after you left?

I went back to my job. I drive a taxi. I put gas in my car.

Do you have a receipt?

Yes. I can locate it if you give me a minute. I grabbed my wallet from the kitchen table. I went through a bunch of receipts until I located the one from that day and I handed it to the detective, who was already snooping through my books.

Do you mind if we hold on to it?

No.

Anything else you did?

I drove all night and picked up customers.

Any customers who might remember being driven by you? Is there a record from a dispatcher we could use to verify your whereabouts?

No, I am an independent driver. I don't rely on dispatchers in my job.

So you drive around...

Yes, I wander and pick up customers off the street. I find it tedious waiting for a call to come to me.

Could you give us the name of any person who could confirm that you were driving that night?

I did drive an old man and his daughter to a seniors' home in Eastmount. I helped the man inside.

Do you remember his name?

No, but I remember that he was crying. And afterwards I drove his daughter back to her place. I could give you that address if you want to check it. We had a conversation and she gave me a good tip and asked me my name. I am known as Fly; she should remember me.

What did you talk about?

Death.

Death as in murder? the inspector asked.

No, death as in old age.

Are you staying here for the next while?

Do you mean here at home?

No, I mean in this town. Would you be taking a plane somewhere soon?

I have no need for airplanes.

Thank you for your help. Oh, one more thing: do you belong to any political party?

No.

If I may ask, do you subscribe to the views of any particular political party?

Like I said, Officer, I am an independent driver.

I see the metaphor, the policeman said. Do you mind if we take a quick look around?

Not at all, but please watch your head.

THE KILLING OF the French journalist was all over the news. The police were looking for a person of interest, they said, and they mentioned Otto's name. And it didn't look like a robbery, they added, because the wallet of the journalist was found, untouched, in the victim's pocket.

Later that evening, while I was driving and following the news, I heard a reporter conducting an interview with Otto's roommate. The old lady was under the influence and her husky voice had the sound of smoke and relentless cigarettes. She called Otto an angry man and a loner. She also said they'd had an argument about God. Which god? the lady reporter asked. None, she replied: he hated them all and he never respected me because I am a believer. Every time one of those good people on TV began preaching the gospel or asking for donations, he cursed and called them quacks, slammed the door, and went to his room. He was an angry man, like I said.

RAIN

I LEFT MY lantern in the trunk and drove through the town of celebration. I looked for a clown, hoping to recognize Otto among the dancing crowds. There is no better place for an exile to hide, I reasoned, than among a horde of humans in masks re-enacting the periodic cycles of life and death.

And it rained and the city's garments danced under the rain. I left my window open as I drove. I smoked in defiance of the signs in my own car, and the water ran down the side of my face. I parked my boat a small distance from my home and walked under the deluge. I stopped and laughed at the memory of Bunzy the clown, who in every performance was showered with water from the elephant's trunk. I wanted to peek again, from inside the tent and behind the curtain of the dressing room, at the laughter of other kids, the covering of faces with hands, the uproar of the crowd. It rained and I stood like a sad-faced clown waiting for the applause. I waited for the elephant to come and lift me up onto her back so I could stand there and tell every soul that the clown who lit the cannons was innocent, lost, distracted by the circle shape of the world, by the gestures of ancient monkeys and the dangerous swinging of women and men and their animal-like acts; that his intention was never to step on the elephant's feet, never to sing in such a horrible voice, never to wobble in clothing that was not his own, shoes that could never be tied, flowers that spat in the crowd's face. His real intention, ladies and gentlemen, was to bring the audience to their senses, let them realize that soon all would be coming to an end, and that all shall disappear to no return.

The rain fell and seeped into my clothing and passed through me, and I stood watching the currents of water convulsing on the peripheries of sidewalks and fleeing to nowhere. I saw an umbrella floating, and I saw a woman rushing towards me, balancing a stick of impermeable colours in the fist of her hand, to shelter me from the elephant's waterfalls. I laughed. She covered me with her umbrella and put her arms around me and said, What are you doing, Fly? Come, let's go inside. All seemed like a silent rehearsal without applause.

We walked back. Her arm around my shoulder felt warm, and her scent under the water brought water to my eyes. I stood in the entrance of the building and I said to her, We are capable of harm.

Why don't you come upstairs? Zainab said. Come, Fly, come with me.

I walked, and the wetness in my shoes made me want to leap, jump, and splash the puddles like a skipping child.

Where are your keys, Fly? The keys, she repeated, practically having to shout in my face.

Somehow I found my keys and I opened the door to my apartment. Zainab followed me in. She started to undo my clothes. She ran to the bathroom, found a towel, dried my hair, wrapped my head in it, and led me to bed. I felt exhausted and weak, and the ceiling and my walls of books spun at an unimaginable speed and I must have passed out.

SALT

THE NEXT MORNING, Zainab knocked at my door. She wanted to know how I was feeling. Now that she had seen me living inside my library, she was intrigued to come again.

I made her tea and she seemed overwhelmed by the volume of volumes and books. All I hoped was that none of the mice would stroll between her feet and scare her into leaving again.

Fly, Zainab said, you should see a doctor. I mean, someone you can talk to. You were not all there last night, if you know what I mean. You thought that I was someone else. Well, many someones. You had, I think, what could be described as an episode...

And then, suddenly, Zainab switched topics and asked me about the books. I proceeded to explain that my system of classification was very different from the one used in the place where she worked. My system, I informed her, was more personal and slid along an impressionistic scale.

She smiled and said, I am intrigued, Fly. Go on.

Well, well, I rejoiced, finally I have got your interest. Who knew?

You always had my interest, Fly, but I was never interested...

Nuances... indeed, nuance is the mark of a great mind... so, fiction books, let's say, I began. These are arranged based on a subjective impression of the book and its main characters' lives. Dead protagonists take priority over triumphant, happy-ending characters but are surpassed by books with open endings, books that don't have grand moral conclusions. Novels with open endings I consider to be of a higher rank; hence they are located before novels with happy endings, which I often call religious, or "resurrection," endings. That is why they tend to be conveniently located on the bottom shelves or facing my bathroom door over here...As for historical novels, they are organized based on the name of the winner of the first battle that appears in the book. For instance, *War and Peace* will be found in the N section, N in reference to Napoleon, of course. Much of the other war literature, unfortunately, tends to be filed under H, for the likes of the Carthaginian commander Hannibal and other delusional elephant herders and failed artists.

Seeing that I still had Zainab's attention, I began to explain the most mysterious layer of my classification system, that is, how to arrange the crime novels. These clueless victims are arranged according to my first attempt at guessing the killer. Since I always suspect Winston the butler, the W section might be better placed at the beginning of the shelves...

But let us move on to more serious things. Dearest Zainab, let me confess to you that the most the privileged position of them all is saved for the misanthropic writers...for instance, the writer and dramatist Bernhard, *l'enfant terrible* of Austria, is found on a golden shelf with his fellow literary radicals, writers of conscience, revolutionaries, debauchers, and liberators...these kinds of writers deserve the utmost respect, though in their lifetimes they are often subjected to neglect or contempt. For instance, and to give you an example that might interest you or might not, most of the Arab writers in my collection, such as Munif, who wrote the magnificent *Cities of Salt*, can be found here under a subsection called "Parisian cafés." This section comprises the works of exiled writers who had to leave their motherlands for France and lingered in Parisian cafés for the rest of their lives, smoking and complaining about both cultures, the French and their own. They are the true writers, because they took a stand against their own governments until their American cigarettes stained their teeth yellow and led them to shun laughter and smiles, out of embarrassment or maybe depression, and so they spent the rest of their days in a chronic state of solitary poetic existence. Please follow me, right this way, and watch your head. Here, if you look up above the toilet, you will find the feel-good apolitical literature. The main function of these complacent pages is to act as a sponge to absorb all the sticky humidity that results from my occasional showers and my daily...well, not to get too graphic...Then there is this lot. As you might well notice, they are positioned next to the window. These, if I may introduce them, are the escapist self-help books that I occasionally rescue from the back seat of my car. Naturally, their position here is in accordance with every comedy and slapstick movie that involves the escape of a naked lover through a bathroom window.

Fly, Zainab said, when and how did you amass these books?

Well, dearest Zainab, I thought you'd never ask. Allow me to explain. You see, when the bearded lady of the circus, who raised me after my mother's death, collapsed one day on the floor of our small apartment, I lifted her up and went all over town looking for a doctor. None of those pious souls would come to our house; none wanted to touch the freak woman with a long beard, a penis, and sinful breasts, and we couldn't afford the fees that might have changed their minds. The lady refused to go to the state hospital because, she said, we should all end in dignity. I was sixteen by then, and I was known all over town as the son of the freak. I carried the bearded lady to the poorest neighbourhood and there, finally, I found a doctor who would help us. He was extremely well-read, and one day, when we were talking about books, he gave me a Baldwin novel to read (I still have it: on the first golden shelf from the left, above all the others... *Giovanni's Room*, there it is).

That good doctor took care of the bearded lady for free. She had been sick for years, and I'd left school and worked up in the hills and down in the streets until one day I landed a job as a delivery boy. I delivered food all over town. I peeked into houses with crosses hanging above televisions and on the kitchen walls alongside pots and pans. I watched workingmen rejoice over the hamburger in the box, the fries in the bag, and the soda in the bundle of ice. Until, one day, I met the professor, who ordered everything without meat but with a lot of salt. I would knock at his door and I would wait for him to open up. He was always distracted by things other than consumption, and confused by the counting of coins. And each time he would say the exact same thing: Oh, you're already here, let me put my book down and bring you the change, I think I left it... And the door would close and I would wait again, and sometimes I would have to ring the bell to remind him that I was still standing there.

But once he opened the door and, without looking at me,

he invited me in, ushering me to the basement, saying, The fuse box is this way. And I stood in the middle of his house, surrounded by a galaxy of books. I told him that I would not be able to fix his fuse box and reminded him that one could also eat in the dark.

Indeed, he said, smiling, there is light to be found in the darkest places. Have you eaten? he asked me.

No.

Well then, join me.

And I did. And we became friends. I would bring him food and we would talk about life, the stars, minerals, and books. His real interest was in history and literature, but he was well versed in astrology and cosmology as well. His two favourite pastimes were to read and to search for wandering planets. Such planets are known as planemos, he informed me once while we ate and talked. They are exiled bundles of matter that wander the universe aimlessly. These objects, he said, have no orbits and no host stars to orbit around. Aimless, he said, wanderers, lost. But they get to know more and reach farther places.

But then, after we became friends and because of his poor vision, whoever knocked at his door was invited in for food and called by the name of Fly. First it was an electrician who accepted the offer of some leftovers, then a taxi driver came and ate all the professor's green jelly beans, and then a series of hobo intellectuals started to come and help themselves to things in the fridge and, if provided, a few glasses of wine. The only objection raised by all these beneficiaries was to being called Fly. You invited us, a hobo was heard saying to the professor, no need for insults and name-calling.

Many years later the absent-minded professor said to me, Fly, I have only three months to live. I shall give all my papers and personal correspondence to the university archives, but I want you to have my books.

And so it was. For weeks I carried his books back to my place. The professor who, incidentally, was named Alberto Manuel, told me that he'd always hoped that one day he would die a glorious and poetic death, in the same manner as a ninth-century Arab philosopher by the name of Al-Jahiz, who, like himself, had amassed a huge library. One day a section of the library fell on his head and killed him.

But the important question remains, my dearest Fly, which is: which section fell on his head? And in what manner was his library arranged?

All libraries must submit to a certain order, I answered.

Indeed, agreed the professor, or all will be lost. The fall of nations and empires begins with the fall of libraries.

At the professor's funeral I walked with many of his students and colleagues. They all gave speeches about the professor's life, his accomplishments, and his love for books, learning, and life. Some recited poems and even songs. A blond man stood up and said: I shall read a passage from the professor's favourite poet, Abū al-ʿAlāʾ al-Maʿarrī. Forgive me for mispronouncing the poet's name, the blond man added, before reading a passage that went like this:

> We laugh, but inept is our laughter;
> We should weep and weep sore,
> Who are shattered like glass, and thereafter
> Remoulded no more.

I carried one of the books from the professor's library, *The History of Salt*, and when my turn came to say a few words, I read a passage on the use of salt in the time of the pharaohs, in the mummification of loved ones. My selection was pedantic, but I knew that the professor's love of salt justified my choice. Salt was never taxed by the Ottoman Empire, I read, and the word *tooz*, though it is no longer used in the modern Turkish dialect, survives in the language of a few inhabitants of the Levant now, long after the Empire's retreat from the region. What vanishes from history and what remains, I concluded, is a mystery.

And since then, my dearest Zainab, I've lived with a large collection of books.

Fly, Zainab said, and she looked at me with tears in her eyes. That is wonderful. Then she extended her hands to my face and said, Fly, I can't take care of you. You were not well last night. You should seek help. You should see someone...

FOG

THE NEXT DAY, as I lay in bed under a fog of lassitude, the thought of the killing consumed me and I wondered where Otto could have gone.

To distract myself, I debated whether to rearrange the history section of my library based on the letter S, to give priority to the erotic over the monumental. Just then I heard the Romanian and the doctor shaking their bed to the tune of "The Blue Danube" so I quickly got up and waltzed my way across the hall. I knocked and knocked until finally the Romanian came and opened the door a crack.

What do you want? she screamed at me.

Well, I know that the doctor is here, I saw his car downstairs, and I was wondering if I could have an off-hours consultation.

Who is it? I heard the doctor yell as he lowered the music.

It is me, Doctor, the neighbour who brings gifts.

Wait outside, he called. I'll be right there.

I stood in the hallway. He came out fixing his trousers. Doctor, I began, I hope you enjoyed the package that I gave to our friend here the other day.

He nodded, but did not otherwise acknowledge it.

Anyway, I have a small favour to ask. I have been having what might be called fantastical thoughts.

What kinds of thoughts?

Well, harmless thoughts. Theatrical thoughts that involve ropes, clowns, and even animals.

Sexual fantasies?

No. More like memories. Anyway, I thought that I would see a doctor for my head, and I happened to learn the name of a good one. So I was wondering if you could refer me to him. His name is Dr. Wu.

Sure, sure, he said, but you will have to come to my office for that.

Yes, and I'm sorry to disturb you, but I thought since you were here and all...

No problem. Come to my office in the morning. Dr. Wu, you said? Remind me tomorrow and it will be done. You won't even have to wait.

Great.

Oh, by the way, if you have any more of that prescription, by all means bring it along.

I'll try, I said, and left.

Once I got the referral, I went straight to the psychiatrist's office. I was taking a big chance, but I had to know whether he remembered my face from the night I had driven him under the bridge to his meeting with Otto. I made sure I was well-dressed, cologne and tie and all.

I entered the clinic and asked the secretary if I could see the doctor. The secretary was gracious; she asked if I had insurance. I smiled and said no, I just needed a quick consultation before I left town. I was willing to pay for it. She asked me to fill out a form and wait. So I sat down and slowly filled out the form under a name that was not my own. I ticked off a few items concerning my physical and mental condition. I arbitrarily decided on chronic bladder infections and double vision.

What can I do for you? the psychiatrist said when I was eventually led in.

Well, Doctor, I said, I've been having sleepless nights and a deep feeling of melancholy; indeed, on some days, sadness has confined me to my bed. I am tired all the time and thoughts of suicide have crossed my mind. The only relief I can find is in my chronic acts of masturbation.

He stared at me with a blank face. What do you do, Mister...

I am between jobs at the moment.

What was your last job?

I worked in transport.

Did that involve physical work?

No, I was sitting all the time.

Right. I'll send you for a complete physical. We'll check your blood pressure and so forth. Then I'd recommend some blood tests, a psychological assessment, and perhaps some pills to relax your desires. Do you experience distortions of vision or episodes of delirium?

What kind of episodes?

Like hearing voices.

Whose voices?

God's, maybe?

No, not me, but it seems that everyone around me does.

The doctor frowned and looked at me from above his glasses.

I am not a believer, Doctor.

I gathered that. Anything else?

It's hard to say. I've been remembering my childhood and it's making me sad. This existence of perpetual transitions, of fluctuations between liberty and loss, is consuming me.

That's quite normal; at a certain age we tend to look back at the past. Anyway, as I said, these are things you will be able to discuss at length in our next session. I'll have my secretary make an appointment for you and tell you where to go for the blood test.

Doctor, have we met before? I asked.

No, I don't believe so.

You look familiar, I said.

He glanced down at the form I had filled out. I don't recognize your name. Have you been hospitalized for any mental illness?

No, not yet, I said, and chuckled, but I do have a tendency to accumulate friends and acquaintances who, at one point or another in their lives, have gone through those institutions.

Family members? he asked.

Yes, more or less.

Well then, how about you come and visit me at the hospital next week. And we can see what we can do for you.

Next week? I said. I have to consult my schedule but I will get back to you. Come to think of it, though, I might be flying out of the country.

I see, he said. Well then, we'll have to wait for your return.

It is rather a long flight, I said. And then I headed out the door and into the street to breathe the fresh air of the city sidewalks.

SPIDERS (AGAIN)

I STOPPED BY Café Bolero. These spiders are getting fatter by the day, I thought to myself. They sit and eat those large, greasy portions that make them talk louder and sit tighter in their car seats. I ordered coffee and joined the loudest table. Number 17 was waving his hands and talking about this country and the difference between here and there, but Number 67 interrupted him and said, Listen. Yes, there is no democracy where we come from, but at least things get done fast and, if you know the right people and you know how to talk to the person in charge, you get respect.

Let me tell you this story, 67 said. One night I took a nice-looking lady into my car. She looked very rich and I was driving her to a wealthy area. She asked me where I was from.

I said, I am from Tunisia, the most beautiful country in Africa. We call it "Tunisia the green." Do you know where Tunisia is? I asked her.

She said that she had been there, and that she had made the mistake of trusting a merchant who sold her a carpet in the souk. I said, Tell me what happened. She said she visited Tunis and went to the market to a buy a nice carpet for her house. All the carpet merchants tried to make her come into their stalls. They threw the merchandise at her feet.

Then this man in a nice suit appeared, and he spoke English with a British accent. Please come with me, he said, and he gracefully held her hand and led her into his store. He told her that in his youth he had lived in England and studied history, but that after his father died, he had come home to take care of the family and the family business. He invited her to sit down, he brought her tea and sweets, and he showed her a few carpets. His daughter came with a flower and put it in the lady's hair. His helpers at the store flipped the merchandise one after the other, and after she had seen many, she settled on a red Persian carpet...everyone says they are Persian but they are all made in Turkey...anyway, the problem was that she couldn't carry it on the airplane. It was too heavy and too big. The owner of the store told her that he could send it by guaranteed mail, and he showed her the papers of a shipping company that reached everywhere, even Japan, because many people from Japan came and bought from his store... The owner asked her to leave a deposit of fifty percent and to pay the other half when she received the carpet. He said that he trusted his clients and she could send the balance by money order or wire transfer once the item was safely delivered, and he handed her a business card.

The lady went home. A few weeks passed and nothing came. She called the number but it was not in service. She had given the guy eight hundred dollars. Nothing. The man stole the money, that's it.

I asked her if she remembered the name of the store. She did. We had arrived at her house, and I told her that in a few weeks I'd be going to visit my family, who lived in Tunis. I can get your money, ma'am, I told her. But if I bring eight hundred, I'll keep two hundred for myself. She thought about it and said, At this point, I have nothing to lose. She went into her house, and what a house, a classy lady, and she got me the business card and the receipt, and she wrote down her number. I will call you when I am back, I told her, and then we said goodbye.

When I arrived in Tunisia, it was the end of the month of Ramadan. Everything was closed. So the first week after my arrival I spent Eid with the family. The week after, I put on my good clothes and went to the main headquarters of the police station. I asked for the commander, Mahmoud.

The man at the desk asked, Who would you be?

I said, Tell the commander that I am an old friend of his little brother Mansour.

The commander himself came out of his office and took me to his desk. Mansour, his brother, had left Tunisia and they hadn't seen each other in many years. I knew Mansour because we were roommates here in this country for five years. He is like a brother to me.

The commander immediately sent for tea and sweets. We talked about Mansour and his life. I told him, I don't think your brother has changed a bit since he left Tunisia. He still wakes up every morning and eats bread and salt and olive oil. He still, every morning, puts on Oum Kalthoum, moves his head to the songs like this, drinks his tea, and walks in his plastic slippers. The same slippers he brought with him from Tunisia.

The commander was laughing with tears in his eyes.

That night, he took me to his village to meet his mother and the family. After we had a delicious meal, the mother asked if I could carry some good olive oil from the village to her son overseas. I said, My bag is full but, for Mansour's eyes, I'll carry the world.

Three days before my departure from Tunisia, I visited Mahmoud in his office again. Commander, I said, I am part of the family now, and Mansour is a brother to me. Before I leave, I have a small favour to ask.

If anyone is bothering you, if there is anything you need done in this town, just say the word! the commander said.

I handed him the business card and the receipt the lady had given me and I told him the story of the carpet merchant. I said, Small, thieving merchants like this man make me and your brother look bad in those foreign lands. They throw our names and the reputation of our country in the dirt. Before long, all these foreigners will be telling each other, Don't go to Tunisia, those Tunisians are thieves. In the name of this glorious country and of our friendship, I am asking if there is anything you can do, Commander.

The commander stood up, banged his fist on the metal desk, and shouted through the door to his assistant. Ten minutes later, I was riding in a convoy of five Jeeps with twenty police in them, heading to the old souk. I sat next to the commander and, once we arrived, I saw all these policemen running through the streets and closing all the shops except one.

I tell you, the whole souk was closed in minutes! I walked down the middle of the souk, right beside the commander. Someone called the owner. I saw this old man in a suit coming out from behind a stack of carpets and bowing his head like a dog.

The commander showed him the card and the receipt for the carpet. First he slapped him and then he gave him a lecture on cheating and dragging the country's name down the drain. He slapped him in front of all his employees and his whole family. His wife was wailing and his grandkids were crying. Two minutes, I am telling you, it took two minutes, and the owner of the store came back with the eight hundred dollars. The commander asked the carpet merchant to write a letter of apology to the lady. I said to the commander, Let him write it in English if he is truly what he says he is, a big shot from England. Liar, he was a liar. He probably couldn't even write it in Arabic.

The first thing I did when I came back here was call the lady. She was so impressed that she gave me an extra hundred. I made three hundred dollars, just like that.

WHEN NUMBER 67 had finished his tale, he leaned back and gloated, and I thought that his posture looked pathetic. I looked at the table and saw that his plate was empty, with only a few crumbs lingering on the surface. And now this admirer of dictators and petty tyrants was picking his teeth.

So I turned my face towards him and said, The only person in that story who should write a letter of apology is the banana republic commander of that police state.

What banana are you talking about? 67 replied. You think we are bananas? The only banana I see is the one you are sitting on. And a few of the spiders laughed at me.

That's okay, I said, I don't mind a banana up my ass, because I am just warming it up for your virgin sister. And calmly I took a sip of my coffee.

Motherfucker, faggot! He stood up and shouted, I will show you, motherfucker!

I stood up calmly and went outside. I grabbed the car keys from my pocket, lit a cigarette, and waited.

As soon as Number 67 came out of the café, I surprised him and grabbed him by the collar and started to hit him in the face with my car keys. I landed a good punch on his nose and it burst red. Two other drivers ran out and held me back. One of them got a good grip on my throat. I grabbed his index finger and forced it up until I heard it crack, and then I heard the man letting out brief, devastating moans and he let me loose. The others, seeing the bigger driver holding his hand and crumpled on the sidewalk, pulled back and started to threaten me from behind the hoods of taxis. I walked away and headed straight towards my car, but then I decided to leave it there and walk away. My knuckles, my nails, and my sleeves were covered in blood.

I walked away from the Bolero and took to the streets, aimless, until I reached a bridge. It started to rain again, and I took the stairs up and began to cross over the highway. The cars slid below me, and I watched the city expanding and contracting under the fluctuation of the torrential rain and light. I stood under the water of the god of the seas, the water buffalo's drooling on the world, the thunder of the son of Cronus, the weeping of mother earth, the slippery love of Yahweh for his tribe, the cleansing of prisoners on the ships crossing the Atlantic, the tattooed hands of Rama scrubbing the untouchables at the edge of the river, the offering of virgins to the surging, dripping, splashing crocodiles, and I let the rain wash my bloody hands and bring back the whiteness to my sleeves.

When I arrived on the east side of the city I took cover under the roof of a bus shelter. I watched the buses leave and the rain fall harder, with the thickness of curtains and the opacity of veils. Then I walked again under the rain. My hair was wet and my clothes nestled against the erection of my nipples and the inward curve of my belly. To the drivers who passed me on the highway I must have looked like a grey ghost, hunched, defeated by the damnation of water and floods. But what do those carcasses of metal and glass, those burners of oil and makers of black rain, know about the pleasures of water, the heaviness of drenched bodies, and the flight of the insane.

In my youth, when it rained, the ringmaster would shout to summon us and we would all take off our clothes and run outside to the elephants with our brushes and buckets. We let the horses and the dogs loose in the circles of mud, and then we sheltered the lions, the monkey, and the birds from the cloudbursts and the pouring sky. We monkeyed around, oinked like pigs in the dirt, and clapped for the seals to come and join us under the grey sky. When the rain stopped, we would all go inside the biggest tent and make a fire, and we would play music and dance among the empty benches. But once, after the rain, I walked along beside the soaking tents and below the wet flags of the circus and I went to our trailer and took off my clothes. I was alone, and my thin, boyish body was shivering from cold and happiness. A few minutes later, my mother came in. Her eyes were vacant, her hair was soaked, and her face was painted with makeup that was dripping down her face. She called me some other name. And she laughed when she saw me naked and stared at me. Flying man, she kept on saying, flying man, let me please you. And she drew me close to her bosom and kissed my neck and her hand swept across my skin and touched me and held my erection and stroked me until I came. There you go, she said, now you can leave and march towards your desert and your stone.

TAMMER

AT TIMES, WHEN the traffic lights turn red and all the engines stop, wait, and release the poisonous fumes from behind the drivers' asses, little unexpected sprinkles of water fall on your windshield from the squirts of plastic bottles, squeezed by the dirty fingers of street kids who make you want to call out to the world and scream, Injustice! It is the waste of this clean water that the poor depend on that I object to most. I scream in the face of these squeegee kids and say, I'll give you change but do not obstruct my horizon with your soaked, stained histories of needle-armed mothers and guess-who-done-it fathers.

The next evening, I took the the bus to Café Bolero but I didn't go in. I claimed my car and drove it through the streets of the city. At a light, I saw a harlequin coming my way with a bottle, ready to spray water on my windshield. But before I could wave my hand and tell him not to carry on with his squirting act, the harlequin started to shout my name, saying, Fly, hey, Fly! It's me, Tammer. And he rushed to the driver's side and called to his friend, who was wearing what must have been the worst insect costume I had ever seen.

Tammer, I said, what are you doing on the street?

Hustling like my forefathers, he said, and he and his friend laughed.

Come into the car, I said.

They did and slammed the doors, and by the weight of things, by the imperceptible curve of the seats under their bodies and the look of their cheekbones, I was reminded that famine is no laughing matter. No city masquerade, no costume, smile, or acrobatic act can appease the vacuity of hunger.

Let's eat, I said.

And they both started to giggle and give each other high-fives.

I took them to a fast food joint. I paid for all the hamburgers they could eat, for the buckets of soda they filled all the way to the rim, and for the extra-large French fries they both insisted upon.

I was still trying to figure out what kind of insect Tammer's friend was supposed to be. When I asked him, he just said: A bug. And when I asked what his name was, Tammer said, This is Skippy the Bug! and they both found it funny. They ate like hungry puppies.

How is your mother? I asked Tammer.

He nodded, and then shook his head because his mouth was full. And then he managed to say, Not okay.

Working? I asked.

No, not working.

Fredao?

Gone, Tammer said. The boys looked at each other and laughed. Got rid of him.

How did you get rid of him?

We bit him, Skippy the Bug said. And they both laughed again.

So where is your mother?

Recovering in the hospital, he said. Fredao beat her. Then Tammer paused and said, He won't beat her anymore.

Fucking bastard.

We all stayed quiet for a while. The two bent their heads towards the buns in their hands and ate.

You heard about the killing of the French journalist? I asked.

French fries, Skippy the Bug said, and they giggled.

Then they asked me if I could buy them milkshakes and more food, because they were still hungry.

Are you still living in your mother's place? I asked Tammer, as we went back to the counter.

No, he said.

Where do you sleep?

That place I took you last time, he said. Under the bridge.

We do barbecue, Skippy said. And they laughed and gave each other high-fives all over again.

I asked Tammer if he had seen Otto since that night.

Yeah, he said. He showed up one night but he left.

How long did he stay?

Not long. He needed stuff, Tammer said.

What kind of stuff?

Booze, the kid said, and laughed.

When we left the restaurant, I handed Tammer a few dollars.

He quickly took the money and showed it to his friend. They started to laugh and scream, and Skippy put his arm around Tammer's shoulders. Without saying goodbye, they staggered down the sidewalk, crossed the street, and started running through the street blocks, the buildings, and the traffic lights.

ZEE

I PICKED UP Zee that night. He was quieter than usual. He had a bag and he kept fixing his collar and tucking his hand inside his jacket and shifting.

Where to, boss? I said, sounding like a low-ranking gangster.

The industrial district, he said.

I drove up Highway 41 and all the way to the periphery of the city. Soon the industrial complexes started to show their long chimneys, and the fumes pouring out of their furnaces filled the sky with circular shapes and evasive patterns. On both sides of the highway were old workers' houses the same shades of grey as the factories behind them. All the walls were drenched in that pale, toxic colour of cement and dust.

Take this exit, Zee said.

I went down the ramp and drove along a row of houses. On the narrow road we encountered a truck loaded with what looked like a mountain of sand. The truck driver drove straight towards us without any hesitation or plan to accommodate our passage. Giving way, I veered right and up onto the shoulder, and dust rose from both sides and covered my car and my windows. I turned on the wipers, and they drew two arches in the shape of peacock tails, or two Andalusian fans, and I fancied myself in Moorish Spain walking through bow-shaped palaces and fountains and the smell of orange blossoms...

We passed a series of warehouses, encountering one grocery store that was open but had a doleful, vacant look, and an old metal sign with the fading letters of a soft-drink brand that no longer existed.

Zee told me to stop. He stepped out and stood at the corner. Then he called to me, saying, Come here, Fly. Get some fresh air.

I got out.

Stand here beside me, Zee said. So I stood next to him and we waited until a kid came around the corner and walked towards us. The kid's steps looked crooked; there was a one-sided, leaning dance to his marching. His hat looked one or two sizes too big, pragmatically casting a shadow on his eyes. The kid stood in front of Zee and I saw him slip something into the dealer's hand.

Zee started jawing at the kid, saying, Late again. I am not the one who should be waiting for your coming. Is it all here?

The kid nodded.

At the end of the street, I saw another kid on a bicycle standing in the middle of the road watching us. Zee saw him too.

Who's that?

My brother.

You come alone. And you be here on time. Zee turned and went back to the car and I followed.

Now what? I said.

Fountain Street, number 45, is all Zee said to me. And for the next half-hour he kept quiet and was pensive.

Did I pay you yet? he asked, as we were about to arrive at our destination.

No, not yet.

I was expecting him to say something else but he didn't, and I didn't pursue the conversation. In my oval mirror he had the look of those melancholic killers, or people about to be killed.

The address turned out to be a record store. From the outside, it looked neglected. The record sleeve hanging in the window had turned yellow under the pounding of the midday sun, the changing seasons behind the glass, and the settlement of dust. In the background, a faded, forgotten red curtain, like a trio of backup singers, was barely noticeable. The artists on the record covers looked permanently young and ever-smiling. Who knows, I thought, eternity could well be found in the permanent display of eternity.

I am staying, Zee said. You go in and hand over the bag.

I hesitated. I looked at the bag but I didn't touch it.

What, are you scared? Zee said.

What's in it?

What's in it. Who the fuck do you think you are, mule, to ask me that? You just open the door and go inside and do what I tell you.

My job is to drive you around, I said, not to deliver bags.

What did you say?

I repeated what I had said, but this time I looked him straight in the mirror.

Why do you think I pay you, motherfucker?

Well, I said, I assumed either you can't drive, or that maybe, deep inside your heart, you are an environmentalist who supports the use of public transport.

One funny, big-mouth motherfucker you are.

And in my mirror I saw his upper body extending on one side and his hand reaching to his waist. Then I heard the cranking of metal.

Don't make me waste you, Fly. Think of it as a promotion, he said. New responsibilities for you. Advancement in the company: the company of me. Now don't let me go in that store and drive back home sorry I killed a fly. My girlfriend wouldn't like it. So what will it be, Fly man. This or that?

I grabbed the bag, got out, and walked towards the store.

The store was closed but I could see people inside. I banged on the window and a man approached. With my imaginary whip, I made the sign of the letter Z in the manner of Zorro, and the man unlocked the door and let me in.

There was bombastic music coming from speakers on the wall. Up by a mezzanine window, two guys were watching the ground floor. When one of them spotted me, he came down the spiral stairs, with difficulty, because he was large and limping under the weight of his humongous thighs. We made eye contact, he had sharp eyes, and I nodded without saying a word. He approached me and frisked my waist.

Who's this from? he finally said.

Zee.

It better be good. He took the bag and looked me up and down. It better all be here, or you're going to be listening to your last song.

I stood there while the big man went upstairs. I looked behind me and saw an employee at the door, blocking the exit and frowning at me. Up above, the forms of men walked back and forth and leaned over a table. After a while the big man returned with the same bag in his hand. He handed it to me and said, You tell Zee to bring it himself next time. He gave a signal to the employee and the man moved out of the way and let me pass.

I went back to the car. Zee had put his dark shades on.

I handed him the bag. He opened it quickly and then told me to drive. Any trouble? he asked, once we were on the road.

No, just that the big guy said you should bring it yourself.

Zee paused, looked up, and said, Who told you that?

The big guy, I said.

Mammoth said that?

The big guy, I repeated.

The motherfucker, motherfucker! Zee shouted. I will teach that motherfucker respect. After I'm done here. Now. Get me to the Island fast. You know how to get to the Island? Zee asked.

I told him that I had a previous engagement and wasn't sure if I could get there and back in time.

Engagement? he repeated. You are engaged to me now. And if you walk out, I will fuck you on and before our wedding day. Drive me to the Island, Zee said calmly, don't make me pull my shit again, because this time if I pull it, I am going to use it, Fly.

And so I drove towards the Island, though it was not an island in any way. Maybe it was called the Island because of its seclusion from wealth, its apocalyptic-looking emptiness, its rundown buildings and abandoned stores. We arrived and the streets were deserted. We passed the emptiness and headed towards the train tracks. The headlights of my car slashed through the darkened road until we arrived at a meadow, or what looked like a meadow, with a small shack at the far edge and a big car waiting beside it.

Now what, I said.

You turn off your lights and we wait. The backup is on its way.

Backup, I repeated.

Yeah. Watch the mirror for a Jeep with tinted glass and shut the fuck up.

We waited for a while and then Zee started cursing, saying, Where the fuck are they? And after a few more minutes he said, Fuck it.

Drive forward, he said. Put your lights back on.

So I rolled slowly towards the shack.

Stop here and flick your high beams three times.

I did, and then he said, Give me the car keys.

I hesitated.

I swear I will waste you here and now. Don't make me do it.

So I handed over the keys.

You aren't going anywhere until I get back, you hear? I will walk over there. Don't go forward, just keep your beams on. They will see me and the shit will be cool.

They won't recognize you, I said. Lit from the back, you'll look like a silhouette on a stage. They won't see your face.

But he didn't listen to me.

He slammed the door and walked in front of my car with the bag in his hand. His shadow swayed in the dark.

Ladies and gentlemen, presenting Zee, in his splendid role as the drug dealer. What a marvellous performance, and now here it comes, the back flip after the last delivery . . . and what a delivery!

A pair of headlights shone on Zee from the audience's side, and I saw the car advancing. It stopped and Zee got in. And a few minutes later he got out and started walking back without the bag. A man stretched out his gun through the passenger window and I heard shots and could see Zee no more. He must have fallen to the ground. I saw the car moving towards me. I immediately switched on my lantern. I imagined that everything that started with the letter T could provide safety and emanate neutrality. Terrified, I searched for words that started with T. I recalled *tenderness* and *tears*, then I switched to less emotional, more action-oriented phrases such as *take a breath, take a dive, take a hop, take a shit, take flight!*

But then I realized that Zee had the keys to my car. So I simply ducked under the dashboard and waited for the killer car to pass. Well, I hoped it would, and to my surprise it did, in so great a rush that I knew no man could leap from such a cosmological velocity and land intact with a gun in his hand. It would be impossible, incomprehensible: even killers are not capable of surviving such infinite speed.

I waited until I didn't hear a sound. Like a seal in the ocean, I stuck my head up and peeked, then I opened the car door and walked the muddy road towards the place I'd last seen Zee.

He was lying on the ground with his face buried in the mud. I rolled him over and I saw the whiteness of his eyes inside a face that was covered with soil. I poked him and whispered his name, but he was gone, dead.

I searched his pockets and found my car keys, and then I opened the inside of his jacket and pulled out his wallet. I counted out what was due to me, which I assessed should include insurance, modelling, risk management, entertainment, subordination fees, gas, windshield washer liquid, insults, waiting time, a shoeshine, penalties for damage to the welfare of society, and, naturally, the taxi fare. In short, after a quick mental addition, the total came out to the exact and full amount of money contained in the wallet. I ran to my car and drove in reverse to the next street, then I wove through the town's alleys, aiming for the highway. I sailed out of the Island and into the city.

WREATH

UNDER THE CIRCUMSTANCES, I cut my night short and decided to go home. As I drove up in front of my building, I saw the janitor coming out, wearing a black suit. He had shaved and his windy hair had settled. I almost didn't recognize him without his leather jacket. I stopped and watched him walking towards a long black car that was blocking the garage entrance. Under the illumination of my headlights, he walked to the passenger side of the black car and opened the door. An elderly woman slowly got out, holding his hand. Her thick black stockings and church-lady shoes extended towards the sidewalk, out from under her bell-like skirt. She stood up and reached for the janitor's neck, he bowed his head clumsily, and she kissed his cheek. The old woman was crying. My Kleenex box was about to fly ahead of me, its layers ready to scoop up the tears, but the lady pulled a handkerchief out of nowhere and dabbed her cheeks. The janitor glanced at my car but did not seem to recognize me. Later on, on my way up from the garage, on the first floor I encountered several large wreaths propped up in the hallway.

I went straight to my apartment to lie down on the carpet. I unbuckled my belt, but the presence of death was too near, too vivid to allow me to imagine gladiators, sailors, or women in need of rescue. I stood up and walked to the cupboard, looking for alcohol. Nothing was there. Fuck it, I said. When short of drink, seek the Arab. I will knock at Zainab's door.

As I was buckling my belt, I remembered a Saudi prince I once drove around for a while. I had met him in the pool joint of a fancy hotel. I was sharking at the time, while also driving my cab. I had picked up the game in no time. When I was a kid, the contortionist had taught me how to twist and how to hustle.

I let the prince win a few times and then gave it to him. Soon he was out of cash. He offered me his Rolex, but once I realized that he was a Saudi, I told him that between us brothers material things shouldn't matter and fed him some fraternal flattery, et cetera . . . He immediately bought it. So I drove him to a "refreshment" bar and told him that my taxi was at his service. The man drank whisky like a fish and fucked like there was no tomorrow; as soon as he had exited the Kingdom, the drinking and the orgies had started. That is all these heretic Westerners are good for, he would say. I made a deal with Linda and provided his highness with pleasures, and then, one day, his two royal cousins came from London and business really thrived.

I would pick up Linda and her friends from the corner and wait in the parking lot of their hotel until they were done. It worked out very well because the Bedouins have a preference for women on the plump side, and this brought prosperity and equal-opportunity employment to everyone. In a single evening they would empty the room's minibar multiple times, swap the women between them, and fuck and sing all night.

The girls would come down giddy and drunk and showered with gifts and golden watches. One must admit, the oily nomads are the most welcoming, hospitable people on the planet. They treated those women very generously and the women welcomed it. Sometimes they would all decide to go dancing and I would have to get another taxi. I would call Mani the Sex Spider or Number 79 or whoever was available at the Bolero...One day, three Saudi princesses, the sisters and cousins of the men, showed up to visit. They all decided to go to an expensive French restaurant. I took the boys in my car, and Number 79, a good-looking Nigerian with broad shoulders, handsomely defined, cut biceps, and a big, bright smile, arrived to take the princesses. He opened the door and eyed one of them and smiled at her. Late that night, before he drove away, the princess pretended she had left something in the car, and she leaned over the front seat, gave him a big tip, and asked him to meet her at another hotel.

At the appointed hour, he came back all dressed up, cleaned, shaved, and wearing cologne. Inside the hotel bar, the princess was already seated, waiting for him. The driver didn't recognize her at first, because she was wearing a short skirt and high heels and smoking behind a whisky glass. She waved him over, bought a drink or two, and took him upstairs, where they drank and fucked all night. She was head over heels in love with him. Her screams of ecstasy rang and echoed all over the town. The next day, I brought them cocaine from a dealer on Main Street and they sniffed and fucked all that night as well. Before the princess went back home, she gave the driver a cheque and a postal address and asked him never to call, but to write.

Number 79 wrote to her, each time with a different story asking for financial support or help. War stories, family sagas, the death of his mother, the breakdown of his car, and in no time, he would receive a cheque in the mail to assist him with his troubles. His biggest coup was to ask for lawyers' fees because he was about to be deported, and if he was deported he would be dragged into the army and forced to fight, and he could well be killed. Immediately, a big fat cheque was couriered to him.

One day, the princess sent him a letter telling him that she had decided to leave everything and run away, if only he would meet her at the same hotel where they had first met. He never answered her letter. She sent a second letter and he still didn't answer her. In her third letter, she threatened to kill him by sending one of her royal bodyguards to cut off his balls. He called home to Lagos and instructed his cousin to send the princess a letter stating that, finally, Number 79 had been deported back to his country, in spite of the lawyers' efforts. He had been drafted into the army and killed in the line of duty. His dying wish was to tell the princess that he was sorry and that they would meet in paradise.

SOME MEMORIES MAKE me want to drink even more, so out of sadness or joy I knocked at Zainab's door. She opened and said, Fly, my dear, it is late, and I have a friend with me. I apologized and asked her if I could borrow some whisky or a cognac. I explained that I'd had a long, hard day and that I needed a drink. Just a shot before bed, it will help me fall asleep, I said.

Okay, Fly, come in. I'll introduce you to my friend Gina here, and since we are also having a drink... just come in.

There was a woman there. She stood up and kissed me on each cheek. You must be the man Zainab has been telling me about, who once brought the forest of flowers, she said.

Yes indeed, I am the flower carrier and the people mover.

You do have great taste, the flowers were magnificent. I've heard so much about you, Fly. All good things.

I am honoured, I said. What a relief and a compliment. People live their lives thinking that they are forgotten, and that is why we do the most outrageous things, so as not to have gone unnoticed.

I agree, said Gina, laughing. Our need for acknowledgement is certainly underrated.

People want to be remembered; the burden of impermanence hovers like a sword above our necks, I said, as I showed off my eloquent thoughts and gallant manners. Speaking of death and flowers, what is with the flowers of death outside?

Oh yes, the landlady died, Zainab said.

I'll pass by tomorrow and pay my respects to her son. Or better yet, I will write him a letter of condolence. May I have that promised drink now, please? I asked. Some days can only be concluded with a certain amount of intoxication.

Here you go, Fly, Zainab said, and poured me a glass of whisky.

And so we all drank and continued our conversation about death, histories, and other inevitable matters.

May I use your bathroom? I asked, with a certain urgency. Though I could always return to my apartment and use mine, if you promise to let me in again.

No, we don't want to lose you now that the conversation has gotten interesting. You can go here, Zainab said. We will wait for you.

I want to hear more about the cannon man and his companion, Gina said.

I walked down the long hallway to the bathroom with my whisky glass still in my hand. But then I thought that it might be dangerous to take it with me into the bathroom (drops of the same yellow hue could accidentally mix and be drunk in a moment of confusion or excitement), so I went back to the kitchen to deposit my drink on the counter, and what did I see but Zainab and the woman in each other's arms, kissing and embracing tightly among the garden of dried flowers.

I gulped my drink in one shot and I tiptoed back to relieve myself.

Back in the kitchen, I helped myself to another drink and called it a night, telling Zainab that I would leave the empty glass at her door.

Zainab smiled at me and said, No problem, Fly. Here, keep the little that is left in the bottle. I think Gina and I are done drinking for the night.

I SAT AT my desk, alone, and drank some more. I flooded the walls with light and shone the lamp on the spider web. The light shall bring the looting of blood from the flying cadavers of the night, I recited. The end, contrary to all popular beliefs, never comes to us, I proclaimed. It is we transient creatures who happily, clumsily, philosophically, drunk with the hardness of denial and the cloudiness of faith, walk towards it with open wings. Death is the inevitable net that shall scoop up the last swing, last sigh, and last blink before the last play, the last note in this symphony of chords in the web of nature that shall inevitably wrap us and bite us to an eternal sleep, I concluded.

I woke up the next day and realized that I had fallen asleep on the carpet, in yet another failed attempt to change history and prevent the splattering of blood.

MIMI

THE NEXT EVENING, I went down to my car, and in the thin light of the garage, I saw a shape that looked like a quilt resting on the back seat. I opened the door and picked it up. It was indeed a quilt. I took it and opened my trunk and laid it inside. I didn't remember seeing any quilt the previous night, either before or after Zee's death. There was also a faint smell of alcohol and tiredness and even fear.

I worked steadily for the rest of that night, and towards morning I drove back home. The streets were empty but for the hundreds of plastic cups and beer bottles that littered the ground. From behind the haze of the windshield, the streets looked like an ocean filled with bottles carrying messages. I remembered the letters the bearded lady had received from the dispersed people of the circus. Once in a while she would get a colourful letter from a magician in Germany or a lion tamer in Africa, or photos from the Siamese twins who had married two women and had, between them, four kids. The circus people all kept in touch and, through this network of letters, we learned that it was the animal keeper who was having the worst time making a living. He had tried all the zoos and all the circuses, but nothing had come of his efforts. In one of his letters, he told the bearded lady that he was working in the furnace room of a cement factory, and he eloquently described to her the fires and the baking of the earth. All starts here, he wrote. All these new nations bake the earth to build and make stones. But the weight of progress and the benefits of contractors and the wealth of nations began to take a toll on the man. His skin itched and his lungs were clogged with dust and chemicals, and then, one day, he died from the smoke and the toxic powders and asbestos that make cities and pave their stretches of sidewalks.

Another tragedy was the magician, who had left Germany and retreated to a small village in the Balkans. He lived in a modest house and ate what the villagers sold to him for a good price. Life was good until he made the wife of the baker disappear at night and reappear in the morning naked from behind the bushes, and until he transformed the daughter of the mayor into an adorable rabbit, hopping through the window every evening and into the meadow. After that, he packed his top hat, escaped, and flew with the help of his cape back to the city.

And then there was Mimi the dwarf, who got involved in an international diamond-trafficking ring. Mimi was provided with a fake passport stating a fake age and a fake name. She dressed up as a little girl and carried a doll in her hands. She was accompanied by another lady who pretended to be her mother. And then they crossed the ocean in fancy cruise ships, smuggling stolen diamonds inside Mimi's doll. The so-called mother pretended to be a White Russian countess from the Cossack region. She was known as the Contessa Tambbar Koussa. She snubbed everyone as expected and spoke French in the tradition of nineteenth-century Russian writers such as Turgenev and Pushkin. She had schooled Mimi in manners and *le savoir-vivre*, and Mimi was always on her best behaviour in her bell-shaped dress and curly hair.

Mimi would curtsy to society ladies and men and she even played the piano and occasionally tap danced, but when the conversation became unbearably pompous, conservative, and dull, Mimi would throw a tantrum and kick the women in the ankles and punch the men in their groins. On deck, the Contessa Tambbar Koussa, whose main conversational tack was to reminisce about her two dogs and the cruelty of not allowing animals in the dining hall, would call out to Mimi, Precious, don't get yourself wet! A coded phrase meaning: Don't get too excited about the muscular sailors on board, about whom Mimi fantasized every night, masturbating under the sheets of the top bunk of their cabin.

But then one day, Mimi got very drunk and saw the handsome ship's doctor, and her eyes were transfixed, her lips quivered, and her thighs wiggled against the lower metal ramps of the ship. She forgot the doll and her age and smiled, held her doll under her arm, lit a cigarette, and made rings of smoke sail above the ocean winds. Dolphins jumped inside the white hoops, to the delight of the passengers, and a few clouds magically descended to join the circle of smoky sighs trailing through the tropical heat.

The doctor, who saw Mimi's provocative gestures, was alarmed and perturbed by his own desires for the little girl. He kept an eye on Mimi and followed her until, one day, he caught her standing in the engine room beneath the belt of the mechanic, giving him some steamy head. At first he thought it was a case of child molestation, but then, after conducting an investigation into the matter, he realized that Mimi was not the innocent child that she pretended to be, nor was the Contessa Tambbar Koussa a real White Russian. To make things even more insulting, this so-called Contessa was found to be an Arab, with a fabricated Arabic name that, translated, meant "the countess with the swollen vagina." The Contessa was interrogated about her fake passport and her impersonation of an aristocrat, and she was threatened with prison. Fearing a long sentence, she made a deal with the authorities to reduce the charges against her by telling them of the diamond hidden in Mimi's doll.

Mimi was arrested and sent to jail for life. In jail, she was harassed and beaten by the big women in the cell, who made her do the circus dance, as they called it, and walk a tightrope tied between two bed rails. In the showers, a pedophile guard molested her and called her names. Early one morning, when everyone was asleep and before the bell rang and the count of the prisoners was made, Mimi untied the rope that she had walked the night before, to the cheers, taunts, and laughter of her cellmates, secured it to one of the high bars of her cell, and hanged herself. That morning, there was no applause in the room, only silence and the faint squeaking of the rope, and the light, and the quiet swings of a small body.

HAT

WHEN I ARRIVED home, I parked in the garage, then I opened my trunk and pulled out the quilt I'd found lying on the back seat. I took all the cash in my wallet and wrapped it inside my hat, and I neatly folded the quilt and placed it on the back seat with the hat on top.

I slept all morning.

In the afternoon I went down to my car. The quilt in the back seat was unfolded and the hat and the money were gone.

I took my car, left the lantern unlit, and decided to drive to nowhere. It was rush hour, and at that time a driver could pick up passengers easily, but I decided to leave the centre and seek the river. I drove until my wheels took me to the bridge where Otto had once dwelt and drunk and slept. The spot, he used to call it.

But the spot was not his discovery or Tammer's, it was Fredao's. Otto and Fredao used to spend nights there drinking and arguing and even, if one were to take them seriously, conspiring. And Tammer, while he waited for his mother to come back from her walks through the night, would sometimes stay awake with them, listening to them talk politics and power. Once Fredao pulled out his gun and showed it to Tammer. Here, son: I am not your fucking father just because I call you son, but I know who is. You are the bastard son of an Arab. Those Arabs were the first to come and enslave my people and sell us to the Portuguese. You, son, you are one part Spanish genocider and one part slave-driver. Bullshit, all that religious boasting about mercy to the slaves, it is all bullshit. A slave is a slave. There is no such thing as mercy to a slave like those books of revelations will tell you. Here, son, come over here. I want to teach you power so you will always be free. Now hold the gun like that, aim, and shoot the bottle.

The gunshots must have been heard by the sailors on the cargo boats, but either they didn't give a damn or they, like those on the shore, were drunk, wobbling with the motion of the water and waiting with boredom for the departure of their ships.

On the weekends Tammer would watch these sailors from beneath the bridge, stumbling drunk, singing the same songs all together. It wasn't their accents that surprised him most, nor the uniforms with the lost ties and crooked hats, but the fact that they all knew the same songs. No matter how drunk they were, they sang and conformed. Fredao would curse the sailors. Filthy white-trash bastards! he would say. A few hundred years ago, they would have been chasing me to put chains around my neck and obliging me to row their filthy, rat-infested boats.

Some of these sailors would have food in their hands and Tammer would look at them with envy and hunger. Meat, Tammer would say, they are eating meat. He would point, and Fredao would spit and say, Yeah, filthy cannibals, they would eat humans as well.

What are cannibals? Tammer asked.

Humans who eat other humans, Fredao replied.

BEFORE I ARRIVED at the bridge, I stopped at a store and bought coffee and cakes. Then I drove down to the spot, parked, and got out. I saw two boys sleeping in a shelter of cardboard boxes and leaning against each other, sharing a blanket. It was Tammer and his friend Skippy the Bug. In a small barrel beside them, a few pieces of coal were glowing faintly beneath burnt pieces of wood. I stood there and waited, smoking and drinking my coffee. And then I moved closer. There were many empty beer bottles and a large bottle of Johnnie Walker, half gone. I was just about to kneel down and wake Tammer when I saw Skippy flip his side of the blanket open and point a gun at me.

Skippy, I said. It's me, Fly, put your gun down.

He immediately began to giggle, and Tammer, as if he had anticipated everything in his dreams, also started to giggle from beneath the blanket.

Fly, do you have fifty bucks? Tammer said, his voice muffled, and they both laughed.

Wake up, I said to Tammer. And you, Skippy boy, point that thing away from me. Where did you get that gun? I asked him.

My inheritance, Tammer said. What's up, Fly?

Drink your coffee and let's go for a walk.

Too cold for a walk, man. Shit, I got to piss. Fucking booze, a massacre, motherfucking massacre that I have to piss out.

While he was pissing against a pillar, I asked him how his mother was.

Not good, he said. She's still in the hospital. I'm going to visit her tomorrow.

I'll come, I said. Which hospital is she in?

The one on the top of the mountain there, he said, and

flicked himself, buckled up, and asked Skippy to imitate some lady's voice again.

Skippy started to shout in a high-pitched voice, Leave those Coke cans alone, what are you doing here!

Hey, Fly, Tammer said as I turned to walk back towards my car, could you buy us some hamburgers? And Skippy repeated, Hamburgers.

Not today, I said. Got to go back to work.

THE NEXT DAY I went to the hospital to see Linda. And there was Skippy, smoking and juggling rocks in the parking lot.

Is Tammer inside? I asked.

No, he went to buy cigarettes.

Did he already visit?

Yeah.

How is his mother?

Not good.

Did you go in?

No.

Where do you come from? I asked the bug.

The moon, he said, and laughed. I come from the moon.

You have the gun on you?

He laughed.

Is that why you waited outside?

Yeah, outside, he said. Tammer is coming. Tammer is coming, he said, and laughed.

How is your mother? I asked when Tammer had reached us.

He ignored my question. He just passed me and kept going and Skippy trailed along.

THE WORD ON the street had it that Fredao, after damaging Linda, had lost the respect of his girls, and that they had rebelled against him. A new pimp had already taken over Fredao's corner and no one had seen him for days. Rumour had it that he'd gotten ill and nostalgic and decided to go back to Angola with a suitcase filled with money.

I went up to Linda's room. Her teeth were now completely gone. Her jaw was so damaged that she could hardly talk. I had to decode every word she said. When I told her that I had seen Tammer outside, tears went down her cheeks and she reached for my hand and squeezed it. Her eyes and her fingers stayed fixed in the same position for a long time.

Two weeks later, the body of Fredao would be found on the shore of the river. He had been repeatedly shot in the head. The news, in a small article on a back page, would report that three of his limbs were missing. The bites would be attributed to hungry stray dogs, though the report would go on to mention that there were knife cuts and pieces of missing flesh.

BIRDS

ON THE WAY back from the hospital, I saw Zainab on the street, walking towards the bus station. I stopped my car and called to her from across the road. She barely waved at me and continued walking. I made a U-turn and drove up alongside her. I opened my window and asked her to get in. She hesitated, and then she opened the door and sat next to me. I'll drive you to school, I said.

She was quiet. And then she said, There's no need. I am leaving.

Home?

Where is home for us, Fly? My home was taken, occupied. I am moving to another city.

Gina, I said.

You saw us?

Yes. I didn't know.

She was travelling in Jordan and we met and fell in love. And I had to leave. I left everything for her. A relationship like ours is not accepted everywhere.

But Zainab, that is the consequence of those religions you so defend and embrace. I don't understand you.

Fly, religion is here and it will always be here.

Am I going to see you again? I asked.

I don't believe so, Fly.

For once you don't believe.

She smiled and said, Fly, what do you believe in? What do you live for?

What do the stars believe in, Zainab? Where do the dead horses go, what do the birds worship, and what do the rivers live for?

Take care of yourself, Fly.

She leaned over, kissed me, and left, and I've never seen her again.

ACT FIVE

CRIMES

NUMBER 6 WAS found shot in the district of St. Lucas Island. His car was discovered six hours after his disappearance. The first alarm was given by his partner, Number 107. They shared the car in two twelve-hour shifts, seven days a week. Every morning for the past ten years they would meet at the same taxi stand and exchange the car keys and a few words before the night driver went home and the morning driver started the day. When Number 6 didn't show up after his night shift, his partner called the dispatcher, who repeatedly tried to reach Number 6, to no avail. At that point, the police were informed.

His car was spotted by a security guard who heard the repeated calling of the taxi dispatcher coming from the radio. Number 6 had been shot in the side of the head. The shot must have come from the front passenger seat: blood was splattered all over the front seat and the glass. The car was held as evidence and couldn't be driven for months. After fifteen years of driving, Number 107, the partner of the deceased, gave up the taxi business and thought of opening a restaurant.

NUMBER 48 WAS found on his knees, beaten by a rock, down by the train tracks. He was discovered by two hobos who said they heard the loud buzzing of the flies and saw a stray dog escaping with a human limb in its mouth. As they approached the car, they smelled and then saw the dead man. The police came and the newspapers went on a frenzy of photographing the crime scene. The hobos were asked to pose for a photo next to the car. They both smiled and everyone in the editorial office commented on their missing teeth.

Number 48 had a young wife and two young children. His wife, who had no other means of income and no family in this land, decided to go back to Algeria and live with her brother and his wife.

NUMBER 96 DIED of a broken neck. His car was found in a hayfield by a farmer. The radio in the car had been left on and played loud music all night. In the early morning, the farmer took his shotgun and drove his pickup truck to the murder scene. The farmer later complained that the loud radio had echoed all the way back to the barns and scared the cows, depriving them of a good night's sleep.

The victim's four brothers, who were, like him, recent immigrants from the Eastern bloc, stayed up all night drinking. Two of them wanted to bury the body in the new country, as they called it, and the other two wanted to ship the body back to the victim's place of birth. They argued, then they drank, sang, cried, and fist-fought among each other. The fight turned violent and the police came and arrested them all.

THE LAST TIME Number 72, also known as the Sex Spider, was seen, he was walking into a hotel with a prostitute on his arm. He drove mostly in the evenings because he preferred the quiet night shift to the traffic jams of the daytime. He also had a few regular travellers whom he drove in the early mornings to the airport, which was always a good fare.

Every evening, Number 72 waited for a big, voluptuous lady at the door of a corporate headquarters and drove her back to her house. Through the years they had gotten in the habit of teasing one another and sharing sexual fantasies over the seats, and then she would leave him a big tip and get out of the car. Once, after many years of these erotic, sexless games, she invited him in to her apartment. She chained him to her bed and left. He was chained there for two days without food or water. When she came back, he was dehydrated and delusional. When he asked her why she'd done it, she simply replied: You asked for it.

His car was found under a bridge with five bullets across the door and the windshield. The killer, the police deduced, must have stood outside the car and shot inside. At his funeral there were quite a few women, and most of the men in attendance were taxi drivers. The victim had no family and no one knew much about his life. Number 92 said, I wish we had asked. We were too busy listening to his sexual escapades. He was a funny man.

Earlier, however, at the wake, five transvestites and two women had shown up and surrounded the coffin. One, by the name of Larry, or Limo, wept the most. Limo stood up and walked into the middle of the gathering and said, Please, please, turn off all the lights. I will show you what

Mani thought of us all. And she stood in front of the coffin and glowed. Little sparks of light began to appear on many of the attendees' chests. Beside Limo, the two women glowed brightly, and, in the corner, a male taxi driver glowed lightly as well.

NUMBER 18 WAS found floating in the city's main river. His car turned up six miles north of the place where the body was spotted. The autopsy showed that he had been stabbed and then thrown into the river alive. The current carried him away from the original crime scene. The stabbing must have occurred on the boardwalk. Little patches of blood were noticed on the wooden deck, not too far from the car. He must have swum for a while before his wounds spilled too much blood and weakened him and he drowned. His cousin, Number 59, said that they had grown up on the Caribbean shores and they were both fishermen and good swimmers. The official death certificate stated death by drowning. The victim was a born-again Christian, and everyone at the church he had attended seemed to believe that his next life would be better.

ALL FIVE CRIMES were committed over the course of two days. It was established that all the rides must have originated in the city, somewhere between downtown and the riverside.

The dispatchers' records showed that none of the drivers had picked up the fatal call from a house or a specific address. Most likely the passenger or, more appropriately, the killer, had hailed the taxis off the street or off the stands. Which led the police to deduce that the killer must have chosen his victims at random.

YET THERE WERE common threads. All of the victims were male and newcomers, also known as immigrants. They all worked the night shift, and none of them bore any marks of fighting or physical confrontation. As a matter of fact, it was thought that the victims must have conversed with their killer; each of the last cigarettes smoked by the drivers turned out to be the same brand, so it appeared that the killer had offered them a cigarette.

Another detail in common was that all the cars had their radios tuned to the same spot on the dial. The frequency in question was a hip hop station, which led one policeman to let slip that they suspected a young black man or men to be responsible for the killings. The odds, they reasoned, that five middle-aged immigrant men had all been listening to this station were slim.

The killings caused panic among the drivers. The taxi commission organized a protest drive through the city. About seven hundred cars drove through downtown, resulting in a great gridlock. Flags of the countries of origin of the victims, black ribbons, and photographs of the dead men dangled from taxi windows. The families of the deceased rode at the front of the parade, and some walked alongside the cars. Some of the victims' children carried their father's photographs. The kids were swamped by journalists and photographers.

Young black men suddenly found themselves unable to flag a taxi off the street. Some of the drivers who used to wait, at the end of the night, at the doors of bars and dance halls that played hip hop and R&B and even jazz didn't wait there anymore. After two in the morning, when the public transport had stopped, and the dance clubs shut their doors, one could see black kids walking in the middle of the road, waving and blocking the path of taxi drivers, even banging on their windows and hoods to try to get a ride. The police were called in one night when, after a few young black men tried to force their way into a taxi, a small riot took place. Several arrests were made.

The taxi commission blamed the mayor for the murders, because he had refused to authorize glass buffers between the front and the back seats. A buffer would limit the passenger capacity to three, and since the mayor was all about attracting families and visitors to town, a four-passenger capacity was perceived as more hospitable. The anti-discrimination league accused taxi drivers and the taxi commission of discriminating against black men. A taxi driver from a Middle Eastern country was caught on camera saying that all the problems came from them, blacks. The footage was aired on the six o'clock news. When the taxi driver was confronted by activists and people from the black community, he stated that, as a Muslim, he never differentiated between races, since the Prophet, peace be upon Him, urged good Muslims to treat all races equally, but then the driver stressed that the young blacks in the city were dangerous and immoral.

During the funeral of Number 18, the church reverend accused the local radio stations of spreading hate and corrupting the youth, and said that such stations should not be allowed to broadcast violent music that called women bitches and whores.

And then, in the course of a televised debate, a music producer replied to the accusations of a campaigning politician by stating that hip hop was listened to by everyone, regardless of race, and he cited sales statistics to prove his point. When the politician condemned the violent language, the producer reminded him that none of the lyrics was any more or less violent than those of the colonial song "Rule Britannia."

It came to light that one of the victims, when he first entered the taxi business, had driven illegally for years. Having failed the taxi commission's written exam because of poor language comprehension, the victim had resorted to using his cousin's licence. Their similarity in looks could easily have fooled any inspector. At last, only six months before his death, he had finally passed the exam and been assigned the number 48. In the aftermath of his death, the taxi union representative raised the issue of exclusion and demanded that taxi permit exams be permitted in many other languages.

At the taxi stands, drivers were urged to look out for each other and to be leery of customers who hailed them from the streets. Many of the drivers decided to stop working the night shift and switched to mornings. Of course, the owners of the cars hiked the rental fees for morning shifts. The Carnival was still on and some taxis refused to take people with masks on. Those who did made sure to look at the skin colour of the passenger's hands before unlocking the doors. A gay couple who were dressed in matching cowboy suits and hats were refused entry to a cab because of the plastic guns that rested at the sides of their exposed hips. When they complained to the commission, the driver stated that he had also refused them for hygienic reasons: one of the cowboys wore leather pants that left his ass completely bare in the middle.

Headlines such as Are Taxi Drivers Racists? flashed across the news. "The Newcomers Who Discriminate," a special report, was repeatedly aired on various radio stations. "Should We Tolerate Those Who Don't?" was another variation on the same theme. The only woman taxi driver in the city, a butch named Baby, was pursued by three different producers to be interviewed.

Is taxi driving dangerous for a woman? she was asked on air.

Not if the doll is riding with me, honey, Baby answered, and laughed.

And then a young graduate from the creative writing department of the local university, who had driven a taxi for two years, was contracted by a publishing house to gather taxi stories. The book was to appear in the fall, in time for the national awards season. The title of the book was *Taxi Stories.*

INDEED THE TAXI killer, as he was called in the news, triggered a new interest in the romantic and dangerous side of the taxi profession. Journalists and producers would hire a taxi for a whole day for a flat fee, or simply let the meter run while they asked the driver questions or rode with him through so-called dangerous neighbourhoods. Taxi drivers were ushered into the labyrinths of the TV stations for interviews. They were offered cups of water from the cooler and called by their last names, which were mispronounced by secretaries and producers alike. The anchors would often come out of their glass rooms and shake the drivers' hands, and they would ask them the correct pronunciation of their names, repeating it to themselves many times on their way back to their high chairs and microphones. In many sound studios, wires were passed underneath the drivers' jackets, all the way up their necks, and down inside their ears. Sudden voices saying things like Can you hear me, sir? elicited fierce head shakes by some South Asian drivers, which made it hard for the technicians to detect the meaning of the answer as a yes or a no. Makeup was applied to the drivers' foreheads and below their eyes to cut the flare and shine. Some drivers, though, refused to wear makeup, stating that it was a woman's affair.

Nearly overnight a reality TV producer introduced a new show, *The Longest Ride*, which consisted of celebrities driving taxis equipped with hidden cameras. The show was almost cancelled after a passenger attempted to mug a celebrity driver at gunpoint. The television crew that was following the taxi in a separate car saw the gun in the kid's hand and alerted the police. It could well have escalated into a hostage-taking situation if the celebrity hadn't informed the mugger that he was without cash because, he said, This is *The Longest Ride*! The mugger, who happened to be an admirer of the show, was ecstatic to discover that he was on television, and he agreed to sign a modelling contract before he surrendered to the police.

CRIMES (AGAIN)

MORNING. AFTER THE burial of the latest victim of the taxi killings, a psychiatrist was slain inside his clinic as he was about to leave his office. The doctor's coat was found hanging behind the door. According to the police report, the patterns of blood on the coat suggested that the killer had worn it while he slashed the doctor's throat.

Many of the patients who were being treated by the psychiatrist got sick reading the news. A computer was missing, as well as a radio, two hundred dollars, and a box of Cuban cigarillos, but the rest of the place was untouched except for the blood that had splattered all over the room. The police confiscated all the doctor's files as part of the investigation. Patients and privacy advocates protested, stating that the police were violating citizens' rights to privacy.

A PROMINENT CEO was found shot next to his car, in the parking lot of the gym where he worked out three times a week.

The CEO was the head of a large mining company. A few years before, the company had been involved in arming rebels in an African country in order to overthrow a left-leaning regime that had demanded the nationalization of the mining company. After the scandal, the then-CEO resigned and a younger CEO, by the name of Edward Stain III (in certain disco circles known as Eddie), was promoted to the job. The young CEO's first proposal to the shareholders was to hire a PR company to conduct a campaign that would highlight the company's social responsibility programs, including job creation for third-world workers and new, advanced environmental technologies to foster better and more environmentally conscious mining practices. The "step technique," one of the new techniques was called, since the excavation and stripping were to be done in a series of steps that would allow future plants and new vegetation to eventually cover the sites. The CEO invited environmental groups to discuss the new procedures.

At the funeral of Mr. Stain III, many honourable guests were in attendance, and the populist mayor promised to henceforth be even tougher on crime. The late CEO had left behind two beautiful daughters and a wife.

THE NEXT DAY a professor of political science at the local university was found, with his wife, mutilated and burned in the woods outside the city. The camping equipment and clothing of the victims had all been stolen. The couple, it was determined after forensic analysis, had been chained together and stabbed. In a gruesome statement, the police revealed that acts of cannibalism had been performed. Some of the limbs had been barbecued on the spot, and traces of human saliva were detected on the victims' arms and thighs. The car of Edward Stain III, the young CEO, was found parked in the woods close to the scene. It was clear that the killer or killers must have switched cars. He, she, or they had arrived in the first victim's car and left in the second. Both crimes appeared to have taken place on the same day.

The news about cannibalism caused renewed panic and debate all over the city. It even made the international news. Experts on cannibalism and satanic rituals were seen on every channel. A panellist who said that the act of cannibalism was justified in times of famine was condemned by the religious establishment, and the news channel was inundated with complaints and threats. The expert later stated that he had merely been referring to human history, and that cannibalism was an undeniable part of our past. He stated that there was proof of cannibalism by First World War soldiers, not to mention incidents as recent as the Vietnam War and after certain plane crashes. Journalists expanded on the topic, chairing panels on devil worshippers, Masonic lodges, and the demonization of Jews in Europe through false accusations by the Church and the Nazis alike.

In a lengthy obituary in one of the local newspapers, the professor was remembered for many of the conservative policies he had helped introduce through the current government. He had been, behind the scenes, an effective adviser on such policies as the abolishment of the gun registry, the dismantling of the census, and other deep cuts to the governmental bureaucracy. The life and work of the victim stirred another debate over the role of academia in the government, and vice versa. Political talk shows on radio and on television suddenly began to question politicians' competence. Is the prime minister a mere front for ideologues and think tanks? Who are the brains that run this country? What is the role of academics and policy-makers in the forming of our values?

NEITHER THE INVESTIGATORS nor the journalists could find any kind of link connecting these latest victims to one another. Judging by their life histories, one could easily assume that the killings had a political motivation; yet, since the murders appeared to be the work of a psychopath or a serial killer, the focus of the investigation fell on the psychiatrist's files, with a secondary focus on patients with possibly radical political affiliations.

The detectives estimated that, out of hundreds of bureaucrats and government employees who had been the doctor's patients, seventy-five percent were on antidepressants and anti-psychotic medicines. Many at police headquarters began to joke that the country was being run by drugged-up zombies and potential mass murderers masquerading as bureaucrats. A chief investigator, discussing the case with his superiors, lit a cigar and said, What happened to going to a bar and getting drunk, getting a prostitute and waking up to go to work in the morning? No one can handle a drink anymore. Pills are the easy way out, and that is why this country is going down the tubes.

The head of the Episcopalian Church demanded the abolishment of the Carnival, stating that its pagan origins were an incitement to debauchery and violence. The Catholic Church was in a precarious position: carnivals had a long history in Church functions and, through the ages, these festivities had never been suppressed or condemned. In an eloquent act of defence, the spokesman for the Catholic Church invoked Francis of Assisi, who had spoken of "spiritual joy" and been known to call himself and his companions "God's jugglers." The spokesman blamed a few decadent elements for transforming the Carnival from a community affair into a drug-infested gay pride parade that was taking over the decent essence of the celebration.

When a task force was formed, ultimately recommending that the city shut down the Carnival, a counter-committee of local merchants, large corporations, and sponsors threatened to withhold their financial support for the mayor during the upcoming election, should the task force's recommendations be followed.

THE LINK BETWEEN the killing of the taxi drivers and the murders of the psychiatrist, the professor, and the CEO continued to baffle the investigators. Ultimately, they came to suspect that two separate serial killers were at work. While the gruesome Corporate Murders, as they became known, had a clear psychotic element to them, the taxi murders were of a different nature. Those killings were not as spectacular and deranged as their corporate counterparts.

Yet both cases remained very puzzling to the police. In the case of the Corporate Murders, though, one breakthrough came from the fact that the killers had been sloppy and reckless. Security cameras had captured images of two men driving the CEO's car out of the gym parking lot. Detectives were able to match a set of fingerprints in the car to those of a minor who had previously committed a felony.

TWO SIXTEEN-YEAR-OLD BOYS by the name of Tammer Gonzalez Othman and Billy Bloom (known as Skippy the Bug) were identified as murder suspects in the corporate cases. They were caught and dragged to police headquarters for questioning.

"Skippy," to the officers' surprise, admitted to all three murders without hesitation, reciting the names and addresses of each of the victims, accurately describing the killings in precise detail, and even mimicking the victims' reactions. He identified Tammer as his partner. When asked why they had chosen those people, he said that they had followed a list. When asked where they got the list, he said they found it at the house of a man named Otto.

The kid was incapable of lying or of feeling remorse, the police psychologist reported. During his questioning he had asked for a hamburger and a Coke. His statement was punctuated throughout with chuckles and even laughs.

Tammer was interrogated separately.

When the investigators asked him why they had gone to Otto's house, Tammer said that it was to get some special suitcase for Otto.

Where is the suitcase now?

Under the bridge.

What was in the suitcase?

Papers.

What kind of papers?

Just papers.

What was written on them? the inspector asked.

Names of rich people, Tammer said.

How did you know that they were rich?

Tammer said that Otto had noted down the income of all the people on the list.

When asked if Skippy had looked at the list, Tammer answered, Skippy can't read.

When questioned about the last time he'd seen Otto, he said Otto had shown up in a clown outfit under the bridge.

When they asked him to list the people he had killed, he named the three men that Skippy had described, and also added a fourth victim, Fredao Mwalila. He said that they'd used Fredao's gun on the CEO.

Meanwhile, in the other interrogation room, Skippy asked if he could go to the bathroom. His feet were shackled and he was escorted by two officers. In the bathroom, he took off his shirt and started to wash his hair and face over the sink. There were still traces of blood on his undershirt. On the way out he stole the soap. Soap, he mumbled to himself, and smiled.

When Tammer and Skippy were brought together in the same room and asked if they had affiliations to any political group, they said no.

Do you go by any other name? the inspector asked, and Skippy said, The Savage Capitalists, and the boys looked at each other and laughed.

When asked if Otto had ordered the killings, they said no, they'd thought of them on their own.

When asked if they'd killed any taxi drivers, they said no as well.

Who, then, was responsible for the killing of the taxi drivers? an inspector asked.

God knows, Skippy said, and chuckled.

MUD

I STOPPED BY Café Bolero. All the spiders had their newspapers spread out on the tables like a pageant of butterflies in
a collector's attic. They murmured and showed each other the
photos of the Killer Kids.

I recognized Tammer and Skippy and I ran across the
street and bought as many of the day's papers as I could carry.
I sat at the counter and I read. Their photographs were on
the front page of every single newspaper and tabloid. Inside
were stories about Skippy's history inside juvenile detention
centres and psychiatric institutions, and articles on the effects
of prostitute mothers on kids' lives. All of it was paraded in
the local, national, and even international news. Otto's picture was in many of the papers too. A prime suspect in the
killing of the French journalist, he was mentioned as a foster
parent to one of the Killer Kids. The link between the two
raised multiple speculations and made for a convoluted story
that left many unresolved ends. It was reported that Otto was
on the run and was being actively pursued by the police. He
was labelled a dangerous ideologue and extreme left terrorist
with ties to anarchist organizations.

Once again, experts, this time on the history of anarch-
ism, found their way into the news. The story of the Serbian
Gavrilo Princip and his band of anarchists, which, one expert
stressed with evident spite and delight, included a mysterious Arab who was later hanged—and their assassination of
the Archduke Franz Ferdinand of Austria, consequently trig-
gering the First World War, was trotted out for the public like
a history lesson explained to kids in an elementary school

class. The life of the famous anarchist Emma Goldman was cited as a lesson in the failure of the movement and its practices of sexual liberation, which, they said, led only to promiscuity and debauchery. Clichés and misconceptions about the movement were revived and repeated. "Anarchist on the Run," read the photo captions, and "The Resurgence of the Anarchist in the West" and "Why a Good Citizen Was Killed by an Anarchist" and all those words made me go to my car, leave the lantern off, and drive aimlessly.

I drove all evening. I watched the delinquents two surface at night and the partygoers two walk like dancers, impersonating movie stars and mobsters, straightening their collars, pulling down their hats, and reapplying their fading lipstick. I drove ignoring all the creatures who bumped their heads on my glass like blind birds and soundless bats trapped in a world devoid of insects. Then I drove up the mountain and gazed at the streets down below, searching. Futile, I thought: in the chaos of the Carnival, a clown could vanish like a laugh. And then, towards morning, I decided to go back home. I opened the garage door and I parked my car.

I saw the vague shadow of a man standing in the corner. The shadow approached me and I recognized Otto with a quilt over his shoulders. He looked like a defeated bat: his beard had grown, the wrinkles on his face had multiplied and traced deep lines that reached the corners of his eyes. His back was hunched and his face had the look of an old black-and-white photograph that had found its way out of an attic.

I didn't want to come up, he said. They might be looking for me there.

Are you hungry? I asked.

I'm okay, he said.

I could go and grab something, I said.

No need, we will pick up something on the road.

Where to? I asked.

To Aisha's, he said.

WE DROVE TOWARDS the limits of the city. Otto rode in the back seat and lay down for fear of being seen. He covered himself with the quilt as I drove through back alleys and into deserted streets. I sailed my boat in the manner of the black and golden ships bringing pharaohs to their burials down the Nile. Once the city was behind us, I stopped at a gas station and I bought water, food, and alcohol.

Otto moved from the back seat to the front. He reached for the bottle of alcohol, opened it, and drank as I drove.

This has to end, he said.

All ends, I said, and then I kept quiet because all was quiet. The roads narrowed and the trees swayed in the silence of dawn. A few cars passed us but no one seemed to be going anywhere. All was still except for the road that curved and passed and disappeared underneath our wheels. Trees appeared suddenly at the edge of the road; they grew in front of our eyes only to pass and shrink again in the frame of the rearview mirror. Otto opened the window and froze his face against the cold wind. Fresh air, he said. Fresh wind for the rodents and the cavemen, he said, raising his voice through the whistle of the open window. Then, to make a fire, he closed the window, lit a cigarette, opened the window again, and blew into the rushing air.

The ground is wet, Otto said. Look how all has turned grey. How I hate that pale colour. The colour of evenness and submission, the colour of dormitories and hospitals and jails. For the funeral of my father, my mother bought us grey suits. She said, Kids shouldn't wear black. Kids should be in grey, and then one day she left us. I can't even remember where she's buried. Do you remember where your mother is buried, Fly?

Beside a river, I said. Somewhere between the Danube and the Italian heel. There was a band playing, and everyone wore bright colours.

Bright colours, lucky you.

We passed by a river. Otto suggested we stop to look at the water. There is a good view here, we can reach it by going behind the truck stop, he said. Pull over. There are no trucks at this hour.

I parked the car and stepped out. A cold wind was coming up from the water. Otto didn't seem to mind. He saw me shivering and handed me the bottle. Here, this will keep you warm, he said. I took a sip and we walked through an opening in the bushes. The soil was indeed wet and muddy. We stood on the edge of the river and we looked at the currents rushing towards an old bridge and a few rocks standing on the shore.

This should end, Fly, Otto said again.

This? I asked.

This, me. This person here. This small universe. This insignificant star. This ephemeral river. All of it should end.

WE ARRIVED AT the cottage. The door was unlocked.

There must be another bottle around here somewhere, Otto said. Aisha had stopped drinking and worried about my habit, so I hid it from her. He went to the kitchen and came back with two glasses and a bottle of rum.

We poured ourselves drinks and we drank.

I asked Otto, What did you and Aisha talk about before she was gone?

Many things, he said. Her family, her childhood. She remembered reading *The Iliad* to Mrs. Rooney, the neighbour. She said that, during the battles, the Greeks burned their dead but the Trojans buried theirs. They all feared for the well-being of their corpses and wanted to protect them from birds and hungry dogs ... Once she asked me to find a jazz station on the radio, but there are none in this area. We laughed about that ... We talked on the days when she didn't feel as bad, we had conversations about music and dance. She remembered a short story about a black jazz musician who played across the Atlantic in Paris for years, then one day decided to return home, only to be pursued and lynched by a mob ... She remembered us dancing, she talked about her father. One day I asked her how she was feeling and she said she finally felt at peace, now that everything was about to end.

Let's light a fire, Otto said suddenly, and got to his feet and went outside. He disappeared and came back with two logs in his hands. He laid them in the stove and started to make a fire, using some leaves as kindling.

We sat across from it and waited for the fire to appear. There was only smoke coming out.

The leaves are wet, Otto said. They'll dry out soon.

It was cold and damp inside the cottage.

When the fire starts, it will warm up, Otto said.

Do you remember that tune, Fly? "Between the Devil and the Deep Blue Sea"? The great Thelonious, you used to call him. It went like this... Otto hummed a bar and swayed a bit. He always swayed gently when he drank.

What album might that be, Fly?

Straight, No Chaser, I said.

You know it, brother. *Straight, No Chaser*, he said, and smiled. There is no one left but you, Fly.

And you, I said.

Otto didn't reply. The conversation stopped when the fire started to take off, and we sat quietly, looking at the smoke.

Then I suggested we eat.

Otto waved his hand and raised his drink and I understood his gesture. He raised the glass because he preferred to maintain the quietness of the place.

You can sleep on the bed if you are tired, he said.

I shook my head in negation. But when the flames started to dance inside the chimney, my eyes felt heavy and I slept on the chair with the empty rum glass in my hand.

Otto woke me up gently and said, Lie on the bed, Fly. It is more comfortable there.

And without resisting I stretched myself out on the bed and Otto took his quilt and covered me with it.

When I heard the gunshot, I must have been dreaming, because for the past few weeks I'd been having the same disturbing dream, which always struck me as very real and vivid. It was a chaotic dream, involving cars and a rundown place that I would struggle to escape from. There were always people chasing me in the dream, though I had never once seen their faces. But this night, I remember turning to confront them and to fight and then chasing them in return... I woke up sweating, thinking, *They've killed another man.* In my dreams, the victims were always nameless men.

It took a while to make the transition back from sleep and to return to the cottage. The stove helped me reorient myself and I looked around the room, but Otto was not there. I went outside looking for him and I saw him lying in the shadow of the tree. I ran towards him, and I held him. I knelt on the ground and held his head and my hands slowly filled with blood.

I stayed there with Otto's body in my arms. I must have knelt motionless for hours, maybe even days. I can't remember. The hours and the minutes were speeding by at a velocity that I couldn't comprehend. It all seemed like a swift flight of time.

I left Otto and I walked back to the cottage to get the sheet off the bed and I grabbed a shovel that was lying at the end of the porch. I covered Otto's body and I dug into the soft earth.

I buried him and it started to rain. I went back to my car and watched the water slipping down the glass. My muddy hands steered my wheel back towards the city. I drove past meadows and trees yielding in reverence to the passage of rain. Ravens flew through the sky in many directions. Their blackness paled against the dark clouds and their sizes varied with the distance of their flight. I drove and everything around me spoke of disappearance and decay. Everything ends with a flight, I thought... the images of passing meadows in rearview mirrors, the dance of a bird towards the light, a horse's last sigh before an end...I drove and I felt the sluggishness of my car against the cadavers of mud. I heard laughter and I laughed.

CITY

I ARRIVED BACK in the city and drove through the last night of the Carnival. It was the last day of the month, tomorrow it would all end, but today everything seemed to hover and soar. My car flew over the Carnival streets and from above I saw men in women's dresses. Kids in Gothic attire splattered fake blood on their faces and clothes and walked like killers. Vampires proudly showed their fangs as they crossed against the lights. I saw men with long hats, canes, and capes impersonating magicians and flying heroes. Homo sapiens with animal heads walked the alleyways with beer in their hands and sang old tavern songs in villagers' rough voices. And on my way back towards my home, towards the east side of the river, I spotted a camel walking behind a bearded man. And I saw the city occupied by deserted tents, and the caravans of vagabonds and domesticated animals leaving.

Here they are, I said. It is time too for me to descend and say goodbye, and wander again.

I arrived at my building, landed my car, and ran up the stairs. I rushed inside and banged on all the doors, but no one opened. So I went inside my apartment, sat at my desk, and decided to write a letter to the janitor and the neighbours. I relayed my condolences for the loss of the janitor's mother and I informed him that I was leaving this place immediately and for good. I included the next month's rent cheque because it was the end of the month, and I urged everyone not to chase away the mice or throw away the books in my library. I invoked death, knowledge, and the importance of books, and then, as an added incentive, I hinted that the library had a financial value and, in case even that didn't work, I threatened the janitor with the poetic justice of fire and arson, elucidating my hint with an extravagant drawing of a large explosion and menacing men wearing rodent masks, long tails, and no clothes.

But I knew that all would be futile. I signed my letter and took up my father's carpet. I closed the door and went downstairs to deposit the letter in the janitor's box. And then I unrolled my flying carpet and I flew above the city. I veered into a side street, went through an alley, and finally escaped the crowd.

Once I reached the river, I flew under the bridge. So long! I cried as I steered the carpet towards the narrow road and headed south to a small town of factories and workingmen. I landed safely. I left my carpet hovering at the doorstep and I entered the motel where the Magdalena girls once offered themselves to the killers of beasts. The Turk at reception was still there, in the same position as the last time I had visited this place. I asked him if the tall Arab was upstairs. Yes, he said. It is the end of the month. He is smoking at the window and the door of his room is always left open.

I took the stairs up. I stepped inside the room and saw the Arab at the window. I told him not to wait anymore, not to grieve, because she was dead and she was not coming back, and I left the room and flew again.